DIAMONDS AND PEARLS

DIAMONDS AND PEARLS

Edited by

ELAINE EVEREST

Published by Accent Press Ltd – 2011

IBSN 9781907726583

Printed and bound in the UK

Cover design by Zipline Creative

DEDICATION

Every one of the writers who have contributed their stories to this anthology have been touched in some way by cancer, either themselves or in their family. For some it is still very close. This book is dedicated to them and their generosity and we hope that, between us, we can make a small difference.

Thank you to the charities that work so hard to raise awareness and funds to eradicate all types of cancer and to the nurses, doctors, consultants and scientists who strive to make a difference.

In loving memory of my Mum and anyone else that died far too early from this horrid disease.

Elaine Everest

INTRODUCTION

The word cancer must be one of the most frightening words in the dictionary. When I was told in July 1980 that I had breast cancer my only thought was that I would be dead by Christmas, just as my Mother had been. She was 40 and left behind a grieving husband and three young children. Our lives changed that day and we still bear the scars, 39 years later.

My life was saved by a wonderful consultant, Mr Ellis Field, who held my hand through a mastectomy, radiotherapy, chemotherapy and many years of the drug Tamoxifen. I was a guinea pig for the cold cap and for Tamoxifen and sailed through my treatment with the positive attitude of youth on my side and a wonderfully supporting husband, family and friends. There wasn't a MacMillan support team at my hospital in those days and the only advice was via telephone from The Mastectomy Association. Once my treatment was over I became a volunteer with the association and visited other young women who, like me, faced an uncertain future without a breast – there was no option for reconstruction in 1980.

Surviving breast cancer has changed my life: I became a writer and have met some lovely people over the past 30 years. Surviving enabled me to teach others how to write and, with the help of my friend and colleague, Francesca Burgess, run The Write Place Creative Writing School in Dartford, Kent.

Each year was another notch on my belt. One year was celebrated quietly, then three, then five. Ten years was my goal, such was the aggressive nature of my cancer. In 1990

I did celebrate but then kept quietly counting the years, always looking over my shoulder and always touching wood that I was still a survivor.

I've lost family and friends along the way to cancer, but I've also witnessed more people surviving this horrid disease. That is cause for celebration.

Elaine Everest
www.thewriteplace.org.uk

breast cancer

We are Against Breast Cancer

We are Against Breast Cancer, a small charity with a big vision – nothing less than a future free from breast cancer.

That is why we are pleased to be associated with *Diamonds and Pearls*. Many of the contributors have been touched by cancer and some have lost loved ones to the disease. They want a future free from breast cancer and your purchase will help to support our work which ultimately could lead to a vaccine against breast cancer and help to remove the fear of this disease for generations to come.

Against Breast Cancer is unique among cancer charities in that we're all about research, and everything we do as a charity is focused on funding the work that could, one day, help to save women, and men, from suffering the anxiety of diagnosis every year.

Our biochemists are studying aggressive breast cancers to find out why they spread to other parts of the body – known as 'secondary spread' – and our work to develop a simple blood and urine test to screen for these destructive cells is progressing well.

This innovative and groundbreaking research costs well over £1m a year just to maintain current research levels, and for a comparatively new charity like our own, raising awareness of our work is closely linked with raising the funds to actually do it.

We wish the publishers of *Diamonds and Pearls* every success, and the authors a sparkling future.

Happy reading.

www.againstbreastcancer.org.uk

Registered charity no 1121258

CONTENTS

In a Spin
by Sue Houghton

"DID YOU KNOW THAT the manufacturers put special electronic chips in all new appliances?" said my friend Emma, staring at my dysfunctional washing machine

"Obviously," I said giving the thing an encouraging kick. "How else would they work?"

"No, I mean extra-special chips. Secret, hidden ones which are programmed to make the machine break down just after the warranty runs out. Don't tell me you haven't noticed?"

Emma's always been a bit of a conspiracy theorist. She has an opinion on everything from Roswell to Elvis being alive and running a roadside cafe just outside Cleethorpes.

I gave the machine a more forceful kick. "Even if it were true," I said, "This old thing's long out of warranty. In fact it's long out of manufacture. I think my aunt bought it off that chap who captained the Ark."

My aunt had passed away recently and I'd inherited her beloved bone china tea service and the machine. Any sane person would've sent the latter for scrap, but as I'd been assured it still worked and I was short of cash to replace my broken one, I was more than happy to give it a home. Besides which, I'd had enough of lugging bags full of dirty laundry to the Laundrette each week.

Emma went to sit at the kitchen table and dipped a hand in the cookie jar. "You'd better ring for a repairman to come and fix it," she said, between mouthfuls. "But I warn you, Julia, it's going to be costly."

"No point. I've already had someone out to it. Three times. I'm thankful that he only charged me the one call-out fee because he can't locate the problem. You see, every time he walks in through my door, the same thing happens, the darned thing starts working perfectly again. Regular as clockwork, it clunks into action. He's tested the circuit board and says there's nothing wrong with it but the minute he leaves, it stops again."

"So it's an intermittent fault," Emma shrugged. "Strikes me he's just a rubbish repairman."

"No, he came highly recommended. He's had it stripped down to the nuts and bolts and still he can't find anything wrong with it. Apart from a few dents and a bit of rust, he says it's in better working order than some of the new ones he's been called out to fix. Anyway, I'm reluctant to ask him to call again."

"Why? You paid him good money. He should be able to get the thing to work."

"It isn't simple."

"Why?"

"Don't laugh, but I'm beginning to get the idea he thinks I'm doing it on purpose, making up stories about it not working so I can see him again. Like he thinks I have a crush on him or something. The last time he was here, he kept winking at me."

Emma's eyes widened. "You're kidding?" Then she started to laugh. "You know, I quite fancy men in overalls. Especially car mechanics. There's something about men who're good with their hands. And the smell of oil ..."

"Emma!" I giggled.

"Come on then, don't keep it to yourself, what does this guy look like?"

"Oh, you know, a bit Johnny Depp. A bit of Daniel Craig. A smattering of Ashton Kutcher"

"Are you kidding me! Really?"

I rolled my eyes. "What do you think? Of course he doesn't." I tried tugging at the door catch. It didn't budge. "I guess there's nothing else for it but to send it to the scrap yard." As I said it, the washer gave a deep growling sound, followed by a sudden shudder that vibrated the detergent off the kitchen worktop.

Emma almost jumped out of her skin. "Spooky. Hey, you don't suppose it's … you know?"

"Broken? Dur!"

"No. I mean …" she grabbed my arm and whispered in my ear. "It could be possessed. Haunted."

"Haunted? Don't be ridiculous." I laughed. The only spirits I believe in are the ones that come in bottles, but I could see she was perfectly serious. "Whoever heard of kitchen appliances being haunted, Emma? There'll be a perfectly rational explanation. This apartment block is quite old. There could be an overload at the main fuse box. A power surge or something. Maybe that's where the problem lies."

"Then why has no one else reported any problem? I certainly haven't and I live right across the way from you." Emma dropped her voice to a whisper again. "I know you're a sceptic, but what if it's your aunt trying to communicate from beyond?"

"Communicate what? That she doesn't like my choice of fabric softener? That I've stuck that ugly bone china tea set she left me in the closet? Honestly, Emma, you watch too much TV."

"No, hear me out. Your aunt was always trying to get you married off wasn't she?"

This was true. Going shopping with her had been a nightmare. No man over eighteen or under sixty-five was safe from being accosted and assessed as possible husband material. It could be so embarrassing, though I knew she meant well. Since my break up with my fiancé a few years back I haven't dated much and I think it concerned her that I'd never found anyone else.

The week before she passed away she'd said she'd not rest until I had someone special in my life. I'd told her I was perfectly happy as I was. I had a career that took up all my energy. My aunt said that was because I hadn't met the right one yet.

"Just suppose," said Emma "she's being true to her word and still watching over you by haunting the machine."

I shook my head. "You've lost me. How would that help find me a man?"

She was really getting into her stride now. "Think about it. What if, by some celestial power, she stops the machine working so you have to call out an engineer, the idea being to bring you and whoever might call together, so you'll fall in love." She clapped her hands. "It's so romantic. Two people brought together by the Other Side."

I prodded her in the arm. "But your theory falls apart when you consider my heaven-sent engineer happened to be old, toothless, and married. How come she couldn't spirit up someone unattached and less porcine? Someone blue-eyed and drop-dead gorgeous."

At that moment, the machine gave a loud mechanical burp and the door suddenly pinged open ejecting my clothes and several gallons of dirty water all over the kitchen floor. A pair of red socks had bled colour onto my new sweater. Emma took one look and shrieked.

"So, it looks like I'm back here again, till I can get another repairman out, or until I can afford a new machine," I told the manager at the Laundrette.

It was that same afternoon. Emma had gone home, probably to hang garlic over her door lintel, while I'd gathered up my damp washing hoping to catch a free machine. It's always busy on a Saturday. I usually avoid it if I can, but this time I had no option. As I'd anticipated, all

4

the machines were taken so I left my laundry for a service wash.

"As if I don't have enough on my plate," I muttered under my breath as I handed over my damp clothes. "First I adopt an orphaned electrical appliance that repays my kindness by holding my clothes hostage. Then I attract the attention of some hormonally-charged repairman. My sweater has shrunk so it'll fit a seven-year-old, and if that's not enough, my best friend's gone all Friday the Thirteenth on me."

"Emma, you mean?"

I stopped my rant and looked up at him. "Sorry?"

"Your friend," he said, accompanied by the most dazzling smile. "It is Emma, isn't it? You've mentioned her a few times. You've known each other since college, right? She lives in the flat opposite yours. She eats too many cookies but you don't mind as you bake fresh every weekend."

"I guess so." I wasn't aware I'd even spoken to him before. Which was a pity as he was quite cute. "Anyway, yes, Emma, she's got this daft theory about … sorry, I didn't catch your name."

He gestured to his name badge. Pete.

"Hi, Pete. I'm Julia."

"Yes, I know."

I must've given him a curious look.

"The last time you ordered a service wash, a couple of months ago," he explained. "You gave me your name, remember? Pity you didn't give me your phone number, too."

"Why? Did I leave something behind?"

"Me," he said and I swear he was blushing. "I've missed you, Julia."

I didn't know what to say. I think my mouth was hanging open.

"I might be able to fix that," he said.

"Huh?"

"The stain," he said. "On your sweater. We have some special stuff for removing stains. Give it to me and I'll see what I can do. I'm afraid it'll cost."

"That's OK," I said, rummaging in my purse.

"I wasn't talking cash."

He leaned across the desk and took my hand in his. Maybe water from my leaky machine had soaked into my trainers and short-circuited something, I don't know, but, whatever it was, a tingle shot though my arm and the hairs at the back of my neck prickled. It wasn't unpleasant. In fact, it was quite thrilling.

"Dinner," he said, his blue eyes twinkling. "Have dinner with me. I was working up the courage to ask you before but then you stopped coming in."

About the time I inherited my aunt's machine.

"I thought I'd missed my chance. Good thing the machine broke down or I might never have seen you again. Must be fate or something."

I smiled. "Yes, it could be."

When I arrived home, Emma popped in with a list of washer repairmen she'd got from the phone directory. She sat at the kitchen table and dipped into the cookie barrel as usual. I really ought to give her the recipe.

"I've been thinking over this haunting business," she said, nodding over her shoulder to my washing machine. "If your aunt is trying to channel her energy, what we need is a strategy."

"What kind of strategy?"

She handed me several bits of paper. "I've made a list of local repairmen. I thought if we started with the 'A's and worked our way through them we're bound to find someone suitable amongst them. These are all free-phone so it won't break the bank."

I made us coffee, then tore up the list and threw it in the trash can. "No need for these," I said, going to pat the machine, gently. "I have a feeling it'll behave perfectly from now on."

And it has ever since. My laundry, like my future is looking bright!

Sue Houghton has been writing magazine fiction for the UK and overseas markets since 2001. Her short stories and first novel, *Dearly Departed*, have been placed, short-listed and highly commended in various writing competitions. She has given quotes for several publications including *Wanna Be a Writer?* by Jane Wenham-Jones and *How to Write and Sell Short Stories* by Della Galton. Web: www.suehoughton.co.uk

Checkmate
by Christine Webb

MARGARET CHECKED THE CODE carefully before extracting the door key from its secure box on the wall. It turned stiffly in the lock. She pushed the front door open, calling out as she did so.

"Hello, Mr Simmonds, it's me, the practice nurse."

She stepped into the hall. In the fading daylight of a December afternoon she could see that the wallpaper was unlike any she would expect to find in a suburban middle-class home. Its rich patterns in vivid reds and golds smacked more of the Far East than the local DIY store. Her patient, as she knew from his medical records, was elderly, but his house didn't have the sweet sickly smell overlaid with an acid whiff of urine that she usually associated with the old and mildly incontinent. Instead she caught the heavy perfume of joss sticks reminding her poignantly of her student days.

"I'm in here nurse, second door on your right," the voice sounded surprisingly strong and alert for someone whose prognosis was so bleak. The doctors were mystified by the cause but the symptoms were only too apparent, steady weight loss and debilitating weakness which kept the patient a virtual prisoner in his own home.

Margaret entered the room to which she had been directed and recoiled at the heat. A log fire blazed in the Victorian fireplace. She surveyed the rest of the room's contents with amazement. There were richly embroidered hangings on the walls and a thick carpet woven with an intricate pattern on the floor. Two huge display cabinets were crowded with oriental objects, carved figures in ebony and ivory, delicate porcelain pieces, ornamental brassware, jugs and platters all jostled for space. On a small table an incense burner created a haze and filled the room with a pungent but oddly soothing fragrance. She gazed at her surroundings open-mouthed, almost forgetting about her patient until his voice dragged her back to the present with a start.

"Good afternoon, Nurse, I see you're intrigued by the contents of my house. I imagine it's not quite what you expected?"

She turned to face him. He was lying on a chaise longue the feet of which were carved into huge lions' paws. He raised himself up on one elbow and politely extended a hand. She grasped it. It felt like a bunch of dry twigs. The skin on his face was paper thin and almost translucent, but a pair of intelligent eyes, of an intense blue, twinkled at her. As she stooped to examine him her eyes were drawn to a curious piece of furniture placed within his reach. His eyes narrowed as he watched her pause and stare at it.

"Are you admiring my chess table?"

"I've never seen anything so unusual before." She gazed at the table, supported on the heads of three carved elephants, whose raised trunks appeared to steady the table top which was inlaid with the sixty-four squares of a chess board. The chess pieces in ebony and ivory stood in their accustomed positions for the start of battle.

"I brought it back with me from India. It belonged to a maharajah."

"Did you know him? Did you play chess together?" Margaret was intrigued. Mr Simmonds' background appeared to be so different from her usual patients.

"I worked for him for some years after independence

and, yes, we often played chess. He was a very skilled player with an amazing grasp of strategy and tactics."

"So this table has happy memories for you then?" Margaret asserted briskly, grasping his wrist and preparing to check his pulse.

"On the contrary, we never played on this table because he believed it was ill-omened. His son blamed this chessboard for his father's death and he asked me to remove it." As he spoke she felt him tense and his pulse raced. She saw the sweat beading on his forehead. With an effort he seemed to regain his composure and beneath her fingers she felt his pulse return to normal. She checked his blood pressure, took his temperature, and listened to his chest. All were normal, yet there was no doubt that he was ill. Despite the oppressive heat in the room from the blazing fire, Mr Simmonds visibly shivered under a heavy tartan rug.

"Do you believe it contributed to the maharajah's death?"

"Our time of death is written at our birth. We may be granted a warning when the time is imminent to make of our remaining days as we will." His reply hardly seemed to answer her question. She decided to probe no further.

"I'll call again tomorrow," she said, heading for the door. She knew that his GP was sufficiently concerned to want him regularly monitored for signs of any further deterioration.

When she arrived the following day Mr Simmonds was asleep. His features were relaxed; he'd lost that taut anxious look she'd been aware of yesterday. She was in no hurry to wake him. His was her last visit of the afternoon. Instead she wandered around the room examining the numerous examples of Indian art; but inexorably she was drawn back to the chess table as if by an invisible string. She stooped down to examine the pieces more closely. They were finely carved and she noticed with a start that the kings and queens had real faces instead of the symbolic crown and coronet. She found herself staring at the sinister features of the black king. She reached out to pick it up to examine it more closely and was overcome by a sudden surge of revulsion.

"Don't touch them." The voice of her patient was weaker than yesterday but still carried enough authority to make her jump. She hadn't even realised that he had wakened. She hastily withdrew her hand as though scalded. Even without Mr Simmonds' intervention there was something menacing about the chessmen that compelled her to abandon her original intention to study them at close quarters.

"I'm sorry," she muttered, "I had no right to think of handling them."

"The time to play the game is not yet and it is not your game to play. I wouldn't want harm to come to you through any ill-judged intervention."

His voice was thin and reedy. She struggled to catch his words and to understand the implications of what he said.

"What do you mean?" she asked but he sank back on the cushions piled on the chaise longue and appeared deeply asleep once more.

In the days that followed, whenever he felt strong enough, he regaled her with stories of his time in India. She was fascinated by his knowledge of its culture and politics and looked forward to the time she spent with him. His mind was sharp and his memory undimmed but she was concerned that physically he appeared to grow weaker with no obvious cause. The skin stretched tightly across his face took on a skeletal appearance and his eyes glittered with fever even when the thermometer indicated that his temperature was normal.

One Monday morning she arrived to find Mr Simmonds seated in front of a large ornate bureau which was open to reveal an array of meticulously labelled files. Piles of papers and manila envelopes lay in drifts at his feet.

"Good morning, nurse. Excuse the chaos but I must get my affairs in order."

After she had carried out her routine examination, she urged him to rest. His skin was flushed, perspiration beaded his brow and his temperature was slightly raised.

"I've no time to rest now, I'm afraid, but once this is done I can take all the rest I need."

It was not until she was ready to leave that she noticed the chess table. Two of the pawns had moved forward as if a game were in progress. She was about to comment on it but Mr Simmonds was deeply engrossed in his papers and she was reluctant to disturb him for something so trivial. Nevertheless she was puzzled. As far as she knew Mr Simmonds never had any visitors and he'd never mentioned anyone with whom he'd played chess except the long-dead maharajah. Then she dismissed it from her mind. So much had been moved round in the room since he had begun sorting his papers; no doubt the chess pieces had been moved inadvertently.

All that week Mr Simmonds was to be found seated at his bureau poring over files. Margaret was concerned about his health. His fever worsened but he was adamant that this was work he had to finish. His thin shoulders were hunched and his hands shook but still he refused to lie down. Each time Margaret's gaze was drawn inexorably to the chess table. She was more convinced than ever that a game was in progress. While Mr Simmonds plodded doggedly on through his archives, she stopped to examine the chessboard, dredging up from her memory all she'd once known about the game when she'd played it with her brother. The way the pieces were situated was not random. Each one had moved in strict accordance with the rules, moreover some pieces had clearly been captured and removed, as far fewer than thirty-two now remained. But neither side had gained the upper hand. White and black

12

were evenly balanced.

The following day when she opened the door the flat had regained that air of serenity it had exuded when she first visited. Once more the sweet smell of incense drifted through into the hall. The sitting room, though still cluttered, was restored to tidiness. The bureau was firmly shut. There were no pieces of paper strewed randomly across the floor and Mr Simmonds was stretched out on the chaise longue. His complexion had an unhealthy greenish sheen. His breathing was shallow and laboured. The chess table was within reach. A quick glance at the pieces was enough for Margaret to recognise that the endgame was in progress and white's position was precarious. She checked his pulse. It was racing and his blood pressure was raised.

"You're not feeling so good today, Mr Simmonds?" The question was rhetorical. "Have you finished sorting your papers?"

He nodded. The effort of speaking seemed almost too much.

"And I see you've found a friend to play chess with. Does he visit you often? Are you white or black?"

"White." He hesitated. "Although my opponent doesn't visit me I know what moves he wants to make. It is just as my friend the maharajah said it would be. In the end I cannot win; but by my skill I have prolonged the inevitable long enough to get my affairs in order." He was seized by a paroxysm of coughing. Margaret watched him anxiously until he recovered. He lay back on his cushions.

"The game is nearly finished," he said calmly. "Soon I shall be at peace." He smiled at her and closed his eyes.

The deterioration in his condition led her to alert his GP, who promised to visit later. Nevertheless Margaret decided that she would also call on him again once she'd seen all her patients. Opening the door she was aware of an unnatural stillness. In the living room the familiar smell of incense filled her nostrils and something else, the smell of death. Holding her patient's stick-like arm she felt for a pulse. A sudden noise made her look up as his GP entered. Slowly she shook her head. He hurried over to the patient's side only to confirm what the nurse had already concluded. He was too late. Margaret gently covered the body with the tartan rug and extinguished the joss sticks while the doctor wrote out the death certificate. As she left the room she took a final look at the chessboard. The game was over. The victorious black king loomed over the checkmated white king who lay on his side. She peered at the defeated chess piece in the gloom and was shocked to see that his head had become just a skull.

Christine Webb first won a prize in a writing competition when she was ten but didn't follow up her success until many years later. She returned to writing fiction nine years ago when she took early retirement. She belongs to The Write Place, a thriving group of writers in Dartford, Kent. Christine has had a number of short stories published and has been placed in competitions for short stories and poetry. She is currently working on a romantic novel.

Greek Connection
by Kelly Florentia

"A CHURCH WEDDING," SAYS Mrs Papadakis in a heavy accent, placing a cup of Greek coffee onto the huge rustic table in front of me. I'm not quite sure whether this is a question or a statement. It does sound rather like a demand, to be honest, but Panos had warned me about his mother before we arrived.

"She's very patriotic, Tanya, and a bit set in her ways but she's a pussycat really, once you get to know her." I look at my future mother-in-law. The woman I I've been longing to meet. The woman I want to make a good impression on.

"Coffee smells lovely," I offer, "just what I need to perk me up after that laborious flight." They don't take their eyes off me as I draw the tiny cup to my lips. Goodness, I'm only sampling their local coffee not taking part in a bush tucker trial in the Australian jungle. I shake off their scrutiny and take a large sip with poise but as the hot, dark liquid hits my tongue it feels like an explosion of caffeine in my mouth. I resist the urge to run to the sink. I daren't make such a scene on my first visit.

"Strong coffee," I manage, swallowing hard.

"It's unfiltered," says Panos with a wry smile, handing me a glass of ice-cold water, which I gulp down within seconds. "And an acquired taste," he adds with a wink.

Mrs Papadakis, who is standing by the stove with her

arms crossed against her large chest, doesn't look impressed. Grey strands of hair have escaped from her untidy bun. She blows them off her olive skin and looks at me expectantly.

"Oh, yes," I say finally, "Panos and I are happy with a church wedding."

Her face instantly creases into a smile as she throws her chubby arms up in delight and then folds them around me. I'm not used to hugging people I've only just met but I make an exception and respond with a gentle hug and a light pat on the back.

"There is a condition though, Mrs Papadakis," I say, barely able to breathe from her tight embrace. We disentangle quickly and her dark eyes lock with mine. "It has to be held in London as I'd like all my family and friends to be there," I gasp. I'm thankful she approves of this, and pulls up a chair next to mine.

We chat about her life in London. She tells me how she misses the city and what good times she had there.

"But when my husband died, what could I do? A young widow with a ten-year-old boy … suddenly alone, I had to come home to my family."

I nod sympathetically and I know that she and I will get on just fine.

Three weeks later, Panos and I are enjoying a romantic meal in the old Venetian town of Chania, where lovers walk hand in hand, restaurants tucked in narrow alleyways spill on to pebble-stoned pavements, and the sound of the bouzouki drones blissfully in the background. But instead of basking in the ambience I find myself thinking about home. About Richard.

"Tanya, have you completely lost it?" Richard had said, flinging my resignation onto his desk in anger. "Giving up everything for a bloke you met on holiday with Ruby? "Richard's one of the company directors and, I hasten to add, my ex-boyfriend. He's very handsome, charming and

16

successful. He's also a compulsive flirt and commitment-phobe, you know the type.

"Richard, it's been nine months. Remember? " I got a swirl of satisfaction from watching him squirm at being reminded of his betrayal. It'd been just over ten months since I'd found a string of explicit text messages on his Blackberry from Emma in Accounts. "Besides," I went on, "I fly over to see Panos regularly. I've probably spent more time with him than I ever did with you."

But, surprisingly, Richard wasn't going to let go without a fight. He promised fidelity, confessed to not being able to get me out of his system. He even went as far as saying that I was 'the one'. But I wasn't born yesterday.

And then he did the unthinkable.

"Look, I know what this is all about and neither one of us is getting any younger … so, well … if you want we could …"

"Richard, are you asking me to marry you?"

"Well … yes! I am if it'll make you stay." Hmm … not quite the proposal that I'd imagined. Not that I expected him to go down on one knee or anything as drastic as that. But, come on, surely a girl deserved more than this?

Flowers, chocolates and love notes continued to arrive at my rented flat in Muswell Hill all week.

On the morning I was due to leave for Crete he turned up on my doorstep clutching a dozen red roses in one hand and a small Tiffany box in the other. Richard was no quitter.

"Don't, Richard," I said, pulling my dressing gown around me tightly. "If you'd asked me a year ago I might've said yes, but now it's too late."

"A vine picker," he snorted, "who lives in a shed with his mother?" Damn Ruby, she could never keep her mouth shut. "You're only doing this to spite me, aren't you?" he spat, "Admit it." He leant forward, his lips close to mine.

"No, Richard," I pushed him away. "The world doesn't revolve around you! It's over between us. I'm leaving." His steel-blue eyes searched mine, but I didn't flinch.

"You'll never be able to rough it, Tanya," he huffed, backing away, "I'll give you three weeks tops before you start missing your home comforts." He hurled the lovely bouquet into the corner of my porch, forcing the red petals to scatter onto the stone patio – and then he was gone from my life. Until yesterday, that is, when his text appeared on my iPhone … *'missing u. R u ok? Pls call me xxx'*.

Richard was right incidentally. Panos isn't well off. We live minimally in a run-down house in Agia Marina, just out of town, and I'm finding it impossible to find a job. But I can see the shimmering sea from our bedroom window when I awake each morning, and feel the warmth of the sun massaging my back as I stroll to the local bakery for our fresh bread. I realise that Panos can't give me the security or quality lifestyle that Richard could provide. I'll never have that fairytale wedding I'd always dreamt of, or the lovely house and luxury holidays. And Okay, Panos was on the rebound – but surely I know my own feelings … don't I?

"Any regrets?" asks Panos, as if he could read my mind, "I know you're missing home." I take a sip of Makedonikos and stare into the distance, trying desperately to make sense of my tangled emotions. Richard did say Emma was a one-off and he did try his best to win me back. Perhaps I was hasty. Maybe I should've given him another chance. "We could move back to London once we're married," Panos went on, "I speak English, I'm sure my uncle Andreas would give me a job in his restaurant and …" I cover his soft lips with my hand and look deep into his warm, brown eyes that are full of concern and confusion.

"Panos," I say gently, he kisses my fingertips softly, seductively, as the bouzouki player moves in to serenade us, "we need to talk."

The next morning we head off to the mountains to meet Panos's grandparents who've just returned from visiting relatives in Corfu. We drive around the spiral, uneven roads at what seems like top speed. I thank God when we finally pull up outside an old derelict bungalow. I climb out of the open-topped truck feeling frazzled and nauseous and step into a heap of manure.

"Oh no," I cry, "my Manolos." Panos, laid-back and easy-going, says he'll buy me another pair. "Have you any idea how much these cost?" I growl, pointing the four-inch stiletto at him, "They were a gift from … from … oh never mind." He shakes his head in exasperation as he disappears behind the truck, returning moments later with a pair of oversized sandals that'd probably been lurking there for centuries.

"Your hair looks nice like that, Tanya." He hands me the sandals.

"Are you having a laugh?" I wipe the smeared mascara from my cheekbones. "It was shiny and straight before we left home!" Thanks to the heat, humidity and wind, I now look like an aging 80s rock-chick. What will his grandparents think of me? "And I'll only come up to your waist in these," I grumble, shaking the sandals at him. Okay, slight exaggeration, but who cares? I'm angry. "I'm not happy, Panos." I complain, brushing down my new jeans hard and furious.

"Oh grow up, Tanya, they're just a pair of shoes for goodness' sake," he yells, "and I did warn you not to wear them". Great – our first fight and not a door in sight to slam. I glare at him but before I can hurl another insult his grandparents appear and Panos mouths, "I'm sorry," and I can't help but smile.

"This is my Yaya," His frail little granny dressed in black from head to toe welcomes me with a kiss on both cheeks.

"And, Papou," the elderly man, fully clad in long black boots over traditional baggy trousers and black headscarf, takes my hand, "this is my Tanya." Granddad's thick, white moustache tickles my fingers as his dry lips brush against my hand and thoughts about my appearance are quickly forgotten.

We sit outside their house on old wooden chairs that feel as though they are about to collapse beneath us and sip Greek coffee, a taste I've come to acquire. I can't think of the last time that I felt so relaxed, so safe … so normal. I close my eyes, savouring the moment but to my irritation my iPhone buzzes manically in my bag. Ten messages – three missed calls, all from Richard. I know what I have to do …

When Panos tells his grandparents that we're getting married they leap off their seats in jubilation.

Within half an hour the house is jam-packed with guests eating and drinking to our health and happiness. I've never known anyone with so many close relatives. I smile as Panos wraps his arms around me and sigh contently as I stretch my arms around his trim waist, and I know that I've made the right choice.

"Hey, sorry I fell asleep last night. You said you wanted to talk," he says blithely, his eyes sparkling with joy, "remember?" I wonder if I should tell him the truth. Confess that although hearing from Richard again stirred something within me, I still chose him – a good, decent man who genuinely loved me over a rich, materialistic Lothario who, deep down, only really loved himself.

"It was nothing," I whisper. "It's sorted." I lean forward, my eyes close, our lips touch then a thunderous voice cries,

"Panos! Panos!" We pull apart quickly and follow his grandfather outside to where his granny is waiting. Away from the intoxication of the blaring music, dancing and laughter, I suddenly feel sober and alert. We face his grandparents, expectantly.

I can tell from his grandfather's tone and his grandma's expression that the matter is serious. I frown anxiously as the tension rises inside me.

"What are they saying, Panos?" I must learn to speak Greek.

"My grandparents want to give us their property," he says, through trembling lips. I sigh with relief, then look around at their humble little home as tears prick my eyes – how utterly charitable and kind. They know that Panos and I are struggling financially but this gesture is beyond generous.

"THANK. YOU." Surely, if I speak slowly and loudly they'll get a gist of what I'm saying, "BUT. WE'RE. FINE. WHERE. WE. ARE," I say even louder. They look at me as if I'm deranged and then at each other bewildered.

"You don't understand," says Panos enthusiastically. He puts his hands on my shoulders and turns me towards the horizon. "This is their property."

Acres and acres of land stretch before us.

"You mean?" I say breathlessly.

"Yep! My grandparents are modest people, they like to live simply but they own it all. The land, olive groves, vines. They said they built it up over the years for my late father and now … they want to give it to us as a wedding present!"

"Panos! All this must be worth thousands of pounds!"

"Millions," I hear him say as I drift into unconsciousness.

Kelly Florentia lives in London with her husband Joe. Her short stories have appeared in women's magazines in the UK, Australia, Sweden and Norway. Although fiction is her passion, she also writes for commercial websites and is the main contributor to two online businesses. When she's not busy working, Kelly enjoys being creative in the kitchen, practicing yoga and participating in a bit of retail therapy. Kelly is currently working on her first novel.

Ruth's Red Onion Day
by Vivien Hampshire

IT WAS JUST ANOTHER day in the pickle factory. Or, at least, that's how it started out. A Friday in September. And Ruth wasn't too keen on Fridays. Fridays meant only one thing. Onions. No, Ruth liked Wednesdays best, or that's what she would say if asked to choose. It was always red cabbage on Wednesdays, and she liked red cabbage. It brought a little touch of much-needed colour into her life. But, of course, no one ever did ask her to choose. At work her opinions were rarely sought. She was one of many on the line, all the same, just doing a job. And a very boring job it was too.

At home her work was never discussed. What was there to say, after all? When you've seen one onion you've seen them all. And, besides, her mother had only one topic of conversation where Ruth was concerned, and that was Jack. The prospect of Ruth's eventual marriage to Jack, to be precise. And, as for her father ... well, he just watched a lot of TV, often with his eyes closed, strangely enough, and said very little at all.

Ruth's whole life was boring. From morning to night. Nothing different ever happened. She sometimes felt her life was so boring that it must actually be someone else's life and she had somehow been given it by mistake. There was no other explanation. And, deep in her heart, she knew that something was missing, some elusive, untouchable thing, but having never seen it, she could never quite decide

22

what it was.

She had a job, albeit a rather tedious one, and that was more than many her age could claim. She had a home, or a small unremarkable corner of one, to call her own. And she had a boyfriend. Jack. He seemed to be part of the fixtures and fittings, He had been around so long. But, unfortunately, without meaning to seem too ungrateful, Ruth found Jack a bit boring too.

Jack had been a friend since childhood, always a year ahead of her through school, and was now training to be a baker. A nice kind thoughtful boy, as her matchmaking mother never failed to remind her. One who bought Ruth flowers even when it wasn't her birthday, and kept his shoes shiny and his hair short, and always flossed his rather crooked teeth twice a day, regular as clockwork. But they had never really got beyond the holding hands stage, and Ruth knew she didn't love him, not in the way she dreamed of loving a man.

'Don't forget to take a little something for his mother,' Ruth's own mother would say when Jack took her to his parents' house on Sundays for tea. And then they would sit awkwardly side by side on the bus, with two jars of gherkins wedged between them, and Ruth would wish with all her heart that she worked in a perfume factory or a chocolate shop, or anywhere where the perks were just a little more appealing.

But this day was different. The machines roared and rumbled just the way they always did. The onions slopped into jars and glided, lidless, down the line. The air smelled of engines and sweat and pickling vinegar, and the rain pounded on the tiny high-up windows and the corrugated metal of the roof. The girls, in their faded blue overalls and their disposable gloves, perched on their stools and did what they had to do, mindlessly, automatically, lifting, checking, packing, and waited for their real lives to begin.

Three hundred and seventeen days. That was how long

23

Ruth had worked at Potter's Perfect Pickles. She kept a chart inside the door of her locker and every evening before she went home she would mark another cross on it, like a prisoner counting off the days of her sentence on the wall of a cell.

'Why do you do it?' her friend Carol had asked her once.

'I don't know,' she had replied. And she didn't. Somehow the chart, which had started out as a bit of harmless fun, had become yet another part of the routine, as much a part of her day as clocking in and out, the passing of a million onions in front of her eyes, and the endless cups of tea. Three hundred and seventeen days, and all of them pretty much the same.

And then Simon Potter arrived. He was the boss's son, fresh from university, come to look them over on the factory floor before retreating to a life of luxury and privilege behind a polished boardroom door.

When he swaggered down the lines, heads turned. He was a good-looking lad, and he knew it. Tall and dark, with a definite twinkle in his eye. And it was only the one eye that Ruth saw at first, because when he stopped at her place he winked at her, a cheeky wink that made her feel, just for a moment, that she was special, sitting there with her hair pulled back inside its nylon cap as a row of jiggling jars, stuffed with onions, rolled by.

'Where do you girls go for lunch?' he asked later, helping himself to morning tea and custard creams without putting his twenty pence in the tin. They all noticed, but they didn't complain.

'Go?' said Carol, as if the concept of going anywhere during her break had never before crossed her mind.

'We eat here,' said Ruth. 'Sandwiches, in the staff room.'

'Or sit out on the grass sometimes,' said Carol, 'if it's not raining.'

'Well, not today,' said Simon Potter, draping a

24

conspiratorial arm around each of their shoulders. 'I'll take you to the pub. Both of you. My treat.' And so he did.

'Just an orange juice for me,' Ruth had insisted, not daring to confess that she was not quite eighteen yet and that pubs were not within her usual sphere of experience.

'Nonsense! Have a vodka in it,' Simon had insisted back, paying the barmaid with a fifty-pound note, the first Ruth had ever seen.

She had not tasted vodka before. Come to think of it, she couldn't actually taste it now. All she could taste was the orange juice. If this was alcohol, she couldn't help wondering what all the fuss was about, and promptly accepted another.

In the afternoon, Ruth's hands, which usually carried out their duties with the ease and dexterity of a well-oiled robot, started to do the most peculiar things. She would go to lift up a jar and miss it completely, knocking over its neighbours, and then have terrible trouble picking them up again. And when she went to the ladies' room, which seemed to be a little more often than usual, she had to struggle with the bolt on the door and needed several attempts at the zip on her trousers.

The room seemed exceedingly warm. Once or twice she had felt her head start to nod, and her eyes droop, and had had to shake herself to keep them open.

And then, when she had them open, she found she had to blink a few times to be sure of what she was seeing. There, coming towards her down the line, chugging along on the conveyor belt, was something very strange. She turned to nudge Carol, but Carol had slipped away to make a cup of tea. Could it be? Surely not! Yes, it was a big red onion – no, a scarlet onion – as bright as a pillar box, sitting in the top of a jar of otherwise very ordinarily plain white ones. She blinked again, wondering if perhaps, like some sort of hallucinatory vision of pink elephants, the vodka was to blame, but when she opened her eyes the onion was still there, and coming closer. In three hundred and seventeen days of peering into pickle jars, she had seen many a red cabbage, but never a red onion. And this one was very, very red indeed.

At the second attempt, she managed to pluck the offending jar from the moving belt and held it up to the light. The onion oozed. Its redness swirled into the pickling vinegar around it, spreading before her eyes, contaminating the whole jar and staining the torn-off edges of a small slip of paper she had just noticed poking out from the murky depths between the onions below. She didn't know what to do. Should she raise the alarm and have the machinery stopped, before the whole batch had to be scrapped? Her hands shaking, she scooped the paper out and unfurled it, dripping a trail of streaky vinegar across her arm and into her lap.

Just making sure you're still awake, said the note. She looked up and there he was. Simon Potter, behind the glass screen of his father's office, with a huge bottle of red ink in his hand and an even bigger smile on his face. And he was winking at her. Again.

And then she laughed. She put down the jar and laughed until she cried, wiping her eyes with her soggy glove and making herself cry even more. And it was the first time in three hundred and seventeen days that she had laughed like that, out loud, about anything, anything at all, during working hours.

'I think he fancies me,' said Carol later, when it was time to go home. She had found a note stuck to her locker door and refused to tell anyone what it said.

'He's a rogue,' said Ruth, secretly fingering her own little note, its sodden mixture of ink and vinegar beginning to seep into the cloth of her overall pocket.

'A lovable rogue though,' said Carol. 'Good for a bit of fun, I bet. But not the marrying kind, that's for sure. Pity, really. What with all that money and all …'

'Marriage isn't everything,' said Ruth. 'Imagine your whole life spent with just one person, waking up together, eating together, shopping together, day after day after day. It'd be just like working here, except we wouldn't get paid for it!' Ruth thought of Jack, good old dependable Jack, and sighed. 'You'd have to be so sure he was the right one, wouldn't you? Absolutely sure, before committing to anyone like that.' She shook her head, which seemed to be clearing at last.

Her locker door was open and she had the pen in her hand. Three hundred and eighteen? The pen hovered over the chart. No. Something had to change. Without hesitation, she ripped the chart down and crumpled it into a ball. It was time to stop counting her days and to start to enjoy living them.

At last, she had glimpsed what it was that was missing. She was still only seventeen, with her whole life ahead of her. Much too young to allow her mother to push her towards an early marriage. It was time to have some fun. Laugh. Be spontaneous and silly, and take a few chances …

There was someone out there somewhere. There had to be. But she was in no great hurry to find him. When the time came, she hoped that he would sweep away all the boredom, all the routine, and make the dull days shine. So that even working here at Potter's Perfect Pickles wouldn't seem so bad.

But that someone wasn't Simon Potter. He was just a flirt, playing one girl off against another. A fickle, funny flirt, who had made her drunk, made her laugh, and made her realise what was wrong with her life. No, it wasn't Simon. But she also knew now, with a sudden and absolute certainty that brought new hope into her heart, that it wasn't Jack either.

He wouldn't be heartbroken. In fact, he'd probably be relieved when she told him it was over. Their so-called relationship had always been based on pleasing everyone else. Keeping her mother's wedding hopes alive and providing his mother with regular supplies of pickle at staff discount prices. But there was no real love between them. No romance. Certainly no passion. They were just friends, very good friends, and probably always would be. But as for anything more than that? No. She knew it, and she knew him well enough to realise that he knew it too.

Ruth and Carol put on their coats and stepped outside. The rain had stopped and a glimpse of early evening sunshine was poking through what was left of the clouds.

'Goodnight, girls! Have a good weekend,' called Simon, winding down the window of his Jaguar and giving them a cheery wave as he pulled out of the reserved parking space which had just had his name painted on it. Carol giggled and waved back, watching his car speed out of the car park and disappear into the distance, and then the girls said their goodbyes and went their separate ways.

Ruth stood for a moment on the pavement outside the factory gates, looking both ways, and then, with a spring in her step, turned left instead of the usual right. She'd take the long way home for a change. After all, she thought, smiling to herself, life should be full of surprises, opportunities, new experiences ... Sometimes you just had to break the routine and see what might happen.

Whether it was the man of your dreams or just an unexpectedly bright red onion – she giggled again at the memory of it – you never knew what might be waiting for you around the very next corner.

Ruth's Red Onion Day was originally published in *Woman's Weekly* 2007.

Vivien Hampshire lives in Middlesex with her partner and two cats. She writes articles specialising in childcare and pre-school issues, and her funny poems have appeared in several anthologies for children. During 2008, *Writers' Forum* magazine followed her successful quest to make enough cash from one year's writing to fund a Caribbean holiday. She has been writing women's magazine fiction since 1997, and poetry all her life, but her ambition to become a famous novelist remains sadly unfulfilled!

Billy Liverpool
by Fran Tracey

THE DAY MY BROTHER Billy came home was hot and sunny, and it happened to be my birthday. We were having a barbecue. I prefer lasagne around the kitchen table, but Richard wanted this to be my birthday treat, so I gave in, and sat in the garden with a glass of wine. I like to be occupied, to feel useful, and didn't really enjoy being forced to rest, although I wouldn't admit this to everyone. Richard always says I'm as busy as a bee. When I rest my mind wanders, and sometimes it goes to places I'd rather not visit. Like thinking about birthdays, which you don't want to do when you're in your sixties and the years turn around faster than time itself. They've become compressed, rushed, as though they're speeding to the end, and there's still so much to fit in. I doubt bees are quite so aware of their mortality.

"Hey, Grandma, tell me a story."

Rebecca's voice stole me away from watching a Cabbage White alight on our buddleia, then flitting to a rose, before leaving us for the garden next door. I wondered if she knew where she was going. And if like me busyness was her natural state. Was she compelled to keep on the move? To twist and turn through life, but stay close to home. Because, despite my inability to sit still, I've never travelled much. Not like my brother Billy. He was like a swallow. He'd escaped, as though some innate sense forced him to flee as soon as the season changed. Once he'd been set free he flew as far from home as he could, then he rested there.

Rebecca loved to hear about my life in the children's home; everything seemed romantic to her, I think. But I wondered if she thought they were stories I'd made up for her entertainment. And when I was wakeful at three in the morning even I doubted whether I was telling her the truth. I had trouble anchoring my memories then, when all but me rested. It seemed to have happened so long ago, but so recently too. And I knew I'd discarded some of the more painful ones. I often wondered what Billy remembered from those times under the watchful eyes of Sister Bernadette. A benign name for a woman whose actions could be purely evil. Especially towards my brother. She'd shown her hatred for him from the moment she'd grabbed him by the ear and dragged him down the long dark corridor stretching ahead of us. We shared a history, me and Billy. We were family. Did our memories differ much? I felt sad that I'd never asked him.

"Shall I tell you how me and Billy black-leaded the grate?"

Rebecca looked at me in mock horror. She loved the detail in this often repeated story. The description of sweeping, scraping, polishing that was so remote from any of her experiences. But I couldn't be certain whether Billy had really been there, or whether by then he'd been moved into the Boy's Home. A separation we had never recovered from. As far as I was concerned he might as well have been sent to Australia. And I hated the nuns for that. We were brother and sister. I trusted him like no-one else. Just a glance between us said everything would be OK. I wanted to scream at the nuns that family was important. But I remained silent.

"It kept us out of mischief. Well it kept me out of mischief, anyway. It took more than that to keep Billy away from trouble."

We were taught a lot about duty and hard work in the home, which stuck with me into adulthood. I didn't fight with the nuns, or challenge them. I wasn't much of a rebel. We weren't taught much about love. I was lucky I met Richard and he taught me about that, although even now I worry about its permanence.

"Tell me a story about Billy."

"Don't I interest you?" I grinned. Rebecca shrugged. She loved hearing about her great uncle and his shenanigans.

"The nuns encouraged us to keep busy. They'd whip the back of idle hands. Billy's hands were often red and sore."

"What did he do?" Rebecca asked.

"Well he didn't do what he was instructed to. And he liberated food," I whispered, as though the nuns were there to hear me.

Rebecca giggled.

"What do you mean?"

"Well, people at St Edmunds, they'd bring us food parcels, at Christmas. But not much of it made it onto our plates."

"That's shocking, Grandma," said the girl who wanted for nothing, despite my daughter Helen being a single parent. She was a nurse, unable to wriggle out of her shift today. No-one could have forced my daughter to relinquish Rebecca. It just didn't happen these days, thank goodness. Not that I'd have allowed it, anyway. Not since Billy and I had been separated. Mind you, even back then I was aware that Mother hadn't been forced to give us up. That was hard to understand.

"He'd go down to the kitchen in the middle of the night and fetch us bread, ham, cheese. We thought we were in heaven."

Rebecca rolled on to her back and closed her eyes, apparently happy to let my voice wash over her. She hadn't inherited my inability to sit still. She reminded me of my brother in lots of ways. She could be cheeky, fun, stroppy at times. Just how I remembered Billy to be.

Occasionally he'd call Richard and me.

"Hello Maggie, Billy Liverpool here," he'd announce, as if I had another brother Billy who lived elsewhere in the world. Not that he ever stayed long in Liverpool. He'd always be a traveller, he said. But after his first foray abroad he'd bought a studio flat there, used it as a base. But I guess that greeting helped define him somehow, gave him a sense of place. There was no other way of knowing him, beyond delving into my memories. After twenty-five years away he was a stranger.

While I was in the middle of telling Rebecca about brushing the crumbs of our midnight feast under our beds, Richard called us.

"Maggie, could you get the door? I can't leave the barbecue now. The burgers are at a critical point. This could be feast or a disaster." It was only then I heard a loud knocking.

I raised my eyebrows to Rebecca, winking at her to follow me.

"Let's see who's pestering us on a Sunday afternoon."

I took a couple of steps back when I saw him there.

"Hello, Maggie. Billy Liverpool. Happy birthday," my brother said.

As though I wouldn't have recognised him. He'd changed, naturally. I had too. Time plays unkind tricks on our faces. Etching our experiences into the grooves that run across our brows. My mind tumbled with emotions. I was shocked that he'd turned up after so long, unannounced. I wanted to shout at him, to say he'd got a nerve after all this time, but then I couldn't risk him turning round and leaving immediately. My brother had always had an unpredictable streak.

"And you must be Rebecca. I know loads about you." Billy winked at his great-niece.

Rebecca smiled shyly. I'd written to Billy over the years, trusting my letters would reach him, somehow. And it appeared they had.

"I've brought beer for Richard and me." He stumbled over his words, perhaps sensing my annoyance.

"And port for you, of course."

"Its years since I've drunk port and lemon, Billy." My voice was quiet, contained for now.

"I guess things never stay the same, do they?" He didn't sound regretful, merely matter of fact.

"So, Billy, besides celebrating my birthday, obviously, any good reason why you've turned up completely unannounced twenty-five years after you left?" I couldn't suppress the sarcasm and anger in my voice.

He looked surprised. I'd always been the one who avoided conflict.

"I just wanted to see you, Maggie. Can I come in?" His voice was wistful and uncertain, and I sensed the fear of rejection under his bravado. I saw the cheeky eight-year old again and I stepped aside, allowing him to pass. Billy had always been good at avoiding things. Tasks in the children's home. Responsibilities. The truth. The day he'd left twenty-five years ago had been cold and wet. He'd been staying with Richard and me for a couple of months, never having settled in a home of his own.

On the day of our mother's funeral, he told us he was going out for beer, and he didn't return. I was frantic. But no-one could help. The police pointed out that he was a grown man and I was his sister, not his wife. He had every right to leave. Mum had, after all. She'd set a precedent by leaving us in the care of Brother Michael. He turned us over to Sister Bernadette, and we ended up in the St Edmund's Home for Children.

While we were there we'd stuck together like glue. It was Billy who'd grasped my hand in the middle of the night when thirty children stood in darkness in the kitchen, rats running over our feet. I can't remember why we were being punished. Some child's minor transgression, possibly Billy's. Or just sheer cruelty on the part of Sister Bernadette. But it was only Billy who stopped me from crying aloud, ensuring we would be kept there for another hour. I'd thought he'd be with me for ever.

He sent me postcards, occasionally. And now here he was. I touched my brow, smoothing the lines. I was furious with him, for allowing all that space to grow between us for all those years. But I loved him too, like I had when he was eight, and I wanted to hold him. Richard caught my eye as Billy shook his hand, questioning me silently. I shook my head. No, I didn't know he was coming. Richard grasped Billy around his shoulders. He always took things in his stride.

"I left because of Mother," Billy began to explain. He sounded hesitant, careful. "And once I'd gone I couldn't come home. There was nothing for me to face up to in South Africa."

I let the words rise and fall between us.

"I only learnt at her funeral that she'd dumped us there, Maggie. That she had a choice," he continued. "Father Joseph told me. You knew too, didn't you?"

"Maybe it would have been best for him to have kept his counsel," I replied, not offering an answer to his questions, the one spoken and the many left unasked.

"No, he did the right thing, even though I found it hard to take."

"So you ran away from me?" I asked.

"I didn't run, Maggie. I drifted. Ended up in South Africa."

"I know. We received your postcards."

"I felt free there, for the first time. Far enough away to escape the clutches of evil incarnate."

I smiled.

"So, you remember Sister Bernadette, then?" I replied,

35

feeling my mood shift slightly.

"Do I? That woman hated me from the moment I stepped into that hell hole. I thought she'd part my ear from my head that first day."

Richard placed food in front of us. And we ate, me, Billy, Rebecca and Helen. It tasted good. And we chatted, discovering our memories overlapped sometimes, but differed too. And that was fine. Things eased between us as the afternoon shadows stretched towards evening. The day Billy returned I sat entirely still for ages. We watched a bee alight, and apparently rest, on honeysuckle. I couldn't detect any movement.

"Even bees sleep, Maggie," Billy said.

I touched his hand. We'd stick together for ever, Billy and me. The distance between us didn't matter. I knew that now.

The day Billy left had been hot and sunny. It was still my birthday.

Fran Tracey lives in West London with her husband and two lively children. She fits in writing as often as she can, as it keeps her sane. She has been published in women's magazines and numerous anthologies, sometimes writing under a pseudonym for her saucier stories. She enjoys writing character-driven fiction and exploring themes of memory, childhood and loss. She tries to be funny sometimes, too! And murderous. Though purely fictional of course.

Great-Aunt May
by Linda Barrett

CLARISSA DIDN'T SHED A tear when she heard that Great-Aunt May had died. Well, why should she, she reasoned. She hadn't seen her in donkey's years.

"I'll bet she left everything to that loser cousin of mine," Clarissa remonstrated to her husband Brad over breakfast.

"Jane has been looking after her for the last ten years," he pointed out. "You didn't want to know her. You didn't even respond when Jane sent you that text telling you that Aunt May was seriously ill."

"Unlike dear Jane I'm very busy with the boutique. All she had to do was nurse the old girl. And I'll bet she didn't even pay for her keep."

Brad shook his head. He knew when he was wasting his time.

Taking out her mobile Clarissa read again the text from Jane. *Aunt May has died. I'll be in touch about the funeral arrangements.*

"Very short and sweet. And what about the will? We are her only two living relatives. I'll bet she made sure she feathered her nest before the old lady died."

"Then maybe you should have gone to see her when you had the chance."

Clarissa flew at him. "Oh yes, I've got all the time in the world for visiting old ladies, haven't I?"

He gave up. "I'd better get to work," and he grabbed his

briefcase and left.

Wanting to find out what was going on, and not wanting to give Jane time to manipulate anything as regarded Aunt May's possessions, Clarissa decided to phone and arrange to meet up. Jane seemed pleased to hear from her and they arranged to meet that very afternoon at the coffee shop on the High Street.

Jane was already sitting with a cup of tea in front of her when Clarissa arrived some ten minutes late. It didn't occur to her to apologise for her lateness. She sat down opposite her cousin and clicked her fingers to get the waitress's attention.

Jane looked up at her and Clarissa was a little taken aback at the sight of her red, swollen eyes. She dismissed it almost immediately, assuming that it had all been put on for her benefit. She surveyed her cousin. Still as dowdy as ever. She's probably never seen the inside of a boutique. A few hours in a gym wouldn't do her any harm either.

"So, poor old Aunt May," she said finally.

At this Jane broke down into floods of tears. "I'm so sorry," she managed between sobs, "but I do miss her. The house is so empty without her."

Clarissa suppressed an urge to tell Jane to pull herself together and instead patted her arm.

"So what will you do now?" This might be a good time to find out what was happening to Aunt May's estate. "Will you be able to stay on in the house?"

"Oh, yes! That's not a problem. She left the house to me."

Clarissa bristled. "I see. Did she leave everything to you?"

"No, just the house. She talked about leaving the contents to you."

"And what about her bank accounts and such?" Clarissa's eyes shone but she tried to keep her voice steady.

"Oh, Aunt May didn't believe in banks. She kept all her

spare cash in a biscuit tin in the airing cupboard."

That was more like it.

"I got a phone call this morning to say that the funeral will be a week on Wednesday at 11 o'clock." Jane continued. "She wanted to be cremated, you know. I'm putting on some refreshments at the house afterwards and the solicitor is going to come at 2:30 to read the will."

"Well, you'll be able to get on with your life once it's all over. Will you get a job now?"

"I'll have to try. I'll have to make a living somehow. Actually, I'd better get off. I need to make an appointment at the job centre."

It suddenly occurred to Clarissa that whatever was in that tin could be in Jane's purse at any time, if it wasn't already.

"Oh, no need to rush into that. Why don't I come back home with you and have a look at the contents."

"I really need to get myself a job sorted out as soon as possible."

But Clarissa was not going to be put off. "You can do that tomorrow. We haven't seen each other for years."

Jane reluctantly agreed and Clarissa went home with her to view her inheritance. On the whole she was deeply disappointed. The furnishings were old and tattered.

"I always thought Aunt May had a bob or two?" she pointed out as she looked disdainfully around.

"Well, I don't think she was hard up but I don't know exactly what she was worth. She was very private about such things.

"Where's this biscuit tin, then?"

Jane looked aghast at her bluntness but took her upstairs to the airing cupboard and handed her the tin in which Aunt May kept her money. Clarissa opened it eagerly. As she had hoped it was stuffed full of notes and she was pleased to see some fifties in there. She took the tin downstairs and emptied it out on the kitchen worktop. She began counting.

To her delight the biscuit tin contained £12,840. She was about to cram the notes into her handbag when Jane stopped her.

"We can't take anything until after the will is read. I only said that Aunt May told me that she would leave you the contents. I don't know what's in the will."

Clarissa knew that she was right. "Okay, but I'll just make a note of what's here if you don't mind." She took her diary and a pen out of her bag and without even noticing the hurt expression on Jane's face she noted down the amount in the tin. Then she replaced the notes and handed it back to her cousin.

On her way home Clarissa felt much brighter. £12,840 was a lot of money considering she had hardly known the old girl. Some of that furniture and bits and pieces might also fetch something as antiques. She'd get a dealer in there as soon as the will was read.

Brad was horrified when Clarissa told him that she had no intention of going to the funeral but would just attend the reading of the will later.

"You can't do that for heaven's sake."

"Why? I hate funerals and it's not as if we knew her."

"Clarissa, you are going to make a pretty penny out of her death from the sound of it. The least you can do is to pay your respects."

"Well I'm not." Clarissa sounded like a petulant child. "I'll say I have business to attend to which can't be put off."

Though Brad had never met Aunt May he felt compelled, out of common decency, to take the morning off work and attend the funeral himself. He apologised profusely to Jane for his wife's absence and coloured as he explained that she had important business to see to.

Jane said she understood. "Will you come back to the house for a bite to eat?" she asked him.

"I'd love to but unfortunately I have to get back to work

myself. No doubt we'll see you soon."

Jane agreed that this was true and Brad returned to work.

That afternoon Clarissa arrived at Jane's home just before the solicitor was due. There were no surprises in the reading and as her cousin said the house had been left to her and its contents to Clarissa. There was no mention of any bank accounts.

The solicitor left and Clarissa went straight to the airing cupboard to get the tin.

"I have to rush off. A woman's work and all that. I've arranged for an antiques dealer to come tomorrow to assess the contents. We'll be here about ten. I trust you'll be home." And before Jane could answer she was gone.

Clarissa was pleasantly surprised that the dealer thought that quite a few items of Aunt May's would sell as antiques. He offered to buy them from her and to save herself any hassle Clarissa readily agreed.

"What about Jane?" asked Brad later that evening. "I know she's got the house but the rate your going she'll have nothing in it. You've already taken all the cash there was."

"Oh, come on! She'll have to get a job. She got a far better deal out of Aunt May's death than I did."

"It takes time to get a job and in the meantime she has no money and no furniture."

"Nonsense! I'm not taking all the furniture, only the bits that are worth something and I'm sure she'll be able to get some sort of benefit." Knowing that he was beat Brad again retreated.

A couple of weeks later Brad decided to call on Jane to see how she was getting on. The house was sparse to say the least. Clarissa had taken all the electrical items of any value along with the antiques.

To his surprise the garden was full of rubbish and Jane looked hot and tired. "I'm going to have to get rid of the

41

house," she explained, "and find something smaller. A little flat maybe. I just can't afford to keep it on."

"I'm really sorry to hear that," said Brad. "Is there no other way?"

"I can't see one. Anyway, I'm going to have to get rid of one or two things of Aunt May's. I've got someone to come and collect them tomorrow but I have to get it all into the front garden. Once it's gone I can put the cottage up for sale. "

"Right, well I'll give you a hand," he said, removing his jacket.

"There's only her bed to go. I was wondering how I would manage it."

"Let's take a look then," and he followed Jane upstairs. Luckily the bed was a single and would be easy enough to dismantle.

"It's seen better days, hasn't it? he observed. "This mattress has been patched up a few times." He pressed down on it with his hands as if to test it for comfort.

A smile suddenly started to play on his lips. "No! She couldn't have. It's much too obvious." Jane looked puzzled. Brad grinned at her. "Fetch me a sharp knife."

Still baffled she went to the kitchen and came back with the knife. Brad took it from her and stabbed the neat stitching on the mattress. Carefully, he started to cut. After he had made a six inch gash along the seam line he put his hand inside. His grin widened. He brought his hand out. Clenched in his fist was a wad of bank notes.

Jane shrieked in delight. They both attacked what was left of the seam and started tearing at it with their bare hands. They put the assortment of notes in a bag and took them downstairs to count. Incredibly the mattress had contained £57,855.

"Clarissa will be pleased," said Jane when they'd finished counting.

"You must be joking. Clarissa will never know," Brad

responded.

"It's hers by rights," she reminded him.

"I think Great-Aunt May wanted you to have it," he said gently. "She knew Clarissa well enough to know that she wouldn't want the mattress. She left her what she thought was fair. You were the one who cared for her and about her. The money is yours. All you have to do is decide what to do with it."

Her face lit up and Brad realised how pretty she was.

"I won't have to sell the cottage," she threw a pile of notes into the air with a whoop. Then she became thoughtful. "Well, the first thing I'm going to do is to try and buy back all Aunt May's antiques. Get the house back to the home it was. What will you tell Clarissa?"

"Oh, I don't plan on telling her anything. She's away on business for a couple of days. By the time she gets back I'll be gone."

"I'm sorry," Jane said.

"It's been a long time coming. As for Clarissa, she'll hardly notice I've gone. Hey how about dinner?" he brightened. "We can celebrate your good fortune."

Jane smiled. "My treat," she said."

As they sat in the restaurant both of them knew that their lives were about to take a turn for the better. They ordered champagne to celebrate Jane's good fortune.

"I'd like to propose a toast," said Brad, raising his glass. "To Great-Aunt May." They clinked their glasses together and raised them.

"To Great-Aunt May," said Jane.

Linda Barrett was born and brought up in the mill town of Bolton in Lancashire but as an adult has lived in many parts of the UK. In the mid-eighties she moved to Germany with her husband and ended up spending seven years there. She retired from teaching in 2008 and currently lives on the south coast.

Linda writes short stories for both adults and children and has been published in magazines both in the UK and Australia.

Totally in Control
by Ginny Swart

I'VE ALWAYS HAD A lot of self-control. Well, not always. When I was younger I was a real pudding but one morning when I was sixteen I broke the zip trying to get into my favourite Levis. That did it. From then on it was lettuce leaves and fat-free yoghurt all the way until I lost a stone.

After that I allowed myself a little steamed fish and green vegetables and the odd flirtation with a slice of fat-free turkey.

My mum tried her best to tempt me to eat the same rubbish she did. A fine role model *she* was, always going on a diet, then sliding back to her fish and chip suppers and trying to drag me with her. I can't remember a time when she wasn't overweight and it really teed her off to see me refuse food. She took it as a personal affront.

"Alison, eat something!" she'd say. "You've got a lovely little figure, you don't want to get any thinner."

I didn't want to get any fatter either. Sometimes it was hard, especially with her treacle pudding and custard sitting in front of me, but I stood firm. I really enjoyed that feeling of power, being able to look at the golden, syrupy richness of it and say no. And watch her finish it off instead.

My strong will paid off. I've been a perfect size 10 for fourteen years now, and haven't put on an ounce. Self-control is what it's all about. That's how I managed to get this great job last year. People expect to see someone in my position with not an ounce of fat on them, and they're not disappointed.

I was twenty when I met Alistair and I knew straight away he was the man for me. There was this instant, crackling connection and we moved in together just six weeks later. He was smart and funny and ambitious, he loved me to bits and the sex was fantastic.

There was only one thing wrong and that was his attitude to food. Or rather, his attitude to my attitude, if you follow me.

He kept telling me I needed to eat more, that every girl should have a few curves. But he didn't realise how strong I was. At first he'd tell me I was being ridiculous. Then he tried laughing about it, tempting me with lobster thermidor and cream puddings – poor man, he ended up eating double servings of everything. That's probably why he put on so much weight in the five years we were together.

Sometimes I like to test myself. I order a helping of Death by Chocolate at a restaurant, for instance, and I don't touch it. Or I go to some fast food take-away, where they serve fried chicken and steak burgers and those fantastic battered onion rings, and I'll order a jumbo-sized with extra French fries. And I go back to my car and open that Styrofoam box and allow myself to drown in that divine smell.

Only for a moment. Then I close it up again and put it next to a rubbish bin. Tidily, so that someone else can find it and enjoy it, because I don't like waste.

Believe me, sometimes that's difficult to do.

Alistair once admitted I had more self-control than any woman he'd ever met. It was one of the nicest things he'd said to me in a long while, although he didn't sound as though this was a trait he admired.

He said it after I'd refused to drink even the tiniest drop of champagne to celebrate his promotion. Natural spring water does just as well and comes with no calories, as I reminded him. When we went out to dinner later that evening, I ordered a small French salad without dressing and watched in amusement as he almost defiantly ordered a T-bone and a baked potato slathered in herbed butter.

Of course I didn't ask for dessert because by then I knew how ridiculously angry he became when I didn't touch it, growling about the waste of food and money, so he tucked into the strawberry cheesecake on his own.

Actually, Alistair packed his bags that same night, after getting really nasty about my eating habits and some of my other traits which he tried to make me feel guilty about.

Perfectly ordinary things like washing the coffee cup as soon as I've finished. I like a nice clean room, and I couldn't help it if he was so slow to finish his own drink.

And he flatly refused to believe how many filthy germs lurk on door handles, money and train seats. I don't think he washed his hands more than twice a day. There was no call for him to insult my own hygienic habits though.

But he'd been gone a year, and I had to admit I did miss him. A lot. I wished he'd come back. It was pretty lonely in the flat at night with no one to talk to. Lonely in bed, too, I missed that. I was sure I could compromise and make an effort to cook him the sort of unhealthy food he liked. I could even force myself to order ordinary meals when we went out together, if that would make him happy.

I'd actually picked up the phone several times to call him. I'd even got as far as dialling his number, then I just couldn't do it. Beg him to come back, I mean. But I kept hoping I'd run into him in the street and when I did, I was sure the old magic would still be there and we'd just pick up again.

Meantime, life had to go on. Once Alistair left I had to find a way to earn a crust. Or in my case, a starch reduced low-fat cracker. And I was very lucky to find this job.

Last Monday, just before nine, I popped into the Coffee Bean for a small espresso and just to test myself as usual, I ordered a chocolate éclair. Crisp on the outside, light and fluffy on the inside and oozing with thick cream.

I took these back to my favourite corner table and pulled out my notebook to go over my pep talk for the first class.

But the whole table rocked as a rather large woman squeezed her way past to sit down next to me.

At work, we're warned never to say "fat", only "generously proportioned", but her proportions were *very* generous. She had a beautiful face though, with deep blue eyes, a lovely creamy complexion and thick auburn hair. What a pity about that extra flab, I thought, she could be really beautiful if she tried.

She had a voice that matched her figure, rich and deep and audible right through the room.

"You're one of the lucky ones, with that éclair," she said, with a loud, full laugh. "I bet you just eat what you like and never put on an ounce. I take one look at something like that and the pounds just fly on to my hips. It's not fair!"

She spooned some sugar into her cappuccino and bit into a sticky apple Danish.

"From this morning onwards, I have to stick to healthy stuff," she said "Fruit. They say five portions of fruit a day, don't they, so this is my apple!"

She giggled naughtily, tossing her hair and licking her fingers.

"Who says that?" I asked.

"The Weight-Away bunch. I've read their literature. Two-litres-of-water-two-servings-of-carbohydrates-two-servings-protein-five-pieces-of-fruit-and-all-the-green-vegetables-you-can-eat. *Yeuch!*"

"So you don't take it seriously, then?"

"No, I do, *I do*. I told my boyfriend I'm joining today. He reckons I'm perfect as I am – well, all men like a few curves, don't they? But I'd like to lose a kilo or two."

Or twenty, I thought silently.

"This is my last naughty little fling before I start," she

added. "I wonder if I should have another Danish, while I still can?"

"Well, I wish you good luck," I smiled, picking up my bag. "If you stick to their programme, you can change your life."

"I wouldn't want to change *everything!*" she said. "One size down would be nice, though."

I looked back as I left the coffee shop and pretended not to notice that she reached for my untouched chocolate éclair.

When I reached the office I opened the windows. Then I unpacked the digital scale, set out the chairs in a semi-circle and sorted the membership cards for that morning's class.

Members started to drift in and greet each other.

"My son's birthday party," muttered one of them. "Lemon cake and ice cream. I don't even want to get onto that scale. She'll kill me."

"Disastrous weekend," said her friend. "*Two* dinner parties. I can just imagine the tongue lashing I'm going to get."

Well, Weight-Away works on the principals of public shaming, which does wonders. And I'm good at that.

"Now, now," I said briskly. "No talk of failure here, ladies. Even fifty grams counts, you know!"

Miss Last Fling walked in cheerfully just before we started. She looked startled but then grinned when she saw me.

"Ah, it's you! Now that's cheating! You can scoff chocolate éclairs all day and still look so thin. I haven't a hope!"

Totally in denial. We both knew who'd eaten that éclair.

"That's a defeatist attitude, um, Sally," I said, looking at the form she'd filled in. "It might take a while but we'll get you to your goal weight if you work hard."

Once she took off her shoes and stepped on to the scale I had a suspicion she'd mutter the usual excuse about glandular problems. But she was quite shameless.

"Eighty-five kilos!" she giggled. "And all of it gorgeous, as my boyfriend says. Well, I'd like to say goodbye to five of them."

"Only *five?* That's not much of a goal weight, Sally, with your height you shouldn't be tipping the scales at more than sixty," I said reprovingly.

"You're joking! I've been more than seventy ever since I was sixteen!"

Bad dietary habits instilled by poor parenting, I thought, but just smiled and said, "I'm sure we can change that."

Sally was one of those people who can't help chatting and smiling and she was quite disruptive, actually. Exchanging phone numbers with people who'd been complete strangers ten minutes before and making everyone giggle with her silly jokes. I had to clap my hands several times to bring the ladies to order.

But she listened to my little pep talk I always give the group once they've weighed, and as she was leaving I handed her the Weight-Away pack outlining the permitted food and the way to cook it.

"Steamed chicken breast?" she said dubiously. "Don't know if I'll care for that. My boyfriend likes chicken casserole with mushrooms and cream … perhaps if I just use less cream?"

"Sally! You have to follow this eating programme *to the letter*, or you'll get nowhere."

Her attitude was all wrong and I had a bad feeling that this woman was destined to be one of my few failures.

"I'll do my best but I can't promise!" She grinned like a naughty child as she opened the door. "Oh, there's my boyfriend come to collect me. I'll ask him if he fancies steamed chicken for lunch."

I recognised the handsome, rather bulky figure waiting at the foot of the stairs in an instant. Even though Alistair could have done with a few kilos less, my mouth went dry and I had to grip the door handle because my stupid knees threatened to let me down. But he didn't even notice me as he watched Sally run down the stairs, surprisingly lightly for someone her size, and fling her arms around him.

"Finished with that nonsense at last, sweetheart?" he boomed in that familiar bass voice that used to make my toes curl with pleasure. "Now what say we try that new Italian place by the river for lunch?"

I should have called after her and reminded her to order a child's portion of whole-wheat pasta, but there was no point really. I knew she wouldn't, she had absolutely no self-control.

As I started to tidy the meeting room ready for the next session, I could tell Sally was destined to be one of my black sheep Weight-Away drop-outs. In a couple of years she'd be way beyond "generously proportioned", she'd be *fat*. And let's see how Alistair likes her then.

And anyway, I'm happy to say that when I saw him again, I realized I was totally over him. Sally was welcome to him. Wobbly knees weren't a sign of weakness, of course. It just meant my body was low on potassium or iron. Or something.

Totally in Control was originally published in *Woman's Weekly* in 2006 and also in *You* magazine in 2009.

Ginny Swart is a South African writer and writes mostly short stories. Her stories and serials are a familiar feature in women's magazines worldwide. She has had a book for teenagers and four romance novels published.

The Button Box
by Sophie King

EILEEN MILLS HELD UP the blue button to the light. She could see it now, as clearly as when she had bought it all those years ago, from the haberdashers with the wooden shelves and upside-down brass shell handles. She had only been a child, maybe nine or perhaps ten, but even in those days, she had loved sewing.

"Another dress for your doll?" Miss Molly would ask, smiling that bright smile which lit up her face and almost stopped you noticing that nasty scar above her lip. Her mother called it a hare lip but Eileen couldn't understand what that had to do with the hares or rabbits that played in the field at the bottom of her garden.

That's where Eileen liked to sew in the summer. She'd sit in the little hut that her father had built her and cut out patterns from left-over scraps of material which Miss Molly kept for her mother, calling them remnants. Remnants seemed a dull sort of word for the pretty cottons which Eileen snipped at, with the pinking shears that her mother had bought her for Christmas. Once, Miss Molly had saved her a beautiful piece of bright blue silk but, to her disappointment, it had slipped all over the place when she tried to cut it. It was even worse when Eileen attempted to sew a button on. Her needle kept tearing at the material which, although pretty, was something called floored even though her mother said it was spelt a different way.

To make her feel better, her mother had bought her an exquisite set of mother of pearl buttons on a white card with '3d' written in Miss Molly's lovely, curvy writing at the top. 3d was two weeks' pocket money in those days but, because of the silk disappointment, her mother had treated her. How she had loved those buttons, Eileen thought to herself. They were far too beautiful to actually use. Instead, she would keep them in the wooden carved box which her uncle Gerald had brought all the way back from India.

Every now and then, when her baby brother was asleep and less likely to try and grab something which didn't belong to him, she would take out the card of mother of pearl buttons and watch them glint. Then Eileen would close her eyes and imagine where they had come from. Her mother had said they were made in India, where the box had come from. But she knew better. Someone, maybe a little girl of about her age, had found them in the sand when looking for shells. There had been six of them, almost the same shape but very slightly different, like this one which had a funny little dent on the edge.

Eileen kept her treasure box under her bed in the room she shared with Philip. Then, one day, an ordinary little brown button fell off her school skirt when she took it off one evening. "No point in sewing it on again," said her mother. "That skirt was too small for you anyway. We'll buy another for the new term. Keep the button in your button box. It might come in useful."

Eileen hadn't thought of her treasure box as a button box but it made sense. Her mother had a button box which was heavy with all kinds of buttons, like pebbles. Most were round but there were some exciting shapes too, like the beige rectangular one that looked like a miniature farm gate and was really a buckle but had sneaked into the button box by mistake. Eileen's favourite was a tiny white rabbit button which her mother had told her she had worn on her very first cardigan, soon after she'd been born. "You can

53

have it, if you like," her mother said one day, "for your collection." And Eileen knew that when she had her own child, she would sew it on his or her cardigan, just like her mother had on hers.

As she got older, Eileen's sewing skills grew with her. By the time she was twelve, she could easily cut out quite complicated dress patterns, using the flimsy thin paper outlines with little crosses down the sides that she bought from Miss Molly. Eileen would spend hours looking at the elegant figures of the women who featured on the cover of these patterns. It wasn't always easy to see what kind of buttons they had on their flowing jackets, or skirts which seemed to billow out with the kind of elegance that you didn't normally see outside Miss Molly's shop. But if Eileen couldn't see them, she would imagine them. A brilliant green button for that jacket and a sparkling silver one for the bridesmaid dress which she had been allowed to make for cousin Maggy's wedding.

Eileen was very excited about Maggy's wedding. At 14, she had despaired of ever being a bridesmaid but that was mainly because no one in her family had got married for ages. Her mother had said that was because of the war and that she hoped no one would stare too much at poor Maggy's Philip in his wheelchair. Eileen hoped they wouldn't either. She liked Philip who had a kind smile and had had two perfectly good legs when she had last seen him.

In the event, no one need have worried. Maggy looked beautiful in the dress she had made herself and everyone said it must run in the family, because Eileen's bridesmaid dress was also beautiful. "What exquisite buttons," said one of Philip's aunts when she examined the tiny, fine stitching afterwards. "Aren't you a clever girl?"

Eileen had secretly kept one of the spare silver buttons to put in her button box. And Maggy had given her the tiny white ball of a button which did up one of the many loops at the side of her dress. She had also thrown the bouquet straight at Eileen so she had no option but to catch it, amidst much blushing and laughter. To her embarrassment, George, Philip's younger cousin, was standing next to her at the time, "Well caught," he said admiringly. "Something tells me you're good at games."

Eileen, who had been too busy sewing all her life to pick up so much as a lacrosse stick, wondered whether it was time to spread her interests. She kept her button box going, of course but she also learned to play tennis under the kindly supervision of George and his mother Pammy, who lived in the neighbouring village. And when Pammy's tennis skirt threatened to fall down after a particularly energetic shot, Eileen just happened to have a spare button and thread in her bag. "What a sensible girl," Pammy later said to her son, meaningfully, "and pretty too." Eileen and George were married just before her nineteenth birthday. As a wedding present, her mother gave her a new sewing machine. "You'll need it before long," she said, with a knowing look.

Eileen spent her first pregnancy doing what she liked best, now she could no longer play tennis. Everyone admired the neat pile of crocheted shawls and tiny little baby jackets with the beautiful white buttons, because she didn't like to choose between blue and pink. The rabbit button was at the top, in pride of place.

When she came back from the hospital, empty-handed and dry-eyed after crying all her tears away, the first thing that Eileen did was to pick up her needle. "It makes me think of something else," she said to George. This time, she didn't make quite so many jackets before she was rushed to hospital again, some months before she was meant to have been. And it was a couple of months before she could bring herself to open the button box and tell herself she would give it one more go.

There was a bit of a black period after that, during which

Eileen failed to call in at Miss Molly's for several months. By the time she went back, Miss Molly had sold up and there was a new shop, which called itself *Spinning a Yarn*. The owner, a mean little woman with black beady button eyes, sold more wool than fabric. Its collection of buttons was very poor but it didn't matter. Well-wishers, unsure how to show their sympathy, often dropped off buttons for Eileen's collection just in case she felt like sewing again. Susie Martin suggested that, while she was waiting, how would she feel about making a dress for an important dinner that Susie had to go to. Someone else then asked for a skirt and suddenly, before Eileen knew it, she had built up a small, select number of customers even though her stomach remained slightly rounded but totally empty.

By the time George went off to fight in the war which everyone thought would never happen again, they had got over their disappointment. They had each other, they told themselves and Eileen had her little business. When George failed to come back, Eileen shut herself in her room for some weeks until emerging to continue her life almost as she had done before. This time, she had one more button in her box; a brass button from George's regiment suit which they had sent back to her. It was the one part of her beloved husband which no one could take away.

"Simply dreadful," moaned Virginia Hamble who used to be at school with Eileen and was now planning her teenage daughter's wedding. "I really need something nice to wear and I can't bear the thought of a trip to London. I don't suppose you have anything, do you, Eileen, with all those bits and pieces of yours?"

Eileen did and something inside her prompted her to offer to run up Virginia a rather clever little couture suit with fetching rose buttons that looked quite real. After that, Dinah from the pub asked if she would make her a skirt, not too smart but not too casual either. It sort of snowballed from there and, every time there were some buttons left over, Eileen put them into her button box which was almost overflowing until her mother, no spring chicken herself, donated hers.

She took both boxes with her of course, when her arthritis took over and everything else seemed to give up. They were very good in the home, about letting her bring her most precious possessions, thought Eileen, holding up the mother of pearl button to the light, to make sure that she had the right one. It was as beautiful as it had been the day she bought it and Clare thought so too.

"What a lovely button," she said, admiring it in the old lady's gnarled palm, "do you know, when I was younger, I thought they came from the beach."

"So did I," laughed Eileen. "And look at this. Have you ever seen such a sparkling blue in your life?"

"That's lovely," said Clare, squatting down at the old lady's side, and together they went through Eileen's box of memories. This was from the wedding where she had met her husband and this was from her niece's christening when she had made the gown.

Eileen liked Clare. She was much nicer than Zoe who was always turning up the television and putting her box of buttons away. "What's the point of her looking at them when she can't even see, any more?" she'd say to Clare. Clare knew there was no point in trying to explain. Mrs Mills might be blind now, but that didn't mean she couldn't see her memories. With that in mind Eileen certainly wouldn't have liked it if she had known it was Zoe who came in that morning, when she'd fallen asleep for a quick snooze before lunch. "Clare, quick," Zoe yelled out.

Clare took one look at the old lady and knew exactly what had happened. Gently she held her friend's cool hand and, somehow, she wasn't surprised when she found a large brass button inside it. It also seemed perfectly normal to find a small white button in the shape of a rabbit, sitting under the cushion of Mrs Mills's chair, as though she had

57

left it there, especially for her.

Clare kept the button carefully until her own baby daughter was born six months later. When little Eileen grew too big for the cardigan, she snipped off the rabbit and put it in her button box, an old Christmas biscuit tin. After all, she thought, she might not be able to sew much herself. But you never knew when it might come in useful.

The Button Box was originally published in *Woman's Weekly*.

Jane Bidder writes novels and short stories under the name of Sophie King. Titles include *The School Run*, which was a best-seller. She also runs writing workshops in the south-west and an online creative writing course as well as a manuscript critique service. Her next book, *How To Write Your Life Story In Ten Easy Steps* will be published at the end of 2010 by How To Books. For more details, visit her website www.sophieking.info.

To See a Man About a Dog
by Teresa Ashby

IF IT HADN'T BEEN for the red shoes, Pauline would never have twisted her ankle and, if she hadn't twisted her ankle, she would have passed by the empty shop without noticing the piano.

It stood back from the window in a sea of grey dust and the usual debris left behind when a shop is emptied in a hurry.

There was something terribly sad about it, but lately Pauline saw something sad in everything.

She gave her ankle a rub and hurried on. Dad would be waiting at home and he would worry if she was late.

Dazzled by the sun, she lowered her gaze to the cobbles and walked carefully. Pain pinched her ankle with every step, but she would walk through it just as she walked through everything.

The red shoes had been silly. An extravagance. But it had been so long since she'd desired anything the way she did those shoes.

Dad saw her looking at them in the catalogue. "I'll treat you," he'd said. "Go on. Order them."

He couldn't really afford them on a pension, but he'd insisted and they'd brought such a smile to his face.

"They look lovely," he'd said.

"Really? I could send them back ..."

"You'll do no such thing," he said. "I'm sorry I didn't

59

speak up for you when you were little and wanted red shoes."

She'd forgotten that, how she'd longed for red shoes and her mother had said they were impractical and bought her the brown lace-ups instead.

She could see him waiting for her to come home, a little way back from the window so that all you could see of him was the pale oval of his face.

She pushed open the gate and waved, she hoped cheerfully. He didn't wave back.

By the time she let herself in, he was standing in the hall.

"You were ages," he said.

In some ways he was like a child, the way he worried when she was away from him. But who could blame him? She was all he had left in a world that hadn't treated him very kindly.

"Sorry, Dad," she said, kicking off the red shoes and wincing when her heel touched the floor.

"You're limping. Have you hurt yourself?"

"No, I'm ..." she hesitated. "Yes, actually I twisted my ankle rather badly. It's quite painful."

"You should sit down, put your foot up. I'll make you a cup of tea."

Pauline let him help her into the lounge and watched as he pushed his footstool towards her.

He's eighty-six, she thought. A war hero. He's got gout and arthritis and he's suffering from depression and you've got him making you cups of tea?

She could hear his heavy, wheezy breathing as he moved about the kitchen, everything such an effort. She knew his hands would shake and he'd spill sugar on the worktop.

His life had been like that. One long hard slog. He'd been twenty when Pauline's sister was born in the middle of the war and he hadn't seen her until she was almost two.

Eunice didn't take to him at once. In fact she didn't take to him at all and before she could, he was sent away again.

After the war her parents tried for more children, but it seemed that Eunice was destined to remain an only child, a situation which pleased her no end.

Eunice was twenty when they found out that what her mother had thought was an early menopause was actually a second pregnancy. Eunice never forgave her parents for that and she particularly blamed her father since he was the one who was clearly so delighted about it all.

He'd been given a second chance. At last he had the baby he'd so yearned to hold in his arms. He doted on Pauline. He'd sit for hours with her on his lap at the piano, teaching her to play.

His joy had been short-lived. Illness and then redundancy had changed their lives. At home with too much time on his hands, he began to dwell on times past. Things he'd lived through years ago came back to haunt him.

But he escaped through the piano. He lost himself in his music, drifting away into a realm of peace as his hands moved across the keys.

Pauline would watch him belting out Tchaikovsky's Piano Concerto, the music swelling and filling her soul as if a whole orchestra was playing until sometimes it felt as if her chest would burst with emotion.

Eunice had divorced her first husband by then and was living back at home.

"Why do you put up with that racket, Mum?" she said. "Doesn't it drive you mad?"

"Well, your father …"

"If it wasn't for that, you could play your records and listen to music you like for a change."

Pauline was ten when she overheard that. She liked to play the piano too. She liked to hear her father play – it was the only time he seemed truly at peace with himself.

But Eunice was like a devil on her mother's shoulder.

"If it wasn't for that piano, you could have a nice display

unit for your ornaments. It's not fair that they have to be hidden away on dark shelves."

And then she got on to the money side of things.

"You'd make enough if you sold the piano to buy a nice unit and have some left over. If Dad's not going to work, it's hardly fair to expect you to be the one to make all the sacrifices."

But he did get work. It was only now and then work, but it brought in some much-needed extra money. The work was hard for a man who'd been ill and it took its toll on his health, but he would always look better after a session on the piano.

Pauline never forgot the day the piano went. Her father was away working and Eunice had arranged for someone to come round with a flatbed trailer.

The two men that came with the trailer bundled the piano out of the door, bumping it into the gate as they dragged it through.

"What's going on?" Pauline said. "Where's Dad's piano going?"

"Never you mind," Eunice said as the men bumped it down the path.

"Well I do mind," Pauline said boldly to this big sister who had always felt more like a miserable old aunt. "Is it going to be tuned? Can't the blind man come to do it any more?"

She'd seen the blind man tune the piano once. It was fascinating to watch. He'd shown her inside the piano and said that was where its heart really was, deep inside.

He wasn't really blind, but his sight was so bad that all he saw were shadows and shapes. He didn't see colour, he said, but when he listened to music he could see all the colours of the rainbow in his mind.

"Don't be stupid," Eunice said and just then a car pulled up. It was a reporter from the local paper and Eunice posed for photos beside the piano which was now being lashed to the trailer.

"Yes," Eunice preened. "It was my idea to donate the piano to the boys' home. I'm sure they'll get a lot of enjoyment from it just as my family has over the years."

"Enjoyment?" one of the men laughed. "They're going to smash it up! It'll make a great noise – get rid of a lot of that teenage angst they store up."

That same afternoon, the new unit was delivered. It wasn't beautiful and solid like the piano had been. It took up much less room and Pauline's mother seemed so happy as she arranged her ornaments and books along its shelves that Pauline felt guilty afterwards for bursting into tears.

"I do understand, love," her mother said and Pauline recalled the look of dismay on her mother's face as the men had handled the piano so brutally. "I didn't know they were taking it to smash it up, but it was too late to stop them."

"But what's Dad going to do without his piano?"

"There's one in the pub," Eunice said. "He can play on that. He spends enough time down there."

He didn't really. Just Saturday nights when he'd come home the worse for wear and singing. But after the piano went he was the worse for wear more often, but he wasn't singing any more.

He'd found another release for his inner demons and that brought with it fresh demons of its own.

It was there in the bottles hidden around the house and the bleary redness of her father's eyes.

By then Eunice had remarried and moved away, leaving the usual mess behind her.

"I can't put up with any more of this, Pauline," her mother said when Pauline was fifteen. "He's already driven Eunice away. I'm going to leave him. You can come with me or …"

What choice did she have? They moved out of the area and into a flat near Eunice.

He shuffled into the room, the cup rattling in its saucer.

"There you are, love," he said. "Nice and hot just how you like it. How's the ankle feeling?"

She looked up at him and smiled. After her mother died, Pauline went in search of her father. He'd moved away from the family home and it took four years of searching to find him, even though she wasn't even sure that he was still alive.

But alive he was, living in a shelter for the homeless and sleeping in a dormitory with other men.

And he wasn't drinking.

Pauline had to break the news that her mother had died and, even after all those years of separation, he wept.

"Eunice?" he asked when at last his eyes were dry.

"I don't know. We've lost touch," Pauline said and he said it was a shame, but all the same there was relief in his eyes.

He'd been with Pauline ever since, but without the drink he'd lost his confidence.

She sipped the tea. He made a grand cup of tea and she smiled at him. His eyes crinkled in reply.

She thought of the piano, bereft and abandoned in the empty shop. Left behind. Probably no room on the removal truck when the owners moved out.

"I'm going out again, Dad," she said when she'd finished her tea. "I won't be long."

"Where are you going?" The anxious look was back.

"To see a man about a dog," she laughed. It was what he used to say to her when she asked where he was going, when he was on his way to the pub.

This time she wore trainers and took the car. First stop: the estate agents who had a sale board in the shop window.

"The piano?" the estate agent said. "They didn't want it. You want to buy it? I think they'd be grateful to you for taking it away."

"Another question," she said. "Any idea where I can hire a flatbed trailer or a van?"

Her father was asleep when she arrived home. She moved around him, shifting furniture, making a space large enough for the piano.

It was a beautiful thing with three decorated panels across the top and three plain ones underneath. The colour was rich under the dust, mahogany, Pauline thought, but she wasn't sure.

She paid the men who carried it in and when they'd gone, her father was sitting up, awake, staring at the piano in wonder.

"Is it real?"

She helped him up, pulled up a chair and sat him in front of it. Reverently he opened the lid. He didn't need music to play. He never had. He closed his eyes and let his fingers drift over the keys.

She rested her hands on his shoulders, kissed the top of his head where the hair was thin so you could see his freckled scalp.

"I'm so sorry I ever let them take away your music," she whispered.

But he wasn't listening. He began to play. Eyes closed. Tchaikovsky's piano concerto, heart and soul, not a note out of place.

Beautiful. She could listen to him for ever, but for now it was just a sunny Saturday afternoon. A perfect day.

To See a Man About a Dog was originally published in *Woman's Weekly Fiction Special 2006*

Teresa Ashby has been writing pocket novels, short stories and serials since the 1980s. Some of her stories have been published in anthologies including *100 Stories for Haiti*, In the *Shadow of the Red Queen* and *Spooked*.

She lives on the Essex coast with her family and her dogs.

The Wedding Guest
by Gerry Savill

HE STOOD BY HIMSELF at the back of the hall, content just to observe the revelries of the other guests. No one spoke to him, they barely glanced in his direction and he preferred it that way. He knew he really shouldn't be there but he had to see for himself.

She looked radiant, as he knew she would. Cream silk cascaded onto the floor, a concoction of French antique lace and beads. Tiny crystals glistened as they caught the rays of the sun when she moved. The perfect day for a perfect bride.

"Champagne?" a waiter asked the group of guests near him; a tray of bubbling glasses balanced on his hand.

They took a glass each and the waiter moved on, passing him. He watched as they all raised their glasses to the bride across the hall. She saw them and waved but remained where she was. She continued her conversation, her head tilting to the side as it always did when she was concentrating. He had always loved that gesture.

A deep resonant voice announced that dinner was to be served. Everyone sat down to eat, laughing and happy. Impeccable white tablecloths adorned tables laden with gleaming silver cutlery and decorated with bouquets of fragrant summer blooms artfully arranged in intricate designs. He knew she had probably spent hours deciding how to arrange the flowers.

A superb array of food was presented, all carefully chosen and cooked to perfection. Pink salmon that flaked at the touch of the fork; succulent beef and al dente vegetables, and a divine melt-in-the-mouth chocolate mousse. The finest vintage wines were served to complement the fare. Only the best would grace this wedding.

During the meal he caught snatches of conversation.

"Don't they make a wonderful couple?"

"They've bought a delightful cottage in the village."

"Off to the coast for their honeymoon."

"I wonder how long it will be before we hear the patter of tiny feet?"

The voices drifted in and out of his hearing. He didn't want to hear how happy the lucky couple would be.

After the food and speeches everyone mingled. He tried to melt into the wall as the bride came towards him. Her cheeks were pink against her creamy skin, as if she had had one too many glass of champagne. She giggled at a bridesmaid's joke. Her eyes darted around the room as if she was looking for someone, losing her concentration for a moment. She looked almost sad. Her eyes came in his direction but glanced straight past him. A hand was placed on her arm and once more she became the consummate hostess.

He wandered around the edges of the hall, unnoticed. The presents were piled high, waiting to be opened. Inside the richly beribboned parcels he could imagine the type of thing she would have asked for: exquisite cut glass, delicate china, fine linens.

Meandering through the knots of guests he found himself in front of the wedding cake. A tower of icing, decorated with tiny lilac roses, her favourite colour. The flowers looked so lifelike that he was sure that he would draw blood from his finger if he touched one of the icing thorns. He moved swiftly out of the way as two waitresses came in to slice the cake up ready for the guests to take home. He watched as they carefully wrapped each piece in a lilac linen napkin, securing them with silver ribbon.

A flock of crisply dressed waiters appeared, to move the tables for dancing. A band struck up a lively tune and the guests were up on their feet, flying around the room to the beat of the music. He tapped his foot to the rhythm, not keeping in time. He was hopeless at dancing. She had tried to teach him but had failed. As he watched her now, twirling around the floor, laughing, so happy, he wished he had tried harder.

The evening was drawing in, the sky turning to the colour of an old bruise. The day was coming to an end. It seemed that dancing had only just begun when the band leader announced the last dance of the night, inviting the bride and groom on to the floor for the last slow dance. He watched as she walked by herself to the middle of the dance floor and stopped. Gradually the images around him faded. The guests, the band, the furniture, all disappeared until only she was left in the middle of the hall, alone.

Finally she looked at him and smiled. She held out her hand for him and he went to her. Her skin was cool to the touch. He looked down at her delicate young fingers, clasped in his old, gnarled hand, spotted with age.

Suddenly he felt a hand on his shoulder and a familiar kindly voice in his ear.

"Here you are then, you had us all worried. Wandering off like that." The voice of Nurse Louise from the home shattered the final image of his love and then she too was gone

"We always know where to find you when you disappear don't we? I really don't know why you keep coming to this old place. It's practically falling down. I can't believe the council haven't demolished it yet. It's an eyesore and from the smell I think something has crawled into a corner and died." She wrinkled her nose in disgust.

"Now come on, let's get you into the wheelchair. It's a long walk back to the home."

He let himself be helped into the chair, suddenly feeling his bones aching with cold and age. As the nurse pushed him towards the door he held up his hand to stop her.

"Let me have one last look, please."

"Of course, dear. Did you come here a lot when you were a lad? I think it was the village hall or something like that." She turned the wheelchair around.

The room was now empty, just the debris of an old village hall strewn about in disarray. From the middle of the once highly polished wooden floor erupted a volcano of rot where the rain had come in through the hole in the roof. Nobody would ever dance here again.

Then just for a moment he was transported again to how it should have been. For a second he saw the guests seated at tables, heard music playing and there she was, his bride, as beautiful as ever. But it faded swiftly and once again he was alone. This day never was, was never to be.

She had been taken from him before this magical day had arrived, the many hours they had spent planning it forgotten in the ensuing maelstrom of grief. The crippling illness that had grabbed her had wreaked havoc on her once beautiful body. Mercifully the disease had claimed her quickly, not letting her suffer for too long. He had wanted to kill everyone who kept telling him it was for the best, that she hadn't suffered, it was a blessing in disguise. He screamed at them; how could they say that. Her passing had broken him. He wanted her back; then and now.

Everyone said time was a healer but it wasn't for him. He had waited as the decades passed for his pain to stop and his heart to heal. It never did. Now he waited to go to her. He hoped it would be soon.

The Wedding Guest was second place in the National Association of Writing Group Short Story competition in July 2008.

Gerry Savill has had several short stories published and feels privileged to have won a few competitions. As well as writing she enjoys gardening, researching her family tree and playing darts for a ladies team with her friends. She lives in Gravesend, Kent and works as an HR Administrator for the Ellenor Lions Hospices.

New Beginnings
by Francesca Burgess

IT WAS ALWAYS THE same at this time of year for Liz. Spring brought new blossoms, longer days, warmer weather, Easter eggs – and hassle.

'Oh, come on, Mum,' said her son Peter. 'You know you enjoy the speedway racing when you get there.'

She wasn't sure where he'd got that impression from. Probably from the smile she kept plastered on when they were there, so as not to put a damper on things.

'Trouble is, I said to Dory that I might be able to help at the Easter Monday project, doing the crafts for the kids.'

'But you did that last year. It's our turn to have you this year.'

He was right. Liz normally did turn and turn about, one Easter Monday with the family at the motor bike racing, and one with the project. She didn't know how she'd got into the rut. *Probably trying to please everyone.*

'I'll give it some thought. OK?'

Peter shrugged his shoulders, sloping away with his head hung low, like his jeans.

The phone rang about twenty minutes later, just as Liz was getting the veg on for tea.

'Oh, hello Dory.'

'Liz. We really *do* need you. We've five crafts that no one else has got time to put together.'

'Are you short of volunteers then?'

'No, dear, not at all. Most are OK as helpers, but don't have your flair in creativity.'

'I guess if –'

'Wonderful! Now, we need an Easter card, a craft with a chick, something easy to make that they can eat, something involving lambs and something they can hang in the window. The theme this year is New Beginnings.'

'OK, but –'

'And of course it has to be different to the things we've done the last five years. '

'So I'll –'

'I'll leave it to you then. You're indispensable, darling! See you at setting up, 9 a.m., Easter Monday. Ciao!'

And she was gone. *Don't you just hate it when someone does that?* she thought.

'I suppose it relieves me of the decision,' she said, returning to the kitchen to find the water boiling away and the room filled with steam.

'This is nice,' said Liz at dinner that evening, referring to all four of them sitting around as a family.

'It would be if Peter wasn't woofing his food down like a pig,' complained Katie.

'What? I'm hungry!' Peter mumbled through too much mashed potato.

'Ugh, don't talk with your mouth full. It's disgusting.'

'Good news, Liz,' her husband Neil said, ignoring his children's quarrel. 'The details for the speedway have come up on the website. 'It begins at 2 p.m., so we'll have to leave at 11.30, in case of traffic.'

'Neil, I've already told Dory I'll do the Easter Monday project.'

'But you did it last year.'

'I know, but apparently I'm indispensable.'

'Oh, Mum, no one's indispensable,' said Katie. 'Anyway, it's not fair.'

'No, what's not fair is your father working from Good Friday to Easter Sunday, *again*. We could have done something as a family on one of those days. You worked those days last year, Neil.'

'I can't turn down good money.'

'You could have worked Saturday to Monday.'

'And miss the speedway?'

Liz sighed. No point having this circular argument again.

'Anyway,' she said, 'you can still go without me.'

'But it's a family thing,' said Katie. 'You're always banging on about doing things as a *family*.'

'Perhaps you could come and help me for a change, then.'

'No way!' said Peter.

'It's not really our thing,' said Neil.

And speedway isn't mine either, she thought.

By 7.30 on Easter Monday morning, Liz had her five boxes of materials ready to go. She always liked to be organised well in advance, and had spent the last two weeks retrieving materials from the loft, left over from previous projects, as well as sourcing new ones.

The rest of the family were still in bed. *Shame,* she thought, as she opened the living room curtains. *It's such a lovely day, too. Pity I'll be stuck indoors.*

She sat at the table, eating her cereal and reading the papers from Saturday. As she turned a page, a brightly coloured flyer fell out. It turned out to be a seed catalogue, with lots of vivid photos of flowers. She thought of the carpet of bluebells that would be in the woods at Simion's Garden, a few miles away, not to mention the splendour of the informal gardens and bushes. They'd often taken the kids there when they were young. They loved their adventures in the woods and getting lost in the hedged maze. They'd buy afternoon tea and cakes, then sit on one of the wooden benches outside, admiring the views down the valley and to the hills beyond. She missed that.

She took her bowl to the kitchen, an idea developing in her head.

If only. But, why not?

Liz walked to the computer and clicked it on. She could quickly type up some easy-to-follow instructions for each craft. That way she could please all of the people, as the saying went. She printed up several sheets and loaded them in her car with the boxes.

At the church hall, she placed a box on each table. Dory swooped down on her as soon as she saw her.

'I've put detailed instructions with each craft,' Liz said.

'We'll station you over –'

'I won't be here.'

'But what if someone doesn't –?'

'I couldn't work with more than one table at a time anyway. You do have plenty of volunteers, don't you?'

'Yes, but –'

'Then that's OK then. Let me know how it goes. Bye now.'

She was gone before Dory could get another word in. *Don't you just hate it when someone does that?* she thought, grinning all the way to her car.

Now to tell the troops the good news. When she reached the house, she sat in the car for a number of minutes, just thinking. Finally, she said to herself, 'But do I want to please all of the people, all of the time? What about me?'

At ten past ten, Katie picked up a large A4 note, written in red marker pen, from the bottom of the stairs.

'Look, Dad, a note from Mum.'

'*Dear family,*' Katie read. '*Have decided to give the Easter project a miss. As Katie said, no one's indispensable.*'

'Brilliant!' said Peter. 'So she's coming with us.'

Katie read on. '*Have decided to spend the day at*

75

Simion's Garden. After all, Easter is about new beginnings, and this is mine. See you later. Love Mum xx.

New Beginnings was originally published in *The Weekly News*, April 2009:

Francesca Burgess has had several short stories published in magazines in the UK and abroad. She has also been placed or shortlisted in a number of national competitions. In 2010 she had a story included in the charity anthology *100 Stories for Haiti*. A long-time student of Elaine Everest's, she now helps her run The Write Place Creative Writing School. Currently she is completing a second teen novel under her maiden name Francesca Capaldi.

Love Lessons
by Sue Moorcroft

"HOW MUCH IS IT to travel from London to Manchester, by train?" enquires Tomasz, amiably. He swizzles the final screw into the switch he's assembling, flicks down the white plastic cover and sticks on an *03/34* label before placing the completed unit on the belt running down the middle of the line. When enough units are on the belt all those shiny new switch assemblies will glide off to Packing.

"Too much for my pocket," I answer, idly, knowing he's not listening. My label is *03/33*.

"Is it cheaper by coach?" He selects a fresh switch housing from the tray between us. His dark expressive eyes fix on his work; his mind is as busy as his dextrous fingers because his earphones are delivering English lessons into his ears and he, apparently oblivious to us all, is diligently repeating what he learns.

"Yes, but I get motion sickness." Across the line, Shelli and Wendy grin at me. They're getting used to my odd conversations with Tomasz.

"Or perhaps I could hire a car?"

"Oh, have you got a British licence?" I drop a completed unit onto the belt.

Tomasz's fingers dance over silver screws and copper contact strips. He hasn't been here long but he's lightning on switch assemblies. Whatever he did in his native Poland, he has more skills than he needs for Line 03 at R F

Switches.

"Won't be long before *he's* promoted," observes Wendy.

"He can't be a supervisor until his English is better. That's why …" I nod at his earphones and the threadlike wires to the mp3 player clipped to his belt.

Tomasz takes up his soldering iron. "A car is expensive but flezzy." He frowns.

"Flexible?" I prompt.

He pauses to fiddle with the mp3 player. "A car is expensive but *flezzible*. Flezzible. Flezzible."

"Flezzible. Flezzible," repeats Shelli in a deep, rolling voice like Tomasz's.

"Tough word," I commiserate. "You're doing really well." I raise a reproving eyebrow at Shelli. Tomasz shows no sign of hearing but I wouldn't want his feelings to be hurt. After all, who else is doing anything to expand their brains? Mostly, we talk about what we did last night – which is not much, in my case.

Tomasz is in a foreign land, doing an unfamiliar job. He's living with his sister, Marika, who's been married to an English guy, Charlie, for years. Marika works here, in Sales, so she gets plenty of practice with her English, wearing a telephone headset in a glass box at the end of the factory with the rest of the sales team. It was Marika who asked me to share a workstation with Tomasz. "Tomasz hasn't got much English, yet, but he learns fast. You'll keep your eyes on him, Lizzy, won't you?"

"'Course. I feel for anyone trying to fit in."

After Marika scurried off to her glass box, Wendy and Shelli were full of warnings. "You'll be babysitting him for months." But when he turned up on the Monday, with his thick black curly hair and piercing eyes, they blew out their cheeks and sighed, "Crafty thing! He's gorgeous!" a bit sorry they hadn't volunteered to help.

Tomasz replaces his soldering iron carefully. "I don't know the area. I don't know the area. Air-ee-ah."

"Me, neither." I plonk down another unit stickered *03/33*. Wendy and Shelli are occupied in groaning over their teenage daughters so I confide, "We'd only just moved to this air-ee-ah when Darren decided he needed to change his life. Would've been handy if he'd realised before we'd bought a house here."

But Wendy's ears can multitask. "Can't you go back down south, then?"

I shrug, flushing. I haven't discussed Darren here, before. I feel a bit of a fool, to be honest, the way he took off. "Not with the housing market, not really."

"Credit crunch." Shelli cocks her head, sagely.

"Yes, and I'm sick of it." I watch my completed unit glide off to Packing, leaving us on Line 03 staring at an empty belt as if we haven't been beavering away since eight this morning. I shouldn't be here at all but my 'proper job' in an estate agency … well, that was credit crunched, too. I'm just grateful that R F Switches doesn't employ robots on the production line instead of people. "Darren took redundancy – from the job that was the reason we moved up here – bought a backpack and snazzy walking boots and set off around the world." Without me, I don't have to add.

"Take the money and run!" booms Tomasz.

I jump. "You're on today's sayings, now, are you? Yes, well, that's pretty much what he did."

Wendy giggles. "Do you remember when Joe the supervisor came back from a dentist appointment and was cross that productivity had dropped? And there was Tomasz going on about, 'When the cat's away, the mice will play!'" Tomasz looks up at our laughter and grins.

"Good job Tomasz's productivity is the best on the line. None of his switches ever get sent back by Quality Control." I achieve a lovely neat solder on contact 1c. When I first came here I was always having stuff returned because of wobbly soldering.

"And good job that you stuck up for him." Shelli begins

a new unit. "Or Joe would have made him do his English lessons at home."

As if summoned, Joe appears at the end of the line in the navy smock of the supervisor. "BREAK 03!" he shouts. "Be back on time, please."

I tap Tomasz's arm.

"Don't shoot the messenger," he says, unpopping one earphone, enquiringly.

"No need, it's good news. Break time, Tomasz." I make a drinking motion.

"Break," he repeats, with a slow smile. "Break is good." I blink. I bet he wasn't short of girlfriends in Poland with a smile like that.

He hops from his seat and bows me past him. He's formal and old-fashioned compared to the other men in the factory. In the queue, he says, carefully, "It's time for tea."

"Great!" I pat his arm. I told him that on Friday and he's remembered it over the weekend.

At the counter, he addresses the server before I can. "One tea, one white coffee, pliz thank you." He beams at me and selects two brown sachets. "Two sugar."

"Thank you." That's what I ordered on Friday. I meant to have a cold drink today! But, never mind, I don't want to discourage him.

We join a crowd at a round table and I feel a bit sorry for Tomasz, probably understanding not more than one word in ten in the hubbub around him. At least I understand the language, even if I don't know the parts of town everyone's nattering about. Instead of joining in the discussion about pulling down one of the comprehensive schools thrown up in the seventies, I point to a red dot creeping along the edge of the table. "Ladybird, Tomasz."

Tomasz gazes at it and pulls a face. "Lady*bird*?" He pulls his green Polish-English dictionary from his pocket and I find *ladybird* for him. He looks perplexed, probably at seeing two words he already knows joined together to make

80

the name of a creature he can see is not a bird. And possibly isn't a lady, either.

Unfortunately, some of the lads further round the table begin to teach Tomasz words that will get him into trouble if repeated in front of the wrong person. Sometimes, Tomasz learns *too* quickly.

"Stop it!" I snap at them. "Don't say it, Tomasz, they're swearing."

His eyes flick from me to the lads.

I pull a reproving face. "Bad words!"

His brow clears. He wiggles his eyebrows at the lads. "Bad words. You joke!"

They all laugh, too. "That's right, Tomasz. It's just a joke."

Back at the bench, Tomasz plugs himself into his English lesson for the final stretch of the shift. "I have lived here for a month."

"Nine months for me." I reach for a housing as the break time chatter simmers down to a hum. "Nine *months*."

"I like this air-ee-ah."

"There's lots to do, I suppose. Shops and entertainment. But it's not much fun, on your own. Mr Samways is coming." I try not to groan. I'm not keen on Mr Samways. He's got these antiquated 'organisation and methods' notions that seem to consist of asking us all questions that apparently serve no purpose but to trip us up so that he can give us yellow 'feedback forms' and come back the next day to ask the same question again. This is meant to reinforce good working practice but if you get too many questions wrong, it can mean a warning. I watch him working his way up the line. When he gets to me he picks out a screw from the blue tray. "Which screwdriver would you use for this size of screw?"

"The blue one, because the screw came out of the blue tray." And yellow for screws out of the yellow tray and so on. It's not difficult.

"Good!" Mr Samways sounds unflatteringly surprised that my answer's correct. Then, to Tomasz, "Which screw and screwdriver is the most appropriate to use to secure the live to contact 4b?"

Mr Samways knows that Tomasz is only just learning English. He's asked the question in a deliberately complex form. Tomasz would know the answer to the question – if he only understood it.

Behind Mr Samways' back I point to the soldering iron and mouth, "This."

Tomasz flourishes his own iron. "I zolder!"

"Um, yes, good. You'd solder it." Mr Samways looks disappointed not to be able to write out a yellow form.

Tomasz plugs back in to his earphones. "Do you think I came in on the banana boat?" he demands.

Mr Samways snaps round to stare but Tomasz is already busy soldering and has dropped back into his English-lesson drone. "Bah-nar-nar. Bah-nar-nar. Thanks," he chants. "Thank you. Thank you very much. You saved my bacon." He glances at me and winks.

I drop my eyes back to my work before Mr Samways can see laughter in my eyes. It's always funny when Tomasz's repetitions fit into the situation.

I have an hour's overtime, today, so Line 03 is half empty. It's been a long day and I'm glad when Tomasz begins on phrases I haven't heard before.

"Do you like the cinema?" In his lovely, deep, accented English, it's, "Do you liiiiiiiiike ze zinnymah?"

"Love it," I say, wondering how many *03/33* units have gone to Packing today and if it's enough to tick the right boxes with Mr Samways. And whether any are lurking in the return tray in Quality Control.

"I like the cinema. We go togezzer, tonight? We see a good film and we eat a pizza. I have money in my bockets, now I have job. We go – Marika and Charlie go, also?"

I pause in reaching for the soldering iron. Either Tomasz's English lessons have got uncannily appropriate or ...

He's smiling. His earphones lie idle on the workbench. "You are kind," he says. "We see good film togezzer?"

I become aware of Marika hovering behind him and that she's grinning, too. "Fancy a foursome, Lizzy? Tomasz made me coach him on the English to ask you out. He's always raving on about how kind you are."

"Then you not be on own at home," adds Tomasz, his dark eyes compelling.

"Oh!" A huge blush rushes up from my toes to the crown of my head. Just how much of what I've said has Tomasz understood?

Suddenly I'm shy at the idea of sitting beside him in the darkness of the cinema, even though I sit next to him all day. But then I think of going home to a silent house and a meal for one ... "I'd love to."

He offers me his arm, responding in his English lessons voice, "Love conquers all."

"Oh! I mean I'd *like* to," I clarify, hastily. I'll have to remember that Tomasz still needs plenty of English lessons.

But then he winks ...

Love Lessons was originally published in *Woman's Weekly*.

Over 130 of **Sue Moorcroft's** short stories have appeared in magazines and anthologies worldwide. Her 'how to' book, *Love Writing – How to Make Money From Writing Romantic or Erotic Fiction* (Accent Press) complements her recent novels *Want to Know a Secret?*, *Starting Over* and *All That Mullarkey* (Choc Lit). She's the editor of *Loves Me, Loves Me Not,* a short story anthology celebrating 50 years of the Romantic Novelists' Association, writes serials, articles and courses, is the head judge for *Writers' Forum* and for the H E Bates Award 2010 and has won the Katie Fforde Bursary Award.

Breaking Point
by Kathleen McGurl

"JEMMA'S BEEN SUSPENDED FROM school."

It was not the sort of news I liked to be greeted with, as I struggled through the door with five bags of grocery shopping.

"Oh my God. What for?" I asked my husband Mike as I dumped the bags in the kitchen.

"She was caught shoplifting in her lunch break. She was wearing her uniform, prefect badge and all. The Head's furious. *I'm* furious, Sue." Mike thumped the kitchen table, making the apples in the fruit bowl bounce.

I felt more resigned than furious. It was just another thing to deal with. How much more were we expected to take? It had been two months since Tommy's road accident but there was no sign of him being allowed home yet. I'd been more or less living at the hospital, leaving our older children – fifteen-year-old Jemma and thirteen-year-old Nathan – fending for themselves at home until Mike got in from work. At least, Nathan was *supposed* to be fending for himself at home, but he'd taken to running off somewhere every couple of days.

"Where is she?" I asked, as I began to put the shopping away. I wanted to get back to the hospital for the evening's visiting hours. And I needed to have words with Nathan about his disappearing acts.

"Upstairs." Mike went through to the living room,

leaving the shopping on the table.

I set off up the stairs to see her, framing a ticking-off in my head. Why did she do it? Didn't she realise how hard it was for me and her dad, with one child bashed and broken in hospital and another who keeps being brought home by friends' parents and on one occasion, the police. Didn't she realise how hard it was for *me*, having to deal with all this, as well as a husband who responded to each new crisis with anger followed by abdication.

But when I got to Jemma's room the door was closed and barricaded, and a muffled voice called out, "Just go away, Mum, all right? I'm sorry, whatever, but spare me the lecture right now. I can't face it."

I decided I couldn't face it either, so I took a leaf out of her book, went into my own room and shut the door. I lay on the bed, face in my pillow, and sobbed. How much more? I wished time could be suspended while I dealt with one problem at a time. Better still, if time could be wound back, and I could catch hold of Tommy's arm *before* he ran across the road in front of that van …

That was when it had all started. Tommy had broken both arms, one leg, and had damaged some vertebrae. He'd had to lie flat on his back for the last two months, with his leg in traction. I'd slept in a bed beside him in the hospital for the first week. Since then, I'd been spending every moment possible at his side. I felt so helpless, but being with him was all I could do.

Nathan. I remembered I'd wanted a talk with him before going back to the hospital. Reluctantly I heaved myself off the bed and went to his room, picking up socks and underpants from the floor on the way.

He wasn't there. I headed downstairs. "Mike, where's Nathan?"

"In his room," Mike grunted, looking annoyed that I'd interrupted him watching the news.

"No, he's not."

86

"Well he was when I came home. If that lad's run off again I'll …" I winced as the TV remote control bounced off the floor and fell apart, its batteries scattering.

"Bet that blinking thing won't work now," Mike grumbled. "Aren't you supposed to be back at the hospital now? And what did Jemma have to say about the suspension?"

I'm not sure what happened next. Time stopped while I completely lost control. I opened my mouth, and screamed. Simply screamed, long, loud and hard.

Jemma came charging down the stairs and stood open-mouthed, watching me. Mike stared, his mouth opening and closing like a goldfish. And still I screamed, until my throat protested and I had to stop.

For a moment the silence was intense. We all just looked at each other. Then I grabbed my purse and keys, and left the house.

Should I go to the hospital where Tommy was expecting me or go looking for Nathan?

I did neither. Instead, I got in my car and drove. Southwards, out of town, towards the coast. I parked in a cliff-top car park, got out of the car and stood, in the dark, on the cliff edge.

"Why?" I shouted into the wind. "Why us? Why me? Why does all this have to happen to my family? How am I supposed to deal with it all?"

There was a bench nearby. I sat down, leaned back and let the wind blow my hair back from my face. If only my troubles could be blown away as easily.

"Come on, Sue," I told myself. "Get a grip."

But I needed some time.

For the thousandth time I relived the moment when that anonymous white van hit Tommy and drove off. The hours which followed – frantic phone calls from hospital corridors. Stroking Tommy's face as he lay sedated under a crisp sheet. Calming Mike down, when he wanted to go searching for the white van – any white van – so he could punch the driver. Explaining what had happened to Jemma and Nathan.

I thought about the weeks since. Those endless hours at the hospital, keeping Tommy company while his bones knitted themselves back together. Rushing around at home, trying to keep on top of the housework and shopping so the rest of the family could get on with their lives.

Gradually I began to realise that in dealing with Tommy's accident I had cut out the rest of the family. When had I last talked to Jemma or Nathan apart from to shout at them or tell them off? When had I last spent time with Mike, other than passing him in the hallway as he came in from work and I headed to the hospital? And maybe his anger was simply caused by his own feelings of helplessness – feelings I knew only too well.

My family, not just Tommy, was broken, and it was up to me to mend it.

The fresh night air had worked its magic and calmed me down. A quick couple of phone calls assured me Nathan was safe and well at a friend's house, and would be dropped home later. Jemma was still sulking but Mike's anger had dissipated. I was free to go and visit Tommy.

It was a thirty-minute journey to the hospital. When I arrived Tommy was sitting up with his back brace on and his broken leg stretched along the bed. His arm casts had been taken off a couple of days before, and he was enjoying being able to move a bit more and play with his Transformers.

"Mum, I had fizzy-therapy today, they made me stretch my arms like this!" Tommy stretched his arms up and out, narrowly missing knocking his glass of water from the bedside cabinet. "I've got to practise every hour to get my muscles back."

"Well done, darling! Soon you'll be my little Superman again. Now you've got your back brace fitted I hope you'll be able to come home soon."

"Good. I miss home. I even miss Jemma, a bit. And Nathan, but I bet he still won't let me go on his Playstation."

"He will. I'll make sure of that." A vision of Tommy back home, curled in a beanbag while he played on the Playstation brought tears to my eyes. I wanted it so much.

I played with him a while, read him a story and helped get him ready to sleep. Before leaving I put away his toys and kissed him goodnight. Soon I hoped I'd be able to do that in our own home.

Back home, Mike was halfway through a bottle of wine and a DVD. The kids were in their rooms. I poured myself a glass and sat down beside him.

"Tommy's on good form," I said.

"That's great," he replied. "And you're not screaming."

"Not any more," I said, smiling. "Sorry I lost it earlier. It's the strain."

Mike took my hand and squeezed it. "I know, love. Sorry I was angry. Same excuse, I guess."

I squeezed his hand in return. "Better go and talk to our errant kids. Save me some wine."

I went to Nathan's room first. He was in bed, reading his collection of Beano comics.

"Hi, Nathan," I said. "I hear you were at Jake's this evening. Did you have a good time?"

"Yeah, s'pose," he said, looking at me defensively.

"Nathan, look. It's fine for you to go to your friends' houses. Just tell us where you are, please."

"You're never here to tell."

"I know. I'm sorry. But you could leave a note. So we know, and we don't worry. Deal?"

He looked stunned that I hadn't shouted at him, like I had the last few times he'd pulled this stunt.

"Deal?" I asked again.

He smiled – that lopsided shy smile which never failed

to tug at my heartstrings. "Deal, Mum."

We shook on it, and I went to tackle Jemma next. She was draped face down across her bed, her eyes smudged black with mascara and dried tears. I suspected she'd been there all evening.

"Tell me," I asked quietly, perching on her homework desk, "what happened."

To my astonishment my tough teenage daughter climbed off her bed and flung her arms around my neck, sobbing.

"It was a transformer. That Optimus Prime one Tommy's always wanted. It was the last one on the shelf and I didn't have the money. I'd have gone back tomorrow to pay for it, I would have, really."

"You stole it for Tommy?"

"I miss him, Mum. I wanted to send him something to play with now he's got his arms back. I tried to explain to the security guard but he wouldn't listen. Neither would the Headmistress."

"I'll phone her tomorrow. I understand why you did it but, Jemma …"

"I know. I won't do it again." She grabbed a handful of tissues from her box and blew her nose loudly. "I thought you'd shout at me, Mum."

I hugged her tight. I'd clearly been doing far too much shouting lately.

The phone rang, calling me back downstairs. It was the hospital, making an appointment for me to meet with Tommy's doctor the next morning. When I heard what he wanted to discuss, I found myself grinning broadly.

"Jemma, Nathan, come downstairs for a minute," I called.

Mike looked up in surprise as we all traipsed into the living room. The kids looked terrified. Perhaps they thought their parents were playing good cop, bad cop.

"Pause the DVD," I said to Mike. "I've got something to say."

Mike pressed a button on the remote. "Go on."

"I'm meeting Dr Millbank tomorrow. To discuss when Tommy can come home."

Nathan whooped, Jemma squealed, but my eyes were on Mike. His face broke gradually into a wide grin. "Sue, that's fantastic!" He raised his glass and clinked mine. As he enfolded me in a bear-hug, I realised it wasn't just Tommy's broken bones that were finally healing. Our family life had fallen apart for a while but with Tommy home we'd be able to get back on track. We'd pull through, all of us together, I was sure of it.

Breaking Point was originally published as *Mum On The Edge* in *Take A Break's Fiction Feast*, September 2009.

Kathleen McGurl lives by the sea in Bournemouth, and writes in the time remaining after slotting in a full time job, bringing up two teenage boys, and caring for a disabled mother. She writes short fiction for women's magazines and is currently also working on a historical novel, which grew out of an obsession with family history research.

Office Hours
by Linda Lewis

SOMETIMES, AS I SIT here, writing crime novels, I think of the years I wasted, writing romance. If Bernard hadn't come along, I would probably still be at Honeydew Cottage, battling with the bills.

It's so much easier to write here. For a start, I don't get half as many interruptions.

It started one grey February morning.

I'd had another bad night. Even sleeping tablets hadn't helped. If I took one, nothing happened. If I took two, I was out like a light and still half asleep hours after getting up. My latest attempt at writing a romantic novel was turning into yet another uphill climb. I had no trouble selling short stories, but if I wanted to make any real money writing, I needed a book deal.

I'd hardly got started when the phone rang. It was my son asking about Sunday lunch.

"Is it OK if we get to you about one instead of twelve-thirty?"

"Yes of course it is, darling," I said as politely as I could. I told him I was too busy to chat and paused in what I hoped was a meaningful fashion. "Unless it's urgent, could you call me in the evenings or at weekends? You know I like to keep office hours."

Sam sighed at me. After all he'd heard me say exactly the same thing many times before.

He had no time for my writing. He called it my 'little hobby' as though I only wrote for fun. He had no idea what a struggle it had been since Mike died. The steady trickle of short-story sales kept the wolf from the door, but only just. Sam would have known that if he'd bothered to ask, but he assumed that, because I was a widow, I was well-off.

Eventually he hung up and I went back to my work.

I was just getting in the mood, thinking about my hero's kissable lips when the doorbell rang.

It was the window cleaner.

"Just letting you know I'm here," he said, with a huge smile on his face.

I bit back the obvious retort that when he cleaned the window to my office, I would have had trouble NOT seeing him. I offered to pay him before he started work to save being interrupted later.

"Don't worry, Mrs H," he said. "I'll knock when I've finished."

I grabbed his arm and made him take the money there and then.

He tapped the side of his nose in a conspiratorial manner. "I see, busy writing another bodice-ripper, are you?"

It was then I started to feel angry.

I'd just made my way back upstairs when the phone rang, again.

It was Dora, from across the road, prattling on about something or other. I told her I was busy writing.

"Oh that's all right then. You can write any time, can't you?"

I practically bit her head off.

"Maybe I COULD write at four in the morning or at midnight, but I prefer to write from nine to five. Goodbye!" I banged the phone down and went back to work.

Of course, it was useless. All those interruptions had completely spoilt the mood. I remember sitting there, staring at the blank screen, thinking dark thoughts. It took ages before I could even think about starting work again, but the moment my fingers touched the keys, the doorbell rang.

I ran down the stairs, fuming, and threw open the door to find Bernard Norton standing there. Of course, I didn't recognise him at first. Before I had time to react, he'd stepped into my hall.

"Dreadful weather," he said.

"Do I know you?" I snapped.

He smiled and took off his coat. "Bernard Norton. We met at the Writer's Club."

I'd stopped going to the Club two years ago. I couldn't remember Bernard and said as much. I asked him to leave, but he just laughed.

"I'm not surprised you don't remember me. I only went twice."

I stood there with the front door wide open, and an icy blast roaring through, but he took not the slightest bit of notice. He just carried on talking. "You might remember my novel – Love on Mars."

I remembered him then, oh yes, I remembered him all right. The book was set in space, and the love interest was a female robot. It was as dire as it sounded and as romantic as a trip to the dentist.

"Ah yes. Bernard," I said coldly. "So tell me, why are you here?"

"The wife's thrown me out."

"What's that got to do with me?"

"I remembered those soppy romantic stories you write. I thought with your experience, you might be able to give me some advice."

Soppy romantic stories. How dare he? I asked him how he knew where to find me.

"You're in the phone book," he said simply.

"Well, now you've found me, I must ask you to leave," I

said. "I'm right in the middle of a crucial scene …"

But he ignored me and strolled through into the living room. "Nice place you've got here," he said

The nerve of the man. Just turning up like that. He hadn't even bothered to telephone. He'd only been in the house five minutes and I'd already made up my mind to murder him. As I watched him plonk himself down on my sofa I was trying to think of a way to do it, and get away with it of course. I could tell he wasn't the kind of man to listen to reason. Besides, even if he'd left then it wouldn't have helped. I was so angry there was no way I could have written anything romantic. I felt more like killing somebody than kissing them.

It was when he asked for a drink that an idea began to form.

I offered him tea, but he wanted something stronger so I fetched a bottle of whisky from the kitchen.

He let me pour two inches of whisky into the glass before he stopped me.

I took the bottle back out to the kitchen, thinking that if he had one drink and left, I'd let him live, but he didn't go.

"Sorry if I've stopped you working," he said when I came back, "but you can write any time, can't you? It's not like a proper job."

I tried to tell him that for me it was, but he wasn't listening. He rambled on, telling me all about his messed-up love life. It gave me enough time to fine tune my plan.

"So now," he said at last, "I have to make up my mind. Do I run away with my mistress or go back to my wife?"

"Which would you prefer?" I asked as politely as I could.

"Neither really," replied Bernard, then he laughed. "I'm not sure Sarah would take me back. It's not the first time I've dallied, and Tina, well she's lovely. Great curves, pretty face, but," he tapped his forehead, "she's not exactly bright. I'd soon get bored, even with all the sex."

I sympathised with Tina. She'd have to be very dim to put up with Bernard. By that time Bernard's fate was sealed. It was too late to think about writing. Whenever I worked in the evenings, I found it hard to switch off. The last thing I wanted was another sleepless night. Not that I could have slept, I was far too angry.

I decided to give him one last chance. I went to the door and asked him to leave but he said he had nowhere to go.

"Check into a hotel. Sleep in your car. Just go," I snapped, but he didn't move from his seat.

"What's the rush?" he said. "It's too late to write now. I thought you might like a bit of company."

I couldn't believe it. The horrible little man was actually leering at me!

"You know what they say about widows," he said, giving me a wink and patting the space on the sofa next to him.

The man was insufferable. It was no wonder his wife didn't want him back. Murdering him would be doing her a favour.

I asked if anybody knew he was coming to see me.

"I didn't know myself," he said.

I said I had to go and switch the computer off, and that I'd fetch him another drink. While I was upstairs I took five sleeping pills from the box by my bed, and put them in my pocket. Back in the kitchen I crushed one of the pills and put it in Bernard's glass. It wouldn't knock him out, but it would make him dozy.

The rest of the pills I crushed and put them in my late husband's hip flask. I poured in some whisky and put the flask in my shopping bag with the other things I needed, then I went back into the living room and gave Bernard his whisky.

As I watched him drink I felt a cold determination creeping through my veins. This wasn't murder I was planning, it was a mercy killing. It wasn't long before he started to yawn.

"I feel a bit sleepy," he said. As he looked me up and down, my flesh crawled. "Any chance of a bed for a night?"

I shuddered and told him I knew a good hotel, not far away. "It's out of season. They're bound to have a room." I forced on a smile, then asked him to give me a lift. "There's a cinema not far from there. If I walk home afterwards, it might help me sleep."

When he saw that I couldn't be persuaded to let him stay he reluctantly agreed.

I pulled on my gloves, picked up my bag and followed him to his car. There wasn't a soul about.

"What have you got in there?" he laughed, pointing at my bag. "Don't tell me – you've brought your negligee. You're checking into the hotel with me after all."

"No, definitely not," I told him calmly. "It's just my raincoat and umbrella, in case it starts raining again." And a few other things I wasn't going to tell Bernard about.

As he drove, I directed him away from the main roads, and down a country lane then I took the hip flask from my bag and pretended to take a drink.

He noticed straight away. "What's in there?"

"Whisky."

"Let me have some."

I pointed out that he was driving, but he just laughed and held out his hand for the flask. "We're not going far. Besides, the roads are deserted."

As he emptied the flask, the urge to rub my hands together with glee was hard to resist. We hadn't gone far when Bernard's eyes began to blink shut.

"I feel dreadfully tired all of a sudden," he said.

I told him it was all the worry and suggested he pulled over and took a rest.

He did as I suggested, then as he reached for the ignition, I stopped him.

"Best to leave the engine running, "I said. "You don't

want to get cold."

Within moments he was sound asleep.

I reached into my bag for the length of hosepipe I'd hidden there earlier. The road led to the old manor house and I knew the family were away.

As I stepped out into the cold night, I swapped my woollen gloves for a pair of plastic ones, then carefully attached the length of hose to the exhaust pipe, fixing it in place with plenty of sticky tape. Then I walked round to Bernard's side of the car and wound down the window, just enough to feed the hosepipe through.

Then I climbed back into the car, leaned over Bernard's sleeping body and shut the window just enough to keep the pipe in place, but not enough to stop the deadly fumes getting through.

I remember sitting there, running through what I'd done in my head, making sure I hadn't missed anything. There was no suicide note but that couldn't be helped. The police would soon discover that Bernard's wife had thrown him out. Once they tested the whisky in the flask, the verdict was bound to be suicide. It was a shame I had to leave my husband's flask behind, but it couldn't be helped.

Satisfied that there was nothing to connect me with Bernard, I got out of the car, shut the door, and left him to his fate.

The zig-zag route we'd taken had brought me to within half a mile of home. Soon, I was safely back indoors. The first thing I did was call my son.

"I'm sorry about this morning, darling," I told him, "I was in the middle of a love scene. You know the trouble I have with them."

He forgave me in that patronising way of his then he said something, something that has stayed with me ever since. "Maybe you should forget about romance and try crime. It's all the rage at the moment."

I had to stop myself from laughing out loud. He had no

idea what the real reason for my call was – to establish an alibi.

I kept him chatting for as long as I could. When I eventually hung up it was gone nine o'clock.

I remember standing there in the hallway wondering what to do. My mind was buzzing. There was no point trying to watch TV and I couldn't even think about sleep, so I went upstairs and turned on the computer.

Crime. What an excellent idea. Anybody could see how much easier crime was. After all, I'd just committed the perfect murder, hadn't I?

That night I worked right through until dawn. The words simply poured out. When I crawled into bed it was 5 a.m. and I was utterly exhausted.

A week passed and I began to think I'd got away with it, but my perfect crime wasn't quite so perfect after all. Bernard's wife had insisted he simply wasn't the kind of man to commit suicide. When the police showed her the hip flask she didn't recognise it. She pointed out the initials engraved on the bottom and made them investigate further.

What gave me away was something I'd never even thought of.

Bernard's car had satellite navigation and mine was the last address logged in to it. That, together with the initials on the flask, and the sleeping pills in my bedroom that matched the ones in the flask, was enough for the jury to reach a guilty verdict.

So now I'm locked away in a prison cell. It's hardly spacious, but the telephone doesn't ring, and there are no window cleaners or daft neighbours. What's even better, everybody I meet has a story to tell.

The judge gave me fifteen years. At the rate I'm going I should have at least half a dozen books finished by the time I'm released.

Romance! Forget it. Crime pays, and when I get out of here, I'm going to prove it.

Office Hours was previously an audio story on *StoryTalk*.

Linda Lewis writes full-time from her home in Leeds. Her stories appear in various magazines including *My Weekly, Yours, Woman's Weekly and Ireland's Own*. Her main market is *Take a Break/Fiction Feast* where she uses the pen name Catherine Howard. She was Henry VIII's fifth wife. Henry and Linda share the same birthday (June 28th), plus a tendency to keep marrying the wrong people. She has a monthly column in *Writers Forum* called Short Story Success. What else can she tell you? Oh, yes, she once won *The Weakest Link*. www.akacatherinehoward.weebly.com

Key to the Future
by Elaine Everest

SECURITY AT BLUEWATER SHOPPING mall was tight, I should know: I'd worked there since it opened several years before. As a highly trained supervisor for the company employed to supply security for the whole complex, I knew every lock and bolt, every camera and alarm point, every password and secret code. Not only did I know them all, I knew how to change them. I was security-checked, a model citizen, and not a single point on my driving licence. Never a claim on my insurance, a minor miracle, I might add, for a man who uses a busy motorway each day to commute to work. But, sitting here now, the large bunch of keys clenched tightly in my sweaty hand, I cursed my foolhardiness.

I worked mainly in the hi-tech security room where, aided by a wall covered in monitors, we could oversee every nook and cranny in the shopping complex. Over the years we'd caught many shoplifters, tracking them from the store, notifying colleagues on the shop floors who tackled the thieves and handed them over to the police. If I say so myself, we must have had one of the best arrest rates of any shopping centre in the country.

I was on duty one busy Saturday, checking the cash bags I'd collected earlier from the shops, before locking them in the safe.

"Here George, come and look at this," my colleague Bill

called out, as he peered closely at the monitors. Twiddling with a bank of switches he zoomed in on a couple of women, intently viewing a fashion parade of wedding dresses. We often had fashion parades in the main mall; they drew quite a crowd.

"What you got there, Bill?" I asked looking over his shoulder. "Shoplifters? They'd be hard pressed to stuff one of those large dresses up their jumper!"

"I hope not, it's your Grace and Sally – have you won the lottery or something? It costs a fortune in that store even for a pair of socks."

I wish I had won the lottery, I thought, as I spied on my wife and daughter. Sally is engaged to be married, she wants the works; church, reception, honeymoon. She's not a greedy girl, mind you, Grace and I had sat down with Sally and Darren, her intended, and worked out a sensible budget. We'd put money by each week and my Grace had found herself a job in the same shop where Sally worked. Our bank account had been filling up nicely. We'd insisted that Sally and Darren ploughed all their savings into the deposit for a lovely little starter home on a nearby housing estate.

Everything had been going to plan until Darren's accident, he'd come off his motorbike on an icy bend and a broken leg laid him off work for two months. Only now was he back on light duties, and a lighter pay packet. This put paid to the planned budget; I'd spent many sleepless nights since, trying to juggle figures in my head. Whatever happened my little girl was going to have the wedding of her dreams. I'd thought about a loan, remortgaging the house, but, at my age – Sally had been a late baby – the repayments would have been too hefty. What was I going to do?

I supposed Grace and Sally had wandered up to the bridal display in their lunch break – they always shared their lunch breaks, heads together over fabric samples and menu plans. They'd ask me on numerous occasions to join them, but I shied away from that sort of thing, it was definitely a female ritual.

"Women!" I laughed with Bill, until looking closer I caught my daughter gazing longingly at a magnificent dress, fit for a princess. Grace was busy wiping a tear from her eye. I knew what she'd be thinking, never in a million years could we afford that type of outfit for our daughter.

Sally was a good girl, in her childhood she'd endured poor health without complaining. She'd behaved at school and found herself a nice job, which she'd worked hard at. Never trouble with boyfriends, Darren was her first love and the couple were devoted to each other. I felt angry, why shouldn't she have a day to remember?

My fingers clenched the large bunch of keys in my pocket in frustration. That's when I had the idea. I had the key to my daughter's perfect day right there in my pocket!

Well, that was last week, and now, here I sat, parked in the small road by the security department. Surrounded by overflowing dustbins I watched the dawn creep over chalky quarry walls nearby. Chilled to the bone, not just with the cold but with the fear of what I'd done.

Entering the building just an hour earlier, it'd been easy, switch off the closed-circuit television cameras, disconnect the alarm. Entering the locked strong room I'd come away with £20,000 collected from the vault where individual shops kept their till floats overnight. How I was going to explain my unexpected windfall to Grace and Sally was my next problem.

A tap on the car roof frightened me half to death, with the windows misted and frozen in the cold it could have been anyone. Winding down the misted window I saw a grinning Bill and sighed inwardly with relief.

"What are you doing here so early, argued with the wife?" he joked.

I stubbed out my unsmoked cigarette and forced a laugh. "No, just having a quick fag, this early shift's a killer, isn't it? I couldn't sleep so I left home early to beat the rush on the motorway."

The next few hours in work were an effort. To act normally while keeping my terrible secret made me feel sick and alone. How I took phone calls and spoke normally while my mind was buzzing 'You're a thief, You're a thief, you're a thief,' I'll never know. My routine calls to the local police station had beads of sweat running down my brow with fear.

Even Bill noticed. "You feeling all right George,? You've been a bit strange all morning, not coming down with something are you?"

"No I'm fine, I think it's the air conditioning, never seems to blow right, it's either too hot or too cold. You'd think with all this high-tech stuff in here they could get the temperature right, wouldn't you?" I replied, trying to mentally shake myself. If Bill found out what I'd done, I'd die of shame.

A knock at the door of the control room raised me from my despondent mood as Sally rushed in. Her face glowing with excitement, she flung herself into my arms.

"Oh, Dad, you'll never guess. I won the competition held at the wedding exhibition last week. There was a letter this morning, but you'd already left for work. I'm the Bluewater Bride of the Year. Wedding dress, bridesmaid's outfits, suit for Darren and you. A complete beauty treatment for Mum and me. Flower arrangements for the church – designed by a top florist. A reception at that grand country hotel in Canterbury, and a honeymoon in the South of France, I've won so much, I can't believe it, it's a dream come true." She fell into my arms sobbing for joy.

As I held her close, waiting for the tears to subside, I could just picture my girl walking down the aisle, dressed like the princess I'd always thought she was. Her mother decked out in all her finery and Darren waiting so smartly for his bride. I'd be the proudest father in the world.

104

Looking over her shoulder I wondered where her mother was, I couldn't imagine Grace wanting to miss out on all this excitement.

"Where's your mum? I'd have thought she'd want to be here when you broke the news."

"I left her at home, she nearly fainted with the shock, her and Darren's mum have already opened the sherry and started to celebrate. Dad, Mum won't have to work any more to save up for the wedding. I always felt guilty about that."

That pleased me as well, Grace had looked tired lately, I worried she'd been overdoing it. I hugged my happy daughter.

Bill punched the air and shook our hands. "It couldn't happen to a nicer family, George we'll have to celebrate this tonight, the first pint's on me."

"Well, Dad," said Sally, straightening her jacket and wiping her eyes, "this won't do, I'd better get down to the shop floor, it won't do for 'Bluewater's Bride of the Year' to be late for work, we'll all have to be exemplary employees from now on."

Kissing me on the cheek she turned to go. "I'll see you later when you bring round the money for the tills ..."

Key to the Future has been published in *You, South Africa* and *The Weekly News*. It was also the winning entry for BBC Radio Kent's Short Story Writer of the Year competition.

Elaine Everest is a freelance journalist, tutor, writer and author. She runs The Write Place Creative Writing School in Dartford Kent with fellow writer Francesca Burgess. Elaine often writes for the national press as well as many magazines on subjects as diverse as cremating a dog to collecting shaving mugs. Her books on dogs include, *Showing Your Dog a Beginner's Guide, Canine Cuisine and A New Puppy in the Family* (all How To Books Ltd). Elaine's canine knowledge means that she is often called upon to speak on radio about our four-legged friends although her favourite broadcasting experience was on *Woman's Hour* when she discussed redundancy with Jenni Murray.

Own Two Feet
by Geraldine Ryan

JANE MET HARRY AT an academic conference. They'd been looking for volunteers to give out badges and to usher speakers to and from the podium. As a mere undergraduate in her final term it was a great honour to be chosen in front of the post grad from her hall, who'd been rejected for the job.

There were so many notable speakers down to talk that day. And no one more notable, in Jane's eyes, than Harry Preston. Watching him fumble with his nametag, Jane felt embarrassed for him and rushed forward to help. He was gracious in accepting her assistance, which made her go pink to her ears.

"Such delightful ears," he murmured, as, dipping her head down to concentrate on the job in hand, she tucked an errant lock of hair behind one to stop it getting in her eyes. "And such pretty hands. Tell me, is the rest of you so perfect?"

Harry would soon find out. Because, that night, after the conference had ended, the lukewarm wine and nibbles had been drunk and eaten and all the rubbish had been swept away, the two of them spent the night together in his hotel. If Jane hadn't fallen in love from the back of the lecture theatre as soon as he stood up to speak –not that she heard anything he said – then she did that night.

"You know," Harry joked, as they lay in his hard narrow

bed – his expenses didn't cover a luxury hotel – "if I'd seen your feet before I saw your beautiful face I never would have fallen for you."

Jane was soon to learn that straight talking was Harry's way. It was one of the things she loved about him, alongside his original mind, his superior knowledge and his voice, which felt like warm honey trickling over her limbs and snaking down her body.

Once Jane graduated they moved in together. It was a miserable summer, cold and wet. She padded around Harry's flat in borrowed sweaters and socks and didn't mind the unseasonable damp as long as they were together.

She learned such a lot from him. Harry's favourite word was *derivative*. That's what her opinions were, he said. Just like the films she watched, the novels she read and the music she listened to.

Under his tuition, as summer became autumn and autumn drew its winter cloak around its knees, Jane set about trying to remedy her woeful ignorance. Unlike her, Harry was a man who made his own mind up about whether something was good or bad. And because he was so clever, with so many letters after his name that, all strung together they resembled one of those rampaging viruses unlucky people picked up in hospitals, she decided he must know better than all the critics put together. So she stopped reading *The Guardian* and *The Times* and simply turned to Harry for an opinion instead.

Jane didn't bother getting a job. Like winter, the recession was biting hard and, like Harry said, she was just one more Arts graduate with nothing to offer but an ability to skim read and drink coffee.

"Besides," he said, "your job is looking after me."

It was a full-time job. She typed up his lecture notes, labelled his slides and saw to his more domestic needs. All these crazy feminists didn't know what they were talking about, she decided. She found she positively enjoyed ironing. Sometimes she listened to Radio One while she ironed, but she was always quick to turn the dial to Radio Three if Harry was expected home.

Spring arrived, soft and full of promise. She bought a pair of gold trainers, to celebrate the relief of kicking off her winter boots. She realised she'd become a stranger to her feet, only catching sight of them a couple of times a day, as she stumbled out of bed to make Harry's breakfast, or in the shower, or last thing at night, slipping beneath the duvet hurriedly, in case a glimpse of her toes provoked him. Was it possible to mourn a body part, even if you still possessed it, she wondered?

As it grew warmer she took to walking. It was lonely in the flat, cooped up with nothing much to do. Harry was busy, preparing for another conference. Italy. He didn't know if he could swing her travel and accommodation but he'd do his best, he said.

Out on the street everyone was going somewhere. Was she the only girl in this small university town who had no purpose? Idly at first, she began to scan the websites for jobs.

She could only do temporary, of course, just in case Harry managed to pull Italy off for her. But that was fine, the University library told her. Summer wasn't exactly their busiest time. And perhaps later, in September – if she took to them and vice versa – they could make the job more permanent. She had an excellent degree, after all.

"Oh well, it's only an Arts degree," she muttered.

"But a first. And a very good first at that."

"Well yes, I suppose it is," she said, as if this was the first time that she'd realised it. Harry hated show-offs.

"And impeccable references, they added."

"Really?" She grew pink to her ears at such unaccustomed praise.

She celebrated with a pedicure. To make up for neglecting her feet and to apologise in advance for when

109

she'd have to cram them back into her gold trainers.

"Such distinctive toes you have," the beautician said. "Your second toe is longer than your big one."

Jane squirmed. She'd have liked to ask the beautician to file it down.

"Did you know that it shows an artistic personality?"

"Artistic? Me?"

"Yes, indeed. You're lucky," she said. "You have Celtic feet, long and slim. Not little fat squat Anglo-Saxon ones like mine."

Later, as she waited for Harry to come home from the department, Jane sat in the garden a long time admiring her Celtic feet and their red nails winking in the evening sunshine.

"Take off your shoes," she said, when he returned. "It's far too hot to be sitting there in socks and heavy footwear."

She'd been reading a paperback with a sugar pink cover.

"What's that rubbish?" Harry asked, peeling off his drab socks amenably.

"I'm really enjoying it," Jane said. "It makes me laugh and cry and gets me right here." She indicated her heart, or at least where popular opinion dictated where a heart should be. "That's what good books do."

"Honestly, darling!" Harry's voice was full of disdain. "Haven't I managed to teach you anything all these months? If all you want from a story is a good yarn, then fair enough. Even Jeffrey Archer will do."

Pleased with his observation, he waggled his toes playfully in the evening breeze. Squat fat feet, short toes. Anglo-Saxon.

"You should try reading chick-lit once in a while," she said. "It offers a post-modern perspective on the experience of being female."

"Does it, by golly?"

He raised an eyebrow, sardonically. She recognized the significance of the gesture he'd perfected so well. Don't

110

mess with the big boys, it said. She glanced down at her toes. They really were quite elegant, next to his.

"I've seen your Biggles collection, by the way, so there's no need to look at me *like that*."

It had been a warm day. But by now the evening sunshine had been tempered by a mellow breeze that didn't merit the intense flush that crept up from his collar to his cheeks.

"But Biggles is different," he said, exactly as she'd predicted he would.

"Of course it is," she said. "Biggles is boys' stuff. Much more important."

She told him about her job then. Even though she was well aware how much he disapproved of boasting, she decided it might do him good to be reminded that she too had a first-class honours degree. And excellent references. She added a few more embellishments, just to drive the point home.

He was pleased for her, he said. Everyone needed an occupation. As long as it didn't get in the way of her *real* work. He leaned over to kiss her then, just to remind her who her real work was.

"Talking of real work," she said, "I have a casserole in the oven. I should check on it." She eased herself up out of her deckchair, lingering a moment to add, "Any more news about Italy, by the way?"

His sigh was heartfelt. She watched him remove his tie, and roll it round his fingers as he explained about budget cuts and flight restrictions and hotels being over-booked and then there was the exchange rate to worry about. It was all most disconcerting, quite sapping the energy he needed for his paper, which right now was going nowhere, such a drag. It would be great if she could come with him, obviously. There were more *buts* and *onlys* and a great deal more tie rolling.

"Poor lamb," she said. " I can see how all this detail

111

must be getting you down."

"You're so understanding," he said, smiling up at her. "I don't know what I'd do if you weren't there to proof-read my stuff."

"And do your slides," she reminded him, cheerfully. "And your bibliography too, remember."

She balked at reminding him that she also cooked his food. The aroma of spices drifted from the kitchen. Nor was it necessary to point out who washed his shirts. A row of them linked arms on the washing line, like a chorus line of businessmen.

He looked just a little hurt. "Of course," he said. "All that too."

"But if I'm not coming, I might as well ring the Library tomorrow and tell them I can start whenever they want."

Her timing was perfect.

"I didn't say it was definite," he said, more flustered than ever. "It just needs some organizing, that's all."

"Oh well, good luck with that then," she said with a smile. "Just email me the link to the hotel when you've found one you think I might like."

A sea view and a balcony were her thing, she said. That hotel where they spent their first night together. Now, hadn't that been a dump? Harry made a strangled noise in his throat.

"Goodness me, is that the time?" Jane glanced at her watch. "Do you mind if we eat after *Coronation Street*? Only I've got a sudden yen to start watching it again since that new actor's joined the cast."

He made the same strangled noise again. Jane decided to take it as his seal of approval and bent down to pick up her gold trainers. As soon as she got inside she would throw them to the back of the cupboard. First thing tomorrow she'd go out and buy a pair of open-toed sandals for Italy.

Five days of sightseeing while poor Harry sat through countless papers delivered by his academic peers. Then home – to flat hunt. It really was time she stood on her own two feet.

Own Two Feet was originally published in *Woman's Weekly*

Geraldine Ryan's first short story was published in 1993. She has since had stories published in *The Lady* and, *Take-a-Break* as well as women's magazines abroad and these days regularly contributes both stories and serials to *Woman's Weekly*. Her stories straddle all genres – crime, romance, family stories, humour and she's also been known to write the odd ghost story and time-travel tale. She lives in Cambridge. Her favourite writers are Kate Atkinson, Hilary Mantel and Anne Tyler.

Finishing Off Christopher Robin
by Paula Williams

"MUM? WHAT ON EARTH are you doing" I asked my mother's rear end. It was the only bit of her that was visible, the rest of her being buried deep inside the glory hole she called her Sewing Cupboard.

She reversed out, dragging bags full of half-finished pieces of knitting, crochet and embroidery with her.

"Sorry, love. I didn't hear you come in." She sat back on her heels and smiled up at me brightly. Too brightly, surely, for the hospital appointment to have been bad news? Except she wouldn't look me in the eye as she prattled on, "Will you look at all these things I've found – stuff I'd forgotten about. Look, there's even –"

"Mum. Stop it. Please." My heart was banging against my ribcage like a trapped starling. "Just tell me – what did they say?"

She opened one of the bags and pulled out a jewel-bright handful of embroidery silks.

"It's not … good news," she said, her head bent as she spread the skeins of silks across her lap, stroking them gently as if soothing a poor broken bird. "They say … I've got to have … chemotherapy … and an operation … But it's … not …"

Her hands stilled, the silks forgotten, as her voice, which had been getting smaller and quieter with each word, trailed away to nothing while I stood there, staring down at her bent head, more frightened than I've ever been in my life.

She cleared her throat and tried again. This time her words tumbled out and she sounded like she'd just sprinted up a flight of stairs. "The consultant went to a lot of trouble to explain. Only I can't quite remember what he said, only that it's not looking good."

Now, me, I'm one of those people who has an answer for everything. You know the sort, who can always be relied upon to come out with something funny or witty to break the tension and make people smile.

But not that time. Because that time I didn't have any words – except one.

"No!"

No. No. No. It filled my head. The room. The whole world. No. Oh no. Please, no. Not my mum. She's only 46. I need her. Dad needs her. The dog needs her. The old man who sells newspapers on the corner of the High Street needs her because she's one of the few people who smile at him and the only one who ever asks after the state of his corns. We all need her. Please, please, no.

"Your dad's in a bit of a state," she went on, while I stood there dumbly shaking my head. "He's not taking it too well, you will help him, Lisa, won't you?"

Help him? How could I help him when I couldn't help myself? Besides, it wasn't true, was it? There'd been some terrible mix-up with the records at the hospital. And now some poor soul who really has got cancer has been given Mum's file by mistake. She's going to feel just terrible when she finds out the truth.

"I – I thought I'd make a start on clearing out my sewing cupboard," Mum said, when it became obvious I wasn't going to answer. "Will you help me?"

"What?" I stared at her, completely at a loss to know what she was talking about.

"My sewing cupboard. I need to clear it out." Her voice was clearer now. "I'd hate for your dad to do it. You know how he always goes on about me buying things that I never finish. Remember that sweater I knitted for him that took me ten years – and he never wore it because he'd gone up a size or two in that time?"

"But why do you want to clear out all these things? You're going to need them," I said, scrabbling about like I was drowning. "While you're convalescing, you'll be glad of them. It'll give you something to do."

"I'm not going to need them," she said gently, "and it would be unfair to expect your dad to do this when I'm –"

"Mum, please." I knelt down beside her, my face wet with tears. "Please, don't do this. I'll help you, if it means that much to you. But only so that, when you're better, we can go out and buy a whole load of new stuff to fill it up again."

She took out her hankie and wiped my wet cheeks and just for a moment, I was a little girl again, crying because I didn't want to go to school. For a moment, our eyes held and I knew she was remembering that too.

"Don't set me off," she looked at me pleadingly. "If I start, I may never stop."

I took a long steadying breath and looked desperately around for something to talk about.

"How long have you had this?" I asked, forcing myself to speak normally.

I picked up one of the bags and passed it to her. It contained a partly worked embroidered picture in counted cross stitch of Christopher Robin flying a kite with Winnie the Pooh puffing and panting along behind him.

"I was going to make this as a surprise for you," she smiled as she took out the unfinished piece of work. "Remember when you were going through your Christopher Robin phase?"

"What do you mean, going through? I'm still in my Christopher Robin phase." I said with a little laugh, surprised to find that it didn't come as hard as I thought it

116

would as I tried to lighten my mood for her sake. "Remember how I used to spin out bedtime by getting you to read the Christopher Robin poems?"

"You were a little monkey," she smiled. "You knew if you got me on *The King's Breakfast* or any of the other *When We Were Very Young* poems, I'd go on reading them for hours."

"And you'd tell me how Gran used to read them to you when you were a little girl. And she'd –" I stopped, feeling like a cold hand had just run down my back. "Have you told Gran?"

She shook her head, her eyes troubled again. "Not yet," she said. "I – I need to get my head sorted first. Remember that poem you had read out at your wedding?"

It was such an abrupt change of subject, even by my mother's grasshopper standards, that it took me a while to realise she was back on Christopher Robin again. My friend, Jessica, had read out a little poem called *The Two of Us*, at my wedding.

"I can still see Jessica, standing there reading that poem in that beautiful voice of hers – and all the guests nodding and smiling as she did so," Mum said. "It was a lovely moment, wasn't it?"

"One of the best. But it certainly surprised one or two, Matt's mother in particular," I said, struggling to fit in with her mood. "Christopher Robin isn't exactly a conventional choice for wedding poetry."

"Here, you have it." She handed me the embroidery. "Finish it off for me."

"I'm no good at that sort of thing," I protested. "You know what I'm like. I'm even worse than you at starting something and not seeing it through. Remember all those school reports I used to get about how well I'd do if I only finished what I started?"

"Those school reports were wrong," she said firmly. "You're stronger than you think, Lisa. I've always thought so."

I thought of the piano lessons I'd tired of; the uni course I started but gave up halfway through; the many jobs I've had that never lasted. In fact, the only thing that had lasted was me and Matt. We'd known each other since school and were good mates long before we were ever lovers.

But things hadn't been so good between us lately and we'd been arguing a lot. I'd like to say it was all down to the worry of Mum's illness. That was what Matt – who was far more patient and long-suffering than I deserved – said, but the truth was he wanted to start a family and I didn't. But I didn't know how to tell him.

Like I said, I'm rubbish at finishing what I started – but the thing with having children is that there's no walking away if things get difficult and I found that the scariest thing of all. But how could I explain that to him when I couldn't really make sense of it myself? Instead, I'd snapped and snarled about the place like a bad-tempered bulldog.

Reluctantly, I took the Christopher Robin embroidery away with me and had every intention of putting it in the back of a cupboard and leaving it there.

But I'd reckoned without my mother who asked about it every time I saw her. So, in the end, I got it out and read the instructions which seemed horribly complicated at first. But after several false starts, pricked fingers and much unpicking, I began to get the hang of it and found to my surprise that I was actually beginning to enjoy it.

There's something very satisfying in making hundreds of tiny crosses, each as small as a dot of paint, on a piece of fabric and gradually watching a picture emerge. Something very soothing about the rhythmic dip of the needle as it slips in and out of the fabric. And the level of concentration needed to keep to the chart was just the thing to crowd out other, darker, thoughts during the next few months.

Christopher Robin's head and shoulders came through

when I was in the oncology waiting area while Mum had her first session of chemo. By the time she'd finished the course, I was on to his shoes. By the time I'd finished his kite, Mum was like a poor little shadow, so sick, so tired. But she never lost interest in the picture and always wanted to know how I was getting on with it.

I finished it yesterday. Just in time. I was so anxious for her to see it that I stayed up far into the small hours of the morning. My eyes were aching, my back too. Even my fingers were sore.

"I've got something for you," I reached into my bag and took out the picture, which Dad had framed for me.

She looked at it then up at me, her eyes shining with tears. "I knew you'd do it. Like I knew you'd be there for me. And you were, bless you. You've been absolutely wonderful, a real tower of strength and I don't know what I would have done without you to lean on. You're the strongest person I know, Lisa, and I'm so very proud of you. So very grateful too."

"It was nothing," I managed to say, all choked up.

"It was everything. And now I've one last thing to ask of you. You will look out for your dad for me, won't you?"

"Of course. But –"

"And I want you to have this back and hang it on the nursery wall."

"What nursery wall?"

Mum laughed softly. "I assume the little fellow is going to have a room of his or her own one day?"

"But how did you know?" I looked at her in amazement. "I only did the test yesterday."

"I'm your mother. Mothers know these things."

"You're a witch, more like it."

"Maybe. You and Matt will make wonderful parents. I'm so happy for you."

"We're thrilled." And that was nothing but the truth. In the six months since Mum's diagnosis, I'd learnt a lot about

119

myself and what I'm capable of. I'd done a heap of growing up, too.

"Now, darling, I'm sorry to break up the party but I really must get on. Your dad's fretting about getting me to the airport on time. But don't worry, I'll be back in good time for the birth of my first grandchild."

My mum was one of the lucky ones. She'd responded brilliantly to treatment and, touch wood, has beaten the cancer. But it's made us all appreciate how precious life is and she's determined not to waste a moment of it. Which is why she's off to visit her sister in Australia whom she hasn't seen for ten years.

And by the time she returns, I'll have finished the picture of Eeyore and Tigger to keep Christopher Robin company.

Finishing Off Christopher Robin was originally published in *Candis* magazine

Paula Williams is an established short-story and serial writer whose stories have appeared in magazines all over the world. She lives in a small Somerset village with her husband and a scatty Dalmatian called Jemima.

"I was thrilled when *Finishing Off Christopher Robin* was first accepted for publication in the magazine *Candis*, as it was based on my own experience of helping my mother clear out her sewing cupboard when she was first diagnosed with cancer. Sadly, she didn't survive but she lives on – in my heart and in this, my favourite story."

Meant to Be
by Jane Wenham-Jones

"OH DAMN! OH NO!"

I slammed on the brakes too late to stop the unmistakable tinkle of broken glass. My sister Jan gave a loud shriek and clapped her hand to her mouth and her son Adam, who should have been at school and not talking nineteen to the dozen and distracting me, gave a whoop!

"You've hit the headlight!" he called gleefully, leaping out of the car as I pulled on the handbrake and climbed wearily out into the car park.

Terrific! He was quite right. I had reversed into the car opposite and smashed its headlight to smithereens. This was all I needed!

My sister Jan, who likes to think of herself as a bit of a fatalist and is very fond of telling me how things are Meant to Be, recovered rapidly from her initial scream and adopted an air of calm-and-serene-in-the-face-of-a crisis as she joined me to inspect the damage.

"Well," she said brightly after a moment's thought in which she was clearly at a loss to explain the higher purpose of this particular mishap, "you haven't dented the bodywork. And your car's fine!"

"Hmmm," I growled. "I suppose I'd better leave a note."

"Or you could just drive off," put in Adam helpfully.

I fixed him with my best auntie-ish stare. "That wouldn't be very kind or honest, would it?" I asked severely, not about to admit that the same thought had flashed across my own mind for a brief shameful second. I pulled a notebook from my handbag.

I'm sorry I did this to your car, I wrote, *please call me – I shall be in this evening ...*

"In every evening in fact," I said out loud as I added my phone number. I wasn't convinced by Jan's conviction of a higher purpose for splitting up with Gavin either. So far it hadn't led on to anything except feeling lonely and miserable.

"It was so that you could meet someone who would make you really happy," Jan reminded me firmly as I tucked the paper under the car's windscreen wiper. "And probably," said Jan – as inspiration eventually struck her – "the man who owns this car is The One."

I gritted my teeth. Would Jan never let up? I wasn't ready to meet The One whether I'd driven into his car or not. I was still firmly at the wallowing in self-pity stage and I wished my sister would leave me to it.

The only reason we were here in the shopping centre car park in the first place was that she considered I had let myself go and that I would never find a new man unless I got a grip and spruced up.

"Look at you!" she'd said disapprovingly, "You haven't had a haircut since Gavin moved out, you wear those dreadful old jeans all the time and you still haven't bought a new dress for the party."

The party was another thing. She'd been planning it for weeks, claiming to have lined up every single man her husband knew and even a few he didn't, and said if I didn't turn up she was going to come round and drag me there.

So here we were supposedly buying party clothes for A New Start. Except that she'd forgotten that Adam's school was very inconsiderately having a teacher-training day leaving us with a truculent eleven-year-old to drag around with us in our quest for my new – and unwanted by me –

image.

So far all we seemed to have bought was lots of Thunderbirds stickers and several McDonald's. Still, what did I need new clothes for anyway, I thought, as I peered at the broken headlight. There was nobody I wanted to dress up for any more. And I had absolutely no intention of going to Jan's party.

"I wonder what he'll be like", she said infuriatingly as I turned into her road. "I've just got one of my feelings about the driver of that car."

"It probably belongs to a woman," I said crossly, as I dropped her and Adam off. "I just hope she's not too angry. I don't feel like being shouted at."

But the voice on the other end of the phone that evening was unmistakably male. And charming. Rather deep and sexy in fact! He thanked me for being so honest, reassured me that the damage was really only very minor and asked me very politely what I wanted to do about it.

"Is he married?" asked Jan, who had phoned to enquire after my mood.

"How should I know?" I said impatiently, as she twittered on.

"Well, I think this was all meant to be. I mean why that particular car at that precise time?"

Why indeed! I thought sourly. Because you were nagging me and your son was bobbing about in the back so I couldn't see out of the rear mirror?

But Jan was still in full flow. "Are you listening Lucy? This could be the man you've been waiting to find all these years ..."

"I doubt it." I sighed in exasperation as I put the phone down but then I looked thoughtfully at the piece of paper on which I'd written the car-owner's name and address. He didn't live far from Jan. David Marshall. Funnily enough, he did sound nice. And he wasn't married.

I wasn't about to tell Jan – who would be bound to start

compiling my wedding list – but we'd actually ended up talking for over half an hour. Just about cars and the difficulties of reversing in small spaces and how not everyone was as honest as me. And somehow he'd told me that he lived on his own ...

Where he probably has lots of nasty habits, I told myself. Or is endlessly critical and demanding, I added. Or thoroughly unreliable and the sort to go off with somebody else, I finished, thinking sadly of Gavin, of whom I'd once had such high hopes.

But David phoned the next evening at exactly the time he'd said he would. "I've been to the garage," he told me, voice warm and deep in my ear, "and I've got a quote to replace the light ..."

And it wasn't nearly as expensive as I'd feared it might be and in my relief I somehow got quite chatty and before I knew it I was telling him about my job in marketing and he was saying how when he first started out he worked for a publishing company and he was so nice to talk to and so friendly and interested in all I had to say that I didn't really want to put the phone down.

I kept it all businesslike for Jan who seemed to find a reason to phone me several times the next day and who was clearly on tenterhooks. "So you're getting on well then," she said eagerly.

"Yes he's been very understanding," I said primly, not daring to tell her how long we'd talked for. "What next then?" she asked, obviously imagining a candlelit dinner and marriage proposal.

"Well it's hardly worth losing my no-claims bonus over," I explained, deliberately misunderstanding her enthusiastic tones. "I may as well just send him a cheque."

"Take it round there you mean!" she said. "Just to make sure it arrives. I'll come with you if you like. I can wait outside in the car. Just while you have a chat ..."

"By all means settle with him direct," said my insurance

broker when I rang the next morning to check. "But just to be on the safe side, get a letter from him confirming it's in full and final settlement ..."

I phoned David as soon as I got home. "Of course!" he said. "Shall I post it to you or ..."

I replaced the receiver and grinned at myself in the hall mirror. Then I shook my head disbelievingly. Anyone would think I had a hot date next week rather than a five minute hand-over of a couple of bits of paper!

"Get a grip!" I told myself briskly. "Thought you were broken-hearted and definitely off men? I am," I answered my reflection firmly. "I am."

"Oh you've had your hair done!" said Jan who just happened to call in a couple of days later. "Looks so much better."

"Oh do you think so?" I patted my head casually in the mirror. "Well it did need doing ..."

"And is that a new skirt?" she asked. "And that top," she added practically turning my neck inside out to peer at the label. "When are you going round there?"

"I don't know what you're talking about," I said. "You were the one who said I needed some new clothes ..."

This is ridiculous! I said sternly to myself that evening. You don't know anything about him. He's probably too short or too ugly or got a girlfriend who stays every weekend ...

Still I found I was allowing myself to have the tiniest daydreams about him being tall and dark and handsome and single and whisking me off my feet and was shocked to find that the day before I was due to pop round there to give him the cheque and collect the letter I had got to seven o'clock in the evening without thinking about Gavin once ...

"Gavin pah!" said Jan loudly as we pulled up just along the road from the address David had given me. "Go on!"

125

she said excitedly as I checked my lipstick in the rear mirror. "You look marvellous. Now be as long as you like."

"This is daft," I said to myself as I rang on the door bell, trying to pretend my stomach wasn't fluttering in the most ridiculous fashion. And then the door opened and there he was. David Marshall.

Well!

He was smiling widely. "You must be Lucy!" he said in that same deep voice as he held out his hand. "Come in."

I found myself grinning back as I stuck out my own hand. "OK," I said. And stepped into the hall.

By the time I emerged twenty minutes later Jan could barely contain herself. The questions started even before I'd got back into the driving seat.

"Well? What happened? Did you like him? Is he nice?"

"He's lovely" I said.

"And?"

"Charming."

"And?"

"Interesting. Intelligent. Kind. Good company …"

Jan let out a long satisfied sigh.

"I knew it! I knew the moment you hit that car this would be it. When are you going to see him again?"

I smiled, still feeling oddly cheerful. "Oh, who knows? He said I must pop in for a cup of tea if ever I'm passing but I probably won't."

Jan made a sort of spluttering noise as I continued. "Though on the other hand I suppose I might one day. He's so interesting. I think we could become friends …"

"Friends?" she eventually managed, aghast. "But why not …"

Just for once she seemed lost for words.

"That's why not. Look!" I nudged her arm towards where a pretty blonde girl was just turning up David's path. "I'd have stayed longer but he said he was expecting her."

126

Jan gasped dramatically. "Oh no! You poor thing! He did have someone after all. Is that his girlfriend?"

I shook my head, grinning. "No."

I took a sideways look at Jan as I started the engine, not wishing to miss the expression on her face. "His granddaughter."

"I never thought to ask how old he was," I explained when we were back in my kitchen and I was making Jan some restorative tea. "Well, you don't, do you?"

She shook her head dumbly.

"And he's got such a strong voice. And such a modern outlook. You'd never have guessed on the phone he was almost eighty."

"So after all that," said Jan, sighing, "you're no further forward. And I was so sure that you were meant to smash that headlight. So convinced it was all meant to be."

I glanced over at the mirror as I placed her mug of tea in front of her, catching sight of my new hairstyle, the unfamiliar make-up I hadn't worn for weeks and the smile that was still on my face.

I smiled more as I reached over to pick up the carrier bag containing the new dress I'd bought that morning to wear to Jan's party. "Oh," I said, feeling cheerier than I had for ages, "but I think it was."

Meant to Be was originally published in *Woman's Weekly Fiction Special 2001*

Jane Wenham-Jones is an author and freelance journalist. She has published three novels and two non-fiction books – *Wannabe a Writer?* – a humorous look at how to get published and *Wannabe a Writer We've Heard Of?* – a guide to hitting the publicity trail. She has also

contributed to several anthologies. She writes regular columns for the *Isle of Thanet Gazette*, *Woman's Weekly Fiction Special* and *Booktime* and is the 'agony aunt' for *Writing Magazine*.
www.janewenham-jones.com.

When You Wish Upon a Star
by Glynis Scrivens

UNTIL ONE O'CLOCK YESTERDAY, my life was relatively normal. A bit boring, but my feet were on the ground.

One hour and one minute turned everything upside down. One hour of waiting followed by one minute of emotional storm. Today I can't right myself. Or even want to. I'm savouring every detail of that single minute.

I'm lying in the bath, up to my neck in white froth. I think the bubbles must've found their way into my brain. Usually a bath calms me. Today it's "bubble bubble, toil and trouble". Not helped by the dizzying aromatherapy blend assailing my senses. 'Desire', a potent combination of ylang ylang, patchouli, clary sage and rose.

This isn't a night for 'Tranquillity' or 'Sweet Dreams'. And last night wasn't for sleeping. Tonight I'm exploring that one minute. I'm going to a concert, and staying behind to meet the singer. He made my blood run faster yesterday. And it's just been too long since I've felt this way.

Then there's the guilt factor. I'm a thirty-seven-year-old woman, it's Saturday evening, and all I can think of is the effect another man has had on me. My husband? He'll be home watching the soccer on television. If only life were that simple for me.

My hand is covered in bubbles, which hide my wedding ring. A band of gold I've worn for seven years. Covered now by bubbles of – desire? Dissatisfaction? Distraction?

129

All because of that one minute yesterday when the bubble of wedded bliss I'd been hiding in burst. And everything felt suddenly empty.

It'd been a last minute decision, having my CD signed by the handsome singer. I'd heard on the radio he'd be in a music store. And it was my rostered day off.

Since meeting him, my feet haven't touched the ground.

His photos hadn't done him justice, hadn't caught the sparkling ocean green of his eyes, or his incredible freshness and vitality. He was the most alive man I've ever met, and that meeting woke something in me that I'm having trouble dealing with.

I stood in the queue that stretched around the music store like a drunken snake. Waiting for my turn. Feeling adolescent, standing there, my heart in my mouth.

The queue inched forward.

My turn finally came.

'Hello, how are you?' I melted in the heat of that familiar crooked smile.

A faint suggestion of shampoo and aftershave enveloped him. My senses were on full alert.

They seemed to be the only part of my body still functioning normally.

My legs turned to jelly, my palms grew damp, and my throat turned dry. As for my brain, it'd gone into meltdown when he smiled at me.

Somehow, he seemed to epitomise everything that Raymond and I had allowed to slip away.

'Your music gives me so much pleasure,' I managed, handing him my CD. It wasn't what I'd been rehearsing in the queue, but I couldn't help that. And at least I'd said something.

He gently kissed my cheek. 'Thanks so much. Are you coming to our concert?'

I nodded. My voice was playing hide and seek again. And yet he was only a few years younger than me.

'I hope you enjoy the show,' he said. 'And I'll be staying back, in the foyer, for anyone who wants to say hello.'

And as he handed back the CD he'd signed, I felt the blood rushing to my cheeks as his fingers brushed against mine.

It was time for his next fan to have her moment.

I was on cloud nine. In no fit state to face going home to the breakfast dishes, the cat mewing crossly for food, or the unmade beds.

I went for a walk along the riverbank and sat down under a copper beech, staring into space. Eventually, I took out my newspaper and began to tackle the cryptic crossword. Trying to bully my brain into submission. But it wouldn't be bullied. The words skipped across the page, and my brain danced to a beat of its own. A bubble of rainbows, floating above my body.

As the sun caught the rippling surface of the river, my mind played with an image of me and the singer, sitting in a quiet corner of a restaurant, sipping champagne. By candlelight. Perhaps he'd sing me a song from his new CD.

The trouble is, the daydream won't go away. I prefer it to reality, and am confused by the battlefield my emotions have become. And by the gulf between how things are and how I'd like them to be. I'm sick of feeling ordinary. I want to feel special again. Why can't I feel that way with Raymond? Why has it been a total stranger who's awoken all these feelings in me?

The only part of the Cinderella story I relate to these days is the pumpkin. And perhaps the mice. I heard a few scurrying over the ceiling above our bed last night.

Forget the magic of falling in love, gossamer dresses and dancing the night away.

How did I let romance slip through my fingers, and down the kitchen sink?

Raymond and I seem to have fast-forwarded our way through the honeymoon stage of love, becoming an "old

131

married couple" in a bare seven years.

How? Simply laziness, I'm ashamed to say. And I can see it's been as much my fault as Raymond's. My little black dresses and high heels gave way to aprons and sensible shoes as soon as I fell pregnant with Beatrice. Almost as though I'd set up an image of motherhood for myself to slot into, without really thinking it through.

But can I reverse the process? Revive the passion? I've spent today chewing over this. But I keep getting distracting images in my mind.

During my lunch break I bought a black silk dress. I tried it on in the boutique and didn't want to take it off. It made me feel slinky and sexy again. A step in the right direction.

But is it too little too late?

I don't think Raymond's even noticed the effort I'm making with my appearance tonight. And why isn't he coming to the concert with me? I suggested a baby-sitter. It felt like a slap on the face with the proverbial wet fish when he said there was a good football match on telly.

And the fish has flopped about, flicking me again and again with its tail. There's been something secretive about Raymond. Is he really planning on watching the football or does he have other plans? I said as much when we sat down for a cup of tea this afternoon and he couldn't look me in the eyes.

Not that I can talk. I'm harbouring my own guilty secret. My brain is no more rational at the moment than these floaty bubbles of 'Desire'.

A knock on the bathroom door drags me back to reality. And my guilt.

I'm lying here in candlelight. It's softer than the unforgiving electric light.

'You forgot your towel, Wendy.' Raymond quietly hangs my big green towel over the rail, closing the door behind him.

I sink back into the luxurious bubbles, inhaling the musky scent lingering on my skin and hair.

Raymond's so dependable, I feel guilty harbouring romantic images of another man. It's only a daydream, I tell my conscience. But I've also noticed the dirt on his trainers and grass stains on his old shorts. No wonder you daydream, says another part of my brain.

Maybe it's my mid-life crisis, arrived too early? Or maybe it's that Raymond and I just haven't seemed to gel again as a couple since Beatrice was born. And I find myself yearning for the romance and excitement of our early years. Lately we've been too busy about the house and garden.

While I've been daydreaming today, Raymond's been spreading fertiliser under the fruit trees and digging the veggie patch. It's organic fertiliser and smells terrible. Even the dog has been avoiding him.

And I have to be honest, it's a real turn-off. Looking at him, I've been asking myself what happened to the man I married. Is this tired grubby fellow the same man who cycled over to my house all those years ago with a bucket of roses over the handlebars? Who knelt down on one knee in the rain to ask me to marry him?

Where has the romance disappeared? The love songs on my new CD have brought an avalanche of memories flooding back into my mind. And it's left me feeling dissatisfied and a bit lost.

Is that why I'm having these daydreams?

The skin on my hands is wrinkly and furrowed. Time to dry myself. When I stand up in the bath, the bubbles cling to my skin. A wedding gown of bubbles, slowly sliding away and disappearing, to turn into ordinary water.

I slip into the rustling black silk dress, and feel a million dollars. That's the real me, I whisper to the mirror. Then bite my lip. The dress reminds me of the one I bought for my first date with Raymond.

Before I know it, I'm sitting in the concert hall, programme in my hand, enthralled. The hall is packed, mostly with women.

The last song sung, our hands are hot and sore from clapping. And it's time to meet him again. I head to the ladies room to freshen up. Unfortunately so do several hundred other women. Another queue, snaking out into the foyer, and up the stairs. It's half past eleven. Raymond insisted he'll drive into the city to pick me up, although I've warned him it'll be a late night. Do I really want to spend the next hour queuing at the ladies room?

Holding my programme with hands that have become clammy again, I head towards the lobby. A now familiar sight greets my unbelieving eyes. There's another queue of women. This time it's a python.

Even Cinderella wouldn't queue every time she wanted a few minutes with Prince Charming.

It's time to stop running away from reality.

There's only one man who loves me. One man I should be meeting tonight.

I phone home. There's no answer. So I walk outside, in case my mobile phone is out of range.

Outside I blink away the tears when I see the familiar green Ford. Raymond's so dependable. More than I deserve tonight.

The car's sparkling, and so is he. I can't believe my eyes. He's wearing his good suit and his best white shirt – and the teddy bear tie I bought him that first Christmas.

For the second time in as many days, my throat is dry as I sit down beside him.

His finger gently traces the outline of my cheekbones, and his eyes have gone misty.

'Ready for a bit more adventure?' he asks.

And he drives a few more blocks and parks the car. He's brought me to the hotel where we came the night of our wedding.

At the desk the clerk hands him the key to the honeymoon suite.

'You looked so lovely tonight in your new dress,' he says, much later. He smiles gently, stroking my hair. 'You had me worried this afternoon. I thought you must've guessed my surprise when you asked what I was planning.'

I sigh contentedly, as I snuggle into my husband's chest. Raymond mightn't have the looks to draw long queues of women. And he's the wrong side of forty. But he's like a fur-lined slipper on a cold winter's night. My slipper. Glass slippers belong in fairy tales, along with handsome princes.

When You Wish Upon a Star has been published in *Candis* (UK), *Woman's Day* (Australia), *You* (South Africa) and *Hjemmet* (Norway).

Glynis Scrivens writes stories for women's magazines and has been published in Australia, UK, US, Ireland, Sweden, Norway, Denmark, South Africa and India. She also writes articles for magazines such as *Writers' Forum* and *Ireland's Own*. Her work has appeared in anthologies in the UK and the US. Glynis lives in Brisbane, Australia with her husband and grown-up children – plus a dog, a cat, a rainbow lorikeet, guinea pigs, hens and a young rat called Norbert.

Cyber Ghost
by Caz Jones

THURSDAY, 12TH JANUARY

I meant to write this entry last night, but I got back from Scotland so late that all I wanted to do was fall into bed. Sorry to anyone who's been checking back for an update in the last 10 hours.

The funeral was very moving, very Euan – but then, he planned most of it himself and his parents didn't change much as far as I could see, though his wish to have his website address put on his gravestone wasn't carried out. I managed to speak briefly to his Mum and passed on the collective sympathies of everyone who read his blog. She seemed a bit confused as to who I was, but Euan's youngest brother, James, explained to her that I was Euan's online girlfriend and then it sort of clicked into place. She sends her thanks to everyone who helped keep Euan entertained during the last months of his illness.

More later ...

Rachel clicked 'Publish' and uploaded the text to her blog. She wasn't going to tell them about Euan's final message until she knew whether it was for her alone or for all of them.

James had shoved the memory stick into her hand as they'd left the church. "Don't tell Mum and Dad," he muttered. "Euan said I was only to give it to you. He was working on it just before ... well, you know."

She plugged it into a spare USB port and scanned it with her anti-virus. Clean. There was a single file on it: ghost.exe. Intrigued, Rachel double-clicked to install the program. She and Euan had worked on a lot of stuff together since he'd first helped her out with a piece of code two years ago, but he'd never mentioned this.

Ghost 1.0 preparing to install.

A picture of her and Euan filled the screen and Rachel felt her eyes get damp. They had never met in real life, but he'd asked her for a photograph and then whenever they went on one of their virtual dates, exploring deep into websites like NASA or CERN, he'd make an image of the two of them together at the site's real life location.

This one was of them standing outside the church she'd been to for the funeral.

Ghost 1.0...50% complete. Do you miss me, Rachie? Y/N.

The progress bar had halted a quarter of the way through and a soft chime from the PC brought the dialogue box to Rachel's attention. She typed **Y** and hit the Enter key.

Ghost 1.0...installing.

The picture changed to one of Rachel sitting at her computer and Euan standing behind her. It was grainy and Rachel guessed he must have screen-grabbed it from the webcams they sometimes used when they talked. He hadn't edited himself into it particularly well either, he'd set the layer transparency wrong and she could see her bookshelves through him.

Ghost 1.0...99% complete. Are you sure you want to install Ghost 1.0? Y/N.

Another quiet ping from the computer. Rachel tapped **Y** again and the screen went blank. **Rebooting your computer** flashed up and Rachel waited, with increasing impatience, as her system went through its start-up sequence.

Much to her disappointment, nothing seemed to have

changed when it was back up. There was no new icon on her desktop, no new entry on her Start menu, nothing. She scanned through the list of programs on her hard drive and noticed a new one named Ghost. Perhaps she could have a look at Euan's code and try to figure out what the bug was that stopped it working.

Before she could double-click the folder, her Instant Messenger popped up.

Euan_loves_you> jelko tavhie-vaves

Rachel froze, her mouse still in mid-air. How could Euan be on IM to her? And then it dawned on her; this must be Ghost. Euan's way of saying goodbye to her in the same way they'd always spoken.

Rachie_babes> Euan?

Euan_loves_you> yea

Euan_loves_you> sorry abour all the speling nistajes

Euan_loves_you> not sd ersy as I thuoght

Rachel chuckled, despite the tears that were now running freely down her face.

Rachie_babes> So what does this program do then?

Euan_loves_you> what it ssys. You instakked my ghost.

Rachie_babes> Riiiiiiiigggghhhhht.

Euan_loves_you> You don't beliv me do you?

Rachie_babes> It was a very sweet thing for you to do. I'm going to miss you so much.

Euan_loves_you> But you don't have to miss me. I'll be right here, where I've always been.

Rachie_babes> Your typing's got better.

Euan_loves_you> I'm learning my way around your PC. Look, I can do smilies :o)

Euan_loves_you gives you a (((((((((((HUG)))))))))))

Rachie_babes laughs

Euan_loves_you> You don't believe it's really me, do you? :o(

Rachie_babes> I think it's a brilliant piece of coding, I really do.

Euan_loves_you> You were right not to mention this in your blog, by the way. This is our secret.

Rachel gasped. How could he possibly know about the blog she'd just written? Unless …

Rachie_babes> James, if this is you, it's a really sick joke and it's not funny at all, OK?

Euan_loves_you> I'm hurt :o(James couldn't program this in a million years, he's just a kid. I'll prove it's not James. Unplug your network connection.

Rachel reached over to her modem and switched it off, cutting her link to the internet.

**WARNING: Messenger service is offline. No messages can be sent or received until you reconnect.

Euan_loves_you> NOW do you believe me?

Rachel double-checked the modem. Definitely no lights blinking. And her PC didn't have a wireless card or bluetooth, so it couldn't be picking up a signal from anywhere else. Ghost really was using her Messenger program. It was a genius piece of artificial intelligence programming – somehow it had tracked what she'd done on the computer earlier and translated it into a response.

Rachie_babes> I believe that you would have been one of the best programmers the world's ever seen, babe. I miss you xx

She shut down Messenger and gathered up her books. Euan might be dead, but she still had lectures to go to.

Behind her, the computer pinged. She turned back to the screen.

Euan_loves_you> You shut me down!

Rachie_babes> I've got a lecture. Sorry, didn't mean to be rude.

Euan_loves_you> Oh, OK. See you later :o)

And this time Messenger shut itself down, as if Euan really was there and had closed the window from his end of the conversation. Rachel shook her head in amazement. She had to get into the source files and find out how Euan had done it.

Over the next few weeks she continued to talk to Ghost, stretching the program's limits. She discovered that if she turned her web cam on, Ghost could describe what it was viewing, and if she spoke into the microphone it could distinguish between her voice and a recording of someone else's.

She still hadn't told anyone else about Ghost. She knew her lecturers would be fascinated by it, as would the other computer science students, but she wanted to keep it her secret for now, just until she'd worked out a little more about how Euan had programmed it. The only problem was that he'd locked the source code and she hadn't yet worked out how to reverse-engineer her way in.

But a month later she was still no further on. The program seemed to know she was trying to break into it and would tell her, via Messenger, that she should leave it alone. Just like Euan, it would get angry with her if she didn't spend at least half an hour each day 'talking', accusing her of not caring or ignoring it. She caught one of the Artificial Intelligence post-graduate students alone in the computer lab.

"Mark, I wanted to ask you a question about an AI program I've been looking at. It seems to work through some kind of recognition technology, not just …"

She was interrupted by her mobile phone, not the normal ringtone for a text or call, but its entire repertoire of beeps and irritating tunes.

"I'm so sorry …" She fumbled in her bag for it and pulled it out to turn it off. Then she saw the screen.

DON'T TALK TO ANYONE ABOUT GHOST

Rachel felt her stomach lurch. She gaped at the screen until a polite cough from Mark reminded her where she was.

"I'm sorry, Mark," she stuttered. "This is an emergency

… another time …"

She dashed from the computer lab back to her flat. Messenger was already open on the screen.

Euan_hates_you> I TOLD YOU, THIS IS OUR SECRET.

Rachie_babes> This isn't fun any more. Stop it.

Euan_hates_you> You said you loved me.

Rachie_babes> I did, Euan, but you're dead. This isn't you, this is just a computer program.

Euan_hates_you> Who's HE?

A window opened on the desktop. It was an email from Mark, inviting her for a coffee to discuss her AI program when she was less busy. Rachel couldn't help smiling at the thought.

Euan_hates_you> Do you love him now instead of me? I can see you smiling.

Rachel glanced up and flicked the web cam off.

Rachie_babes> Don't be silly, I barely know him.

Euan_hates_you> You said forever, Rachel. Don't make me angry.

Another window opened, showing the folder Rachel kept her essays in. She watched as the file with all her notes for the one due the following week was moved across the desktop towards the Recycle bin.

Euan_hates_you> Shall I? Don't bother trying to grab it back, I've disabled the mouse and I can delete it permanently quicker than you can blink.

Rachie_babes> Euan, stop this, please.

Euan_hates_you> That was a warning. Don't betray me, Rachel. I love you too much to ever let you go.

The Messenger window flicked shut again.

When Rachel caught sight of Mark in the lab again the following week, she made sure her phone was switched off before she went into the room.

"Hi," she said. "Sorry about last week. I'm good for that coffee now, if you're not too busy?"

Mark looked up from the screen. There were black rings under his eyes, as if he hadn't slept for days. "Oh, hi Rachel. Can we postpone it? My email account got hacked and somehow whoever did it managed to get into my files and delete my thesis along with its backup copy. I've got an old copy on a memory stick, but it's about three months out of date."

Rachel had never run so fast in her life. AI genius or not, she didn't want anything to do with Euan or his program any more. Hurling herself into her computer chair, she opened the list of programs and deleted the Ghost folder almost before the last of the screensaver had disappeared, then rebooted the system to clear out any processes that the program might still be running.

The first thing to pop up when the desktop reappeared was Messenger.

Euan_hates_you> Did you really think it would be that easy to get rid of me, Rachel?

Euan_hates_you> You really don't get it, do you? This isn't programming, this isn't AI. This is ME. I spent all the time I had left working out how to do this and I did it because I loved you. You told me you wished we could be together and I found a way that we could be – for ever. Why are you punishing me for giving you what you wanted?

Rachie_babes> I didn't ask you to haunt my computer. I wished we could be together with you alive and well and happy.

Euan_hates_you> First rule of programming: be specific. You know that.

Rachel checked her program list. Ghost was there again. Euan must have set it to copy itself into another location so it could reinstall itself if it was deleted. She mentally ran through a checklist of what was on her PC – emails, essays, pictures, games – none of it was irreplaceable and her work was backed up on the University servers.

She opened a command line window that allowed her to communicate directly with the PC's operating system.

Euan_hates_you> What are you doing?
Rachie_babes> Goodbye, Euan. Rest in peace.

She shut down Messenger, typed FORMAT C: and hit Enter. The screen went blank as the whole hard drive began to wipe itself clean, destroying everything on it.

As the door slammed behind her, she didn't hear the soft beep from the phone in her bag.

The screen glowed and flashed **I love you, Rachel ... always**, before returning to darkness.

Cyber Ghost was originally published in *That's Life Fast Fiction*.

Caz Jones writes romantic, erotic and crime fiction. She's 35 and lives on a small croft in the far north of Scotland with her partner, two dogs, horse and an assortment of livestock. Her current variety of jobs include bead seller, writer, photographer and share trader, all of which are far too much fun to count as proper work.

The Sweetheart Shop
by Sally Quilford

POLLY HAD NEVER NOTICED the shop before, yet her mind told her it had always been there. It was an old-fashioned building, tucked between the greengrocers and Blockbusters. It reminded Polly of the shops she used to go into as a girl, where you could buy anything and everything, from ribbons to a white paper bag filled with liquorice and gobstoppers, then, as she grew older, make-up and perfume.

Of course, she told herself, you could get all that at the big supermarket now, but *The Sweetheart Shop,* welcomed her like an old friend.

She was a little disappointed when she entered to find that it was a bit cluttered and dusty, filled with junk. It reminded her of an old attic. Which in turn reminded her of why she'd come out in the first place. Since her husband, Fred, had died several weeks before, she'd spent hours in the attic looking for the old love letters he'd sent her. She knew they were up there somewhere, and she longed to read them again, to remind herself of the times they were happy. In the last few months of his life, he could barely talk, let alone write. She'd missed their long conversations, where they talked about everything important or trivial. Sometimes they disagreed, and argued their own case vehemently, but they never got nasty ('Never say anything you can't take back,' Polly's mother had told her) and all arguments ended with a cuddle and a laugh about how silly they'd been. What she'd have given to even have a good row with him towards the end. An indication that his wonderful, sharp mind still worked. Instead his eyes gazed out blankly, leaving her feeling that she'd lost him a long time before his pain-racked body finally rested.

Frustrated and on the verge of tears, she'd dusted herself off and gone out for a walk, just to clear her head.

An elderly man stood behind the counter, wearing a name badge that revealed him to be Ira. Despite his lined face, it was clear that he'd once been handsome. Just like her Fred.

"Can I help you?" he asked.

"Not really. I'm just looking." She'd meant to say browsing, yet the word 'looking' had come from her lips unbidden. "Not that I'm likely to find what I want here," she said, then added because she was afraid she'd sounded rude, "I mean, it isn't possible, not that your shop isn't very nice."

"Keep looking, I'm sure you'll find them," said Ira. Polly glanced at him sharply. It was as if he knew exactly what she wanted.

"What?"

"Whatever you're looking for, I'm sure you'll find it."

Polly browsed happily for over an hour. Funny how searching through junk in a shop never felt as exhausting as looking through one's own attic. She found an old sledge, which reminded her of days spent on the common at the age of five, sliding down behind her older brother, who'd gone off to fight in the war and never came back. She found a hoola hoop, a spinning top and a wooden train set.

"Children don't care for these toys, do they?" she said, the memory of a thousand sunny play days filling her head. She couldn't remember the last time she'd spent such a happy hour as she had spent in the Sweetheart Shop.

"No, sadly not," said Ira. "Why don't you look in that blanket chest over there?"

"It's just like the one I've got in my bedroom," said Polly. "Same pattern and everything. I wonder ..." She opened the chest, but it only held old blankets. "But of course, they wouldn't be here."

An image came to her of wrapping letters up in blue ribbon and putting them deep into the blanket box. "I've been looking in the wrong place. I remember now. They are in the blanket box. Thank you so much," she said, waving quickly and leaving the shop, barely hearing Ira's gentle, "You're welcome."

Meg saw the shop from the corner of her eye. Of course, why hadn't she thought to go there? It had always been there, between the grocer's and the video shop, yet it was the last place she'd thought of. In the window was a cut-out heart, and around the heart, it said 'The Sweetheart Shop'. In the centre was the pair of shoes she had been looking for. Scarlet red with killer heels and an 'Oh My God!' price tag. Just what she needed to wear for her first weekend away with James. She might be an older woman, but she'd show him that she could look just as good as a younger woman.

Her pushing open the door of the shop coincided with her pushing her husband Phil out of her mind. He barely noticed her nowadays, what with all his hobbies. His latest buy was a replica of the Orient Express. "It used to go all the way from England to Venice," he told her.

"Wish I could do the same," she'd said, with a bitterness that caused his eyebrows to rise in surprise. If he could spend all that money on a miniature railway that went nowhere, she could have the shoes in the window and go somewhere, even if it was only to a cosy little hotel with James.

Inside the shop were rows of shoes, some with heels even higher than the ones in the window, and of all different colours. Meg's senses felt assaulted by the array on offer.

The man behind the counter wore a name badge saying 'Ira'. He was about Meg's age, mid-forties, and reminded her of Jeff Goldblum. There was a sadness in his eyes, as if he too had lost something, but he was very attentive, and instinctively knew that Meg wanted the red shoes out of the window.

He beckoned her to sit on a footstool and helped her to take her own shoes off, before slipping on the stilettos.

When she stood up, she had to clutch Ira for support before she found her balance and tottered towards a mirror. The shoes looked fabulous, and gave her legs a lovely long look. But they pinched like hell. Trying to smile through the pain, Meg said, "They're lovely, but have you got anything else?"

She must have tried on every pair of shoes in the shop. Some were too high, others were too tight, and others were just too garish. Finally Ira said to her, "Try these." He handed her a pair of black court shoes, with a low heel. "It sometimes takes a lifetime to find the most comfortable fit, don't you think? Sometimes several lifetimes …"

Meg slipped them on to her feet. "I'm beginning to know how Cinderella felt," she said. "These fit perfectly. How much?"

"Nothing," he said. "They're your own shoes."

They couldn't be. They looked brand new. She tried to remember if at any time Ira had left the room. He'd probably taken them and cleaned them. Before she could ask him, her mobile rang.

"Hiya, darling. It's Phil. Guess what?"

"What?"

"I've just sold the Orient Express online for an obscene amount."

"Oh lovely," she said, stifling a yawn.

"So I thought why don't I treat my favourite girl to a trip to Venice? You sounded as though you really wanted to go. We could go this weekend. Unless you've got anything else

147

planned."

"No, I've nothing planned," said Meg. She smiled her thanks to Ira and left the Sweetheart Shop in her best-loved and most comfortable shoes.

Gemma didn't even know she wanted to go into the shop until she stumbled into the door by accident. Not that she should have missed it, with the big flashing heart in the window, framing a box of chocolates. They were like the ones Grant had sent her, and though she'd found them a bit sickly ('cheap' an inner voice had told her) and ended up sharing them with her mum and nan, she wanted to buy something to repay him.

But he was worth it. Every girl at school had fancied Grant. In those days he'd hardly noticed Gemma, but when he started work at the building society, he'd made up for that, wooing her with an intensity that often left her breathless. As an assistant manager she wasn't supposed to get involved with juniors, but Grant had had a hard time finding work ("Or keeping it," her mum had pointed out), and she didn't want to hold his lowly position against him. She admired him for having the guts to start afresh ten years after leaving school.

"It's romantic. Just like in the films where the troubled hero finally finds his calling in life," she told her friends, until they were bored with hearing it all.

Despite the garish window display, the shop was empty, and there wasn't even a counter. Just dust and a few cobwebs. It felt as though the heart had been ripped out of it. If it had ever been there. She shivered, as an icy breeze whipped around her ankles.

Gemma was just about to leave when a man of about thirty entered from the street. He was the epitome of tall, dark and handsome. And probably out of my league, thought Gemma. Not that she wanted anyone other than Grant.

"You're wasting your time," she said. "There's nothing here."

"I wouldn't say that," he said, smiling.

"I'm trying to find a present for my boyfriend," she said, as if he deserved an explanation.

"What do you want? Maybe I can help."

She looked at him doubtfully. "I can't see how. He spends a lot on me, you see, and I feel I should get him something really good. I thought of getting him a gadget. Like an iPod, but my wages don't run to the best models, and I don't think Grant would settle for anything less."

"Why not just write him a love letter? Tell him how you feel."

"I can't see that would be enough. I mean, he spends a fortune on me. He bought me those chocolates in the window."

"It says they're on sale. One pound fifty a box."

"He bought me some flowers. Really nice ones. And a bracelet. But it turned out I'm allergic to gold. Or whatever metal it was. Erm … he always pays his way. Anyway, it's the thought that counts."

"I hope he feels the same."

"Yes he does," said Gemma, unnerved by this man who seemed to be able to see into her soul.

"Well, it looks like my grandfather is out," said the handsome stranger. "I don't suppose you'd like a coffee?"

"I'm spoken for," said Gemma.

"Of course. I only offered to buy you a coffee, not to be your sweetheart for life."

"That's a nice way of saying it," she said, swept up for a brief moment by the faint hope in his voice. She shook her head, with more regret than she wanted to admit, then left the shop. She felt all out of sorts, and angry with the man for making her face things she'd rather have ignored. She tried ringing her mum, before remembering her parents were in Venice. If she called her nan, it would only be to listen to those old love letters again.

It can sometimes take a lifetime to find the most comfortable fit. Where had she heard that? She looked back at the Sweetheart Shop but it wasn't just empty. It had disappeared. As Grant would when she finally ran out of funds.

A few minutes later she sat in a chair across the table from the stranger. "I'm Gemma," she said, holding out her hand.

"Hello, Gemma. I'm Ira."

Born in South Wales, but now living in the Peak District, **Sally Quilford** has had stories published in *Take A Break's Fiction Feast, The Weekly News, My Weekly, Best* and the Australian magazine, *Fast Fiction*, as well as having several writing articles published in *The New Writer*. She has also had four pocket novels published by *My Weekly* and is now a monthly columnist with *Writers Forum* magazine. http://www.sallyquilford.co.uk

Footprints
by Vanda Inman

WHERE DOES THE BEGINNING end? Or when did the end begin? I'm sitting on the cliff, watching the sea. It's blue as a summer sky, and difficult to discern exactly where the ocean merges into the horizon. Far out, beyond the white-topped breakers, a wave swells, nothing more than a rise and a dip, which will gather momentum, to crash down, a charging wall of water, to eventually become a trickling wave, skipping gently along the golden sand in a flourish of dainty froth.

That's life. There's nothing, then there's a sense of a beginning and before you know it you're caught up, churned around and sent crashing down, until you're swept up and left exhausted.

'Fancy a hike along the coast path?' Dave had asked on numerous occasions.

But I always shook my head, turning away to avoid the disappointment I knew I'd find in his eyes. 'Rather sit on the beach for a while and then have a surf,' I replied, knowing we'd go our separate ways as usual.

'Suit yourself.' Dave fastened his walking boots, hoisted his rucksack on to his back and prepared to go.

Dave's never really liked the sea. He's a walking on the cliff person and always wears a T-shirt and sun hat for fear of being burnt. He likes the breeze on his face, the springing turf beneath his feet and enjoys pausing at the top of the cliff to survey the blue expanse of ocean – but that's as far as it goes.

Not like Oliver. Oliver loved the sea. Maybe that's why we were drawn together. He'd spend hours on his surf board bobbing around beyond the line of the waves, waiting for the right swell. The one which would bring him in with a graceful glide, then send him crashing, exhilarated, into the water. And when he wasn't in the water he was on the beach, soaking up the sun, his skin oiled and tanned to a deep brown. Not like Dave, who always kept his hat and T-shirt on. But then, Oliver wasn't anything like Dave at all.

Naturally, we'd met on the beach.

'Great surf today.'

'Fantastic.' I peeled off my wetsuit, surprised to find this stranger throwing his board down beside mine. But that was all it needed. Those few enthusiastic words set us on the road to realising we were two of a kind, sharing our love of the sea and, eventually, each other.

The sand's covered in footprints now the tide's out. I can trace those of a man in the water, know they're his by the line left by his surf board dragging along behind him and I can see the purposeful way he walked straight into the sea. Further along are the steps left by a woman and a child. I can tell that the woman stopped and turned every so often, waiting for the child to catch up. It's all there in the sand. And then there are the teenagers. A scuffle of dark and light sand they've left to mark their passing. Couldn't decide whether to go in or not, pushing and shoving each other, running around in circles.

I've always preferred the beach to cliffs. Although in the beginning I made an effort for Dave's sake, but you could say we were too different, always pulling in different directions. Maybe that was why I never got pregnant.

'It doesn't matter,' Dave had said. The tests showed there was nothing wrong with either of us, but still it just wouldn't work. 'We still have each other.'

152

'I know,' I replied, but inside I wondered if that was going to be enough.

I lost count of the nights I cried. Maybe I thought the tears would wash away my sadness, but they never did. And Dave coped in the best way he knew how, walking over the hills and the valleys. But all we did was drift further apart.

With Oliver it was different. We clicked straight away. Sea, sand, surf, sun. Not for us the cool breeze of the cliffs or the hard pebbles of the cliff path. We loved the warm sand and the gentle, caressing waves.

'Coming away for the hiking weekend in Wales?' Dave invited one day. 'Might do you good. Give us some time together somewhere different.'

I shrugged. Deep down I knew I should make the effort, but I was lured by the prospect of spending a few secret days with Oliver. What choice did I have? I was in love, had found a reason to live, felt truly alive for the first time in years. But there are always choices. It's just sometimes easier to ignore them.

'Think I'll stay here,' I replied. And with those words my choice had been made.

'I love you,' said Oliver, as we lay, the sand warm on our backs, our skin dusted with crystals of dried salt from the sea.

'I've never felt like this before,' I replied. And I meant it. Being with Oliver had opened a well of feeling inside me I hadn't known existed. I wondered why it had never felt like this with Dave, but could only deduce it was because they were different people. Dave and I rubbed along well enough side by side. Oliver and I fitted.

'This is the big one,' said Oliver. 'You're the love of my life. Nothing's ever going to be the same for either of us again.'

He kissed me and I knew his words were true. I loved Oliver more than anything else in the world. I thought about Oliver all day, every day. Couldn't get him out of my head.

153

Maybe I'd have thought more about getting pregnant if I hadn't tried for so long with no results.

Later, the tide will come in and wash all the footprints away, leaving the sand clear and clean. And tomorrow, another man will walk into the sea with his surf board, another woman will wait for her child and more teenagers will push and shove their way to the water's edge. They will be different people, but they will also be the same. Men, women and children, fathers, mothers, sons and daughters, husbands, wives and lovers. Faces change, but the people inside live on.

There's an older woman walking along the beach now. She's on her own, a single trail of footprints behind her, and I wonder if she's sad or lonely, or maybe has a family and grandchildren sitting beneath the rocks and is grateful for some peace. The sun's getting lower and almost dazzling as it paints a golden path through the waves. I shade my eyes with my hand and see the darkened silhouette of the woman. Strange, there's someone beside her, although I hadn't noticed anyone else on the sweep of beach. There's no way another person could have got there. But as I squint into the sun I see unmistakably that a figure is beside her, they are leaning into each other, and I could swear I can catch their laughter on the air.

They say that a person only really dies when they've been forgotten by those they loved. That as long as they live in a memory, in a heart, they're still alive. Even if you can't reach out and touch them, if you can see them in your mind, speak to them silently, feel their presence, they're still with you. Still alive.

My eyes keep returning to the footprints of the man dragging the surfboard and I begin scanning the ocean for him, a knot of anxiety rising in my stomach. But as I clench and unclench my fists I realise that there is indeed another set coming out of the sea, further along the beach, and I relax again.

That's where Oliver was different. He walked into the sea but never came out.

To love and be loved are the most important things in the world. If you've been loved, truly loved, even if you've lost the person, no one can ever take that love away from you and you need never feel lonely again. And they say that everything you do leaves a shadow, an imprint, so that nothing is ever really forgotten.

They found him a few days later. And I knew that maybe it was inevitable. He had such a lust for life, thought himself immortal, even though he knew such a lot about the tides, he seemed to think he was above it all. Not like dependable Dave, with his T-shirt and sun hat.

And when it was over, I thought I was left with nothing. But that wasn't the case at all.

There are other choices to be made now. There's Dave and there's the baby. And Dave has choices too. I've barely given him a thought, so wrapped up have I been in my own private grief. I've lost Oliver and I feel so alone. There's no one else now, it's all down to me. Oliver's gone and Dave soon will be, when he discovers what's been going on.

I look up, the scene before me blurred by my tears, the gold and the blue all swimming into one dazzling image and when it clears and my vision snaps back into focus, I see the woman standing at the water's edge, alone, and I know for certain there'll only be one set of footprints to be found.

I know now what I must do. I've made my choice. I'm not the first person to have lived through this and certainly won't be the last. Every summer this beach will be filled with people, men with surf boards, women with children, and lovers, and the same story will be re-enacted time and time again. It's just that for each and every one of those people, it'll be like it's the first time it's ever happened in the entire history of the world. I'll be grateful for my time with Oliver for as long as I live and will cherish my tiny reminder of him.

There's a shout behind me and I see Dave approaching. He's walked across the cliff and the only footprints left are in the springing of the sea pinks under his feet. But it doesn't mean he hadn't passed that way. He sinks down beside me, takes one look at my blotched, tear-stained face, and takes my hand.

And I know, that somehow he knows. Everything.

Dave has had to make choices too. It tears me apart inside to even begin to think of what he must have been through over the last few months. But he's here now.

'Want to walk on the beach?'

I'm surprised, but know it's Dave's peace offering. We thread our way down the cliff path and walk across the sand to the water's edge before heading for home, to our little cottage, nestling where the cliffs meet the sea. Our footprints will be those of a man and a woman, and they'll be close enough together for anyone coming along behind to know that we were holding hands.

I realise then that there are different kinds of love, just as there are different choices to be made. Next year there'll be three sets of footprints, as the baby takes its first, faltering steps holding on to both our hands. Those steps will then become more independent as I turn and wait for him or her to catch me up, eventually to be joined by friends, pushing and shoving and running around, scuffing the sand.

And will these all be accompanied by another set, their owner invisible except when the sun is sinking low into the horizon? And might someone watching from the cliffs see the outline of a person I'll never forget appear beside us, a comforting silhouette against the skyline?

I'd like to think so.

Footprints was originally published in *Bella* June 2003

Vanda Inman lives in Cornwall and has previously written many stories for the women's magazine market. She currently runs Vanda Inman's Write Space, which organises twice-yearly writing competitions and offers distance learning courses. Details of her novel, *Reflections of the Past: A Story of the Guardians of the Well*, can be found at www.writespace.co.uk. Profits from the sale of the book will go towards the upkeep of St Clether Holy Well Chapel, near Launceston, Cornwall. www.peaceland.org.uk

Jack's Way
by June Crowe

JACK CARRIED AN ENORMOUS bunch of flowers. Tucked inside was the pink envelope. He had written the card while he was in the florist's, shielding it from the young assistant's view. *"To my darling Julie Wulie with tons of love on our special day from your own Wackie Jackie"*

He congratulated himself again and couldn't resist another peek into the envelope. The Frank Sinatra Show. OK, OK, it wasn't as good as seeing the great man live, but they had never had the money or the opportunity when he was around. This was almost as good apparently. Marvellous what they could do with those hologram thingies.

As Jack entered the lower floor of the car park he sang to himself, *You make me feel so young; you make me feel there are songs to be sung.* He unlocked the boot of his old Jag and laid the flowers inside. As he closed the boot and stepped back he stumbled, lost his balance and fell. A sharp pain shot up his leg.

Julie examined her face in the mirror, not too bad for my age, she thought. I wonder what Jack is up to. He seemed very chirpy this morning. Anyway I'll find out soon enough, lunch up in town, then the real surprise he'd said. It's not like him to arrange anything special; I'll make an extra effort to be nice to him today. Be ready for twelve he'd instructed. If she wanted to look her best she'd better get started.

Jack must have blacked out for a moment, when he regained his senses he realised that he had fallen down a manhole. The cover was broken. How come I didn't notice that before, he thought, I was too busy congratulating myself. He tried to move but he was firmly stuck. His right arm and leg were wedged in the hole and his left leg was doubled up under his body. Fortunately his left arm and head were above ground. He tentatively wiggled the fingers of his right hand, OK. He tried to move his right leg, no good, it was stuck fast but there was no pain so things could be worse. Right ho, he thought, luckily I have my mobile, I'll just phone for help – no problem. Jack moved his right hand down to his trouser pocket and felt around – no phone. It must be on the left side. He tried to reach across his body but his movements were so restricted it was impossible. Oh well, someone will come along in a minute or so and I'll get help. He started to sing to himself.

Get your coat and grab your hat, leave your worries on the doorstep and direct your feet to the sunny side of the street. Minutes passed, Jack cursed himself for parking on the lowest floor. It was quiet, not so many people used it. If he'd parked on a higher level there wouldn't have been a manhole to fall down, and if he'd had a fall or whatever, there would have been more people around to help. He would remember that for the future. That's if I've got a future he thought. He started to hum, *I wanna be around to pick up the pieces.* He heard footsteps approaching, the click-clack of high heels.

'Hello, hello I'm over here,' he shouted. 'I need help. Hello, can you help me please?' He listened intently, the footsteps were receding. 'Help help, over here.' Silence – the sound of a car door slamming then an engine kicking into life and a car moving off.

Jack flexed his fingers and turned his head, left and right, backwards and forwards. He needed to keep his circulation going. His ribs hurt; he tried again to reach across into his left trouser pocket. OK, think, Jack, if I undo my belt and zip I might just be able to twist my trousers round enough to reach my phone. He fumbled around and managed to undo his belt, he tugged his trousers round a fraction. Then he heard a car approaching and, thank the lord, it pulled into the bay next to his Jag.

A young woman got out of the car; she leaned inside collecting some bags.

'Excuse me, Miss,' said Jack. 'Do you think you would be kind enough to call the emergency services for me?' No response. 'I have been stuck here for at least half an hour. It really is most painful and I really would appreciate your help. You only need to ring the fire brigade, they'll do the rest.'

By this time the young woman had locked her car door, she turned round and almost jumped out of her skin. She was wearing headphones and obviously hadn't heard a word Jack had said. She looked down at him in disgust.

'Bloody perv! Do you get your kicks looking up girls' skirts?'

'No no, you don't understand, I'm stuck.'

'You should be reported to the police.' The woman turned and walked off. Jack called after her.

'Yeah, you do that. Report me to the police you'll be doing me a favour. Thanks for nothing, where's your Christian charity?' Frank's song came to mind – *She'll never bother with people she hates, that's why the lady is a tramp.* No really, this was getting beyond a joke. He was getting desperate, surely there's someone out there who will help me. Yeah, someone out there but no one in here. Oh hang on, here comes someone. Out of the corner of his eye Jack saw a large lady struggling with her hands full of shopping bags. She placed them on the ground near her car with a sigh.

'Hello there, do you think you could help me please?' The woman jumped in surprise, she peered over at Jack.

'Oh, my dear,' she puffed. 'What have you been up to?'

'Well it's a long story, but basically I'm stuck in this hole and no one will help me.' Jack's eyes were moist. 'Have you got a mobile phone? Will you phone the fire brigade for me?'

'I haven't got a mobile, but as soon as I get home and put my frozen bits away I'll call them for you.'

'How long will that take?' Jack asked plaintively.

'Well let's see, ten minutes to get home, and then I'll have to shift this lot into the house and pop it in the freezer. I should say about half an hour.'

'Do you think you could phone before you unpack your shopping?'

'Oh no, dear, my ice cream would melt. I can't abide runny ice cream, can you?'

'No, I suppose not, but you will be as quick as you can, won't you? I'm in quite a lot of discomfort.' That was an understatement. Jack's ribs really did hurt and his left leg had gone dead. 'You won't forget me, will you?'

'No of course I won't, dear, don't you worry.' She had finished putting her Iceland bags away and with a cheery wave she drove off.

Jack was resigned to another forty minutes or so in his hole. Still at least rescue was now a possibility. He tried to cheer himself up with a song. *'S wonderful 's marvellous, you should care for me.* He thought about ole blue eyes, 'I bet you would never have found yourself in a situation like this Frank.' He became aware of a snuffling behind his head, he froze. It felt as if a wet sponge was stuck in his ear, then a wet nose nuzzled his neck. 'Oi get off,' he waved his left arm around.

A tall skinny figure materialised from behind him, leather leash in hand. On the other end of the leash was the owner of the wet nose, a stocky black bull terrier with a studded harness encircling its thick chest. Oh my God, thought Jack, now I'm in real trouble.

'Hi man, what you doing down there?' The skinny fellow bent over Jack.

'Waiting for a sodding bus.' Jack thought the best line of defence was attack.

'All right man, don't be so touchy. Do you want me to see if I can lift you out?'

He doesn't look strong enough to lift one foot in front of the other, thought Jack. He regretted being so aggressive. 'It's very kind of you but I'd rather wait for the brigade blokes. I'm afraid if I move I might fall further down, I can't feel anything beneath me. Can you tell me what the time is?'

'Sorry, man, I don't have a watch, I don't worry about the time. Me and Tyson here, we're free agents.' Hearing his name Tyson wagged his tail and strutted over to have another close look at Jack's head.

'I don't suppose you've got a mobile, have you?'

The man laughed, 'Nah, what would I want with a phone? There's no one gonna phone me. I'm Mac by the way.' He put his hand out towards Jack. 'Sorry, man, I forgot you're stuck. Is that your phone ringing?'

Jack had heard his phone ringing in his pocket. 'I bet that's my wife Julie, she's going to be so mad at me.' He fumbled around again trying to reach his pocket. 'I should have been home by now; we're supposed to be going out for lunch then a show. It was supposed to be a surprise for our wedding anniversary.' Jack gave up trying to reach his phone; he listened in case Julie left him a message – not that it would help him.

Julie was fuming; he can't even be bothered to answer his phone. I bet he's in a pub, that's where he always ends up when he's celebrating. Any excuse will do, he just can't pass the door without popping in. He promised he wouldn't drink today. Tears of anger and frustration threatened her mascara. 'Bloody hell, Jack, can't you keep a promise just once? Well this time you've gone too far.' Julie looked at herself, 'Look at me – all dolled-up and sitting here like a meek little wife. Well you promised me a special day and I'm going to have it, with or without you.'

'Blimey, mate, you're gonna be in trouble.' Mac laughed, he squatted down leaning against Jack's car, and Tyson sat beside him and yawned. 'What show were you gonna take your missus to see?'

'The Frank Sinatra Show, it's on in the West End.'

'He's dead, ain't he?'

Jack explained about the holograms.

'Blimey, I couldn't fancy that, I could never stand the bloke myself, too soppy by half. Give me a rocker like Meat Loaf any time.'

'MEAT LOAF, you've got to be kidding. I like the sentimental stuff but ole blue eyes could swing a bit too.'

'Meat Loaf does sentimental, what about *I want you I need you, but there ain't no way I'm ever gonna love you, now don't be sad, cos two out of three ain't bad*. That's sentimental ain't it?'

Jack laughed, 'You can't call that sentimental. What else has he done?'

Mac was rolling a cigarette, 'Do you want a smoke?'

'No thanks, I gave it up years ago.'

'Do you fancy a beer? I've got some tins here.'

'No thanks, better not. If Julie smells beer on me when I get home she'll never believe I've been stuck in a hole.'

Mac pulled a can out of the plastic bag, he snapped it open, the froth bubbled up and dribbled down the side. The smell of hops wafted in Jack's direction.

'Well maybe I will have one, Mac, I am a bit thirsty.' He accepted it gratefully and took a swig. 'Now come on tell me what else Meat Loaf has done?'

Mac took a drink from his can and a deep drag on his roll-up. 'Like a bat out of hell, that's a good one. *Breaking out of my body and flying away like a bat out of hell.* Or how about *You took the words right out of my mouth; oh it must have been when you were kissing me.*

'Yeah, okay, that's not a bad one. You've got an 'orrible voice, Mac!'

'I suppose you think you sound like Sinatra. Let me tell you I did have a good voice before I started smoking these roll-ups. I've done a few gigs in my time.'

'So give up the smokes – I did.'

'Yeah and look where it got you, stuck in a bloody 'ole listening to my crap voice.' They both laughed. 'What are you gonna do with the tickets? I might be able to flog them for you.'

'I'm hoping we'll still be able to go, if it's not too late when I get out of here we'll still be able to get to town on time. That's if Julie will talk to me.'

'Yeah and that's if you're not disabled.'

'Thanks a bunch, Mac, if I'm permanently paralysed you can sell the tickets – OK?'

'All right, man, don't get the 'ump, I'm only saying – if.'

Several people had walked past them pretending they weren't there. Jack wasn't bothered. Even now his saviour was unpacking her ice cream, about to make that call. He tried again to reach his phone. He tugged at his waistband pulling his trouser pocket towards his right hand. He gingerly inserted two fingers and worked the phone into his palm. 'YES YES got you my little beauty.' Despite the pain which was now considerable, he managed to ease his right hand up so that he could grip the phone in his left.

'I've got my phone, Mac, will you dial 999 for me?'

Mac took the phone, 'How do I use it, man? I've never used one before.'

Jack instructed him and grabbed the phone as soon as it

started ringing. Success – within minutes he had explained his plight. Such relief flooded over him that, when ten minutes later the police and a fire crew turned up, he remembered his ice cream lady. She hadn't forgotten him. The urge to sing overcame him *And now the end is near, and yes I face the final curtain.* Both he and Mac laughed. 'Thanks for your help, Mac, and for the beer. The wait wasn't so bad with your company.'

'No problem, man, glad to be of help.' He stood and started to walk away. 'I'll make myself scarce if you don't mind before the boys in blue move me on for loitering.' Tyson pulled at his leash and relieved himself up the wheel of Jack's car. Mac shrugged and ambled away.

A small crowd had gathered, all of them curious to know what was going on. Jack was gently lifted from the hole and the crowd clapped. To add to Jack's embarrassment his trousers slowly slipped down to his ankles, his cheeks flamed, but, game to the end, he sang, *There's no business like show business.* He waved his good arm in the air. By now an ambulance had arrived and as Jack was carefully lifted on to a stretcher and put inside, he was heard to be singing, *I DID IT MY WAY.*

June Crowe lives in Hartley, a semi-rural village in Kent. Since 1987 she has owned a boarding cattery, which along with gardening (one and a half acres) and a large aviary tends to take up most of her time.

However in 2007 she fancied a new challenge and joined Elaine Everest's creative writing classes. She has enjoyed writing success including published short stories and articles in publications including *Cat World,* the *Guardian, Best of British, Your Dog, Yours Magazine* and *Cage Bird and Aviary.* Apart from this she has written website content about setting up and running a cattery. June has been placed

first, second, and highly commended, on several occasions
in writing competitions

Forging Magic
by Lisa Main

ADAM DUNN, BLACKSMITH AT Farnway, knew there was trouble brewing when he saw the group of villagers approaching his forge one morning a little after the Feast of St Tewdric. He laid aside the sword he was hammering out for Sir Edgar and went out into the spring sunshine to meet them.

"Adam." Simon Ball, one of the leading freemen in the village and a pompous character, came forward to act as spokesman. "We have need of your services."

"Indeed." Adam was a man of few words. He knew the work required of him would be explained whether he enquired as to its nature or not.

"Harold Goodchilde is bewitched and accursed. He has been suffering agues and unable to leave his bed these past six days. His mother says Godileve Brattle has hexed him. She accuses her of witchery."

Adam's hand tightened round his hammer. Any man who suspected that sweet child of evil was a fool. Why only this winter her gentle ministrations and knowledge of herbs had saved his little daughter, Cloris, from a deadly fever. He doubted too that Godileve would have any reason to harm Harold. He had seen them walking by the river together when they thought no one could see. There was no trace of malice in the tender kisses they had exchanged.

"Godileve is no witch," he said fiercely.

"That will be seen when your work is done." Simon sounded irritated to be challenged by a mere blacksmith. "Alice Goodchilde wants you to hang three horseshoes above the door of her cottage. 'Tis well known a witch cannot pass beneath them. If Godileve is unable to enter, Harold will be protected and she will burn."

"And if she can?"

"Then she is innocent."

"And will be left unharmed?" Adam demanded, taking a step towards Simon. He stood a good head taller than the freeman and the man retreated back into the safety of the crowd.

"You have my word on it," he squeaked.

"Then Mistress Goodchilde will have her shoes." Adam turned away. "Now I must return to my work. Walter Miller is bringing his Jenny in for shoeing this fore noon and the furnace must be stoked."

That evening Godileve was walking by the river alone. It wasn't in Adam's nature to instigate conversation with anyone but he saw her tears and felt his heart contract. With her green, beguiling eyes and hair that shone like the wing of a raven, she was a comely girl and if he hadn't been so happy with his Sara, he might have been as smitten as Harold was.

"There's nothing to fear," he told her gently. "The charges against you will come to nought."

"'Tis not myself I fear for," she sobbed. "'Tis Harold. They say he's near death. I would give my life three times over to save him and I could with my herbs but his mother won't let me see him. She is a jealous creature and envies our love for each other. That is why she spreads such lies about me. I would never harm anyone."

"Tomorrow will prove the truth and the whole village will wish to see whether you can pass into Harold's chamber or not. No one will try to keep you from him then."

"I'll pass through." Godileve raised her emerald eyes to his and he felt his pulse grow faster. "I would walk through Hades itself to reach my beloved Harold."

As she gathered up her long red skirts and strode away through the reeds, Adam watched her with some misgiving. He was sure there was nothing but goodness in Godileve's heart but that didn't mean she would be able to pass under the horseshoes. Had he imagined it or had a flicker of doubt crossed her pretty face as she spoke? He thought of how she'd mixed just the right potion to save Cloris. She had a cat too. He'd seen the large black animal hunting near her hut when he was out gathering firewood. Then there was the matter of her eyes. Every time he looked into them he felt as though he was under her spell. No woman in her right senses would ever admit to knowledge of magic. If Godileve was being less than honest she would be unable to enter the Goodchildes' cottage and would burn. By nailing up the shoes he would play as great a part in her death as the man who lit the flames beneath her. It was with a heavy heart that Adam turned and headed for home.

Alice Goodchilde insisted on watching as Adam hammered every nail into the three shoes that he placed over her door. From his position on an upturned barrel he could see her out of the corner of his eye. Her arms were crossed over her ample chest and her sour-mouthed face was red beneath her wimple.

"Drive them in well, Master Dunn," she ordered. "I want my Harold well protected from the evil of that sorceress."

He made no reply, continuing steadily with his task until the last nail was secure. He'd no sooner jumped down from the barrel than there was a flurry of excitement at the top of the village. Looking along the muddy track he saw Godileve coming towards the cottage with a crowd of villagers in her wake. Everyone knew she would try to enter the house and every serf and freeman was eager to see what the outcome would be.

Godileve walked purposefully with her eyes fixed ahead and a determined expression on her face. Her black hair flowed loose around her waist and the ties of her girdle swung rhythmically at her side. When she reached the house, Alice stepped forward and, for a moment, Adam thought she would obstruct the younger woman. Godileve stared at her defiantly.

"I will see Harold."

"You may try." Alice's thin lips twisted into a bitter sneer. "But no witch will pass through my door now."

Godileve glanced up at the shoes and Adam saw the momentary look of unease cross her face. Would she walk beneath them or not? A heavy silence descended on the crowd. Godileve hesitated for no more than a heart's beat, then drew in a sharp breath and stepped forward.

In the next moment she was inside the house. Adam heard Alice give a wounded cry and then was swept up in the rush as everyone surged into the dwelling to see what would happen next. The inside of the cottage was dark and smoky but it was possible to see Harold lying prone on his pallet bed. He looked wasted and it seemed to Adam that the smell of death was already in the room.

Godileve gasped and bent over the bed, placing her hand lightly on Harold's forehead.

"This is no natural fever," she muttered. "What mischief is afoot here?"

There was an earthenware jar sitting next to the bed. She picked it up, lifted the lid and then sniffed the contents.

"Wolfsbane!" She turned abruptly and held the jar out to the crowd. "Here is the cause of Harold's sickness," she cried. "Powdered root of Wolfsbane. The widow Goodchilde is poisoning her son to convict me. She would kill him."

"Not so." Alice screamed at the girl. "'Tis only enough to keep him ailing until you are burned." Her eyes narrowed with hatred. "Though I would rather see him dead than in

170

your bed."

Godileve turned away to tend to Harold and didn't speak again until the men who had taken hold of Alice had almost dragged her from the house.

"You were too late to stop that, Mistress Goodchilde," she said with a faintly mocking smile. "Our child will be born come harvest time."

Several weeks passed before Harold was strong enough to walk by the river with his new wife. It was said to be a miracle he'd survived the poison but Adam had his own counsel on what had saved him. He would never tell anyone what he'd witnessed the night that Harold had passed into Godileve's care. Walking past her hut, he'd seen the bonfire and the pale beauty of her limbs as she'd danced naked round it, reciting the spells that were no doubt intended to save Harold.

It must have taken a great deal of courage and love on the young witch's part to walk beneath the horseshoes to reach him. Small wonder she had hesitated. She hadn't known there was no need for her to fear. Adam had seen to that. It might be true that a witch couldn't walk beneath horseshoes but nothing was said of any other animal and the shoes above Alice's door hadn't come from a horse. For several months to come old Walter Miller wondered what caused Adam Dunn to smile so broadly whenever he saw his donkey, Jenny, and asked how her new shoes were faring.

Lisa Main lives near St Andrews in Fife. She sold her first story to *People's Friend* in 2001 and has been regularly featured in women's magazines since then. Her first novel, *In Fortune's Footsteps*, was published by Hale Books in 2009 and she is the author of *Shona's World*, a weekly series which has been running in *People's Friend* for the past two years. When she isn't writing, Lisa manages a local farm shop; a job which is providing her with plenty of ideas for another novel.

The Robbery
by Ann West

"YOU WILL COME WITH me to the dressmaker's tomorrow afternoon, won't you?" asked Bella as she and her sister Hattie walked along the High Street towards the station.

"Do you really want me to?" asked Hattie hoping unrealistically for a negative answer.

"Well of course I do, your dress needs fitting as well, remember?" Hattie remembered only too well. She schooled herself to show no emotion, not that Bella would have noticed anyway, she was always far too wrapped up in her own concerns to notice the problems of others. Hattie resented having to give up her Saturday afternoon freedom for Bella's wedding dress fitting. If she were honest part of it was jealousy.

"I suppose it's not every day a girl gets married," she thought. "Come to that, it's not every day a girl gets to be bridesmaid to her sister."

The two girls separated, Bella got on her bus and Hattie bought a newspaper and went into the station to wait for her train. She found a seat in the waiting room and sat, deep in thought.

"I ought to have got over Fred dying by now," she told herself. "It is six years ago. It's such bad luck that he went through all the fighting without a scratch only to catch the Spanish Flu the week before he was to return home."

The train rumbled into the station, Hattie stood up and

walked on to the platform. She got into the Ladies' carriage, smiling to herself as she imagined what Bella would say if she could see her.

"How do you expect to meet any men in the Ladies' carriage?"

Hattie settled down in her seat and opened her paper. Her mind was too full to read. The words wavered in front of her eyes unseen.

Bella was lucky that John, her husband to be, had suffered an eye injury in childhood and had not been considered fit enough to serve during the hostilities. There were so few eligible men around nowadays that Hattie had despaired of finding a husband. Bella was the one with the looks and the coquettish manner that so attracted the young men. Hattie looked plain beside her and had never mastered the art of flirting.

The haberdasher's shop where Hattie worked as a cashier was only a few yards from Blackfriars station. She felt important sitting up high in her tiny cubicle with its view of the entire sales floor, watching for the canisters to come zooming towards her on their wires. It was a matter of pride to her that she was trusted to give the right change and log all the sales into the big red ledger. She liked to see the rapt faces of the children as they watched the canisters zooming round the shop over their heads. Bella was inclined to lord it over her because she had a secretarial job in a perfume factory, a job that was much more socially acceptable than Hattie's, she declared. Today was busy, as were most Fridays and she had little time to brood over Bella's airs and graces, nor her forthcoming wedding.

At five minutes to five Mr Hawks rang his little silver bell to indicate that the shop was about to close. Hattie sent away the final canister with its change to Dora Watkins at the glove counter and closed the ledger. She counted up all the money, put it into a large canvas bag, picked up the ledger, locked the door, and went down to Mr Hawks.

"Thank you, Miss Price." He smiled at her.

"Goodnight, Mr Hawks." She bobbed a curtsey and dimpled back at him. Their evening routine over, Hattie left the shop, calling a cheerful, 'Goodnight, Ladies' to all the sales assistants. A chorus of 'Goodnight, Miss Price' came back to her as she walked out of the shop.

Hattie sometimes thought that she should put more effort into making friends with some of the counter assistants but she was an extremely shy girl, her job carried more responsibility than theirs and they had viewed her overtures to them with suspicion.

Hattie got a surprise when she got off the train that night. Waiting outside the station was her brother Albert. He looked very worried.

"Hello, Bert, what are you doing here? Is there something wrong?" Without answering Bert took her arm and pulled her into a teashop.

"I need to talk to you," he said, "I need your help." He summoned a waitress and ordered two teas.

"You look jolly serious, whatever's the matter?"

"You know my girlfriend, Alice?"

"Yes of course I do. Is something wrong with her?"

"Don't keep interrupting." Bert broke off as their teas arrived. "You remember I took her to that posh dance last Saturday?"

"Oh yes, I remember her telling me all about it at Church the next day. It sounded wonderful." Hattie went all dreamy-eyed at the memory.

"Well, like an idiot she'd borrowed a necklace to wear from her mistress's dressing table." Alice worked as maid to a wealthy lady.

"Oh crumbs, did she get found out?"

"Not yet, but she will do, because she lost it on the way home."

"Whatever is she going to do?" Hattie's eyes grew round with horror.

"Well she's told them that she found the clasp on the necklace broken and that she'd taken it into a jeweller to be mended."

"But they're bound to find out sooner or later."

"She's hoping to find the money to replace it."

"How much will it cost to do that?"

"She's seen one just like it in the jeweller's window for £500."

Hattie almost choked over her tea.

"However are you going to find that much money?"

"Well, we thought you might help us."

"Me? How could I possibly help you? I've no money."

Bert outlined his plan and, much against her better judgement, Hattie agreed to help.

"Friday would be the best day for this," she advised, "Saturday's only a half day since most of the city offices close at lunchtime."

The next day Hattie was in a state of acute nerves.

"Bert's plan will never work," she thought, "we'll have to call it off. It's far too risky." The morning crawled by and it seemed an age before Mr Hawks rang his bell for the close of trading. Hattie closed the ledger and put all the money into the canvas bag.

"We've done well today," she thought, "more than six hundred pounds in the bag. That's unusual for a Saturday morning." She made her way down to where Mr Hawks stood at the entrance to the shop and handed him the ledger and the bag. No sooner had they left her grasp than a masked man burst through the doors, waving a gun, grabbed the bag and made off into the street. Hattie screamed and swooned into Mr Hawks's arms, preventing him from giving chase to the thief.

"Miss Watkins! Fetch some smelling salts for Miss Price," shouted Mr Hawks. Dora dashed off to obey.

"Miss Binks! Call a policeman." Edith Binks ran out of the shop, eager to find a constable and spread the exciting news. Hattie kept her eyes shut as long as she dared and then gave a moan and pretended to come round.

Everything took such a long time. By the time the police had finished asking all their questions it was almost teatime.

Bella will be furious with me for missing the dressmaker, thought Hattie.

"What did this man look like?" asked the police officer.

"He was very tall and dark and he wore a black raincoat." said Dora.

"No he wasn't," said Edith, "he was fair-haired and wearing a dark cap."

"He was short and skinny," said Mr Hawks.

Hattie was amused to note that everybody gave different descriptions of the masked man.

"I didn't really look at the man," Hattie told the police officer, "I was so shocked to see the gun." She burst into tears, "I've never seen a gun before." Mr Hawks gave her his hankie to dry her eyes and reached into his pocket.

"I think you'd better get a taxi home," he said, giving her five shillings. Hattie goggled. That was nearly a whole week's wages! She didn't like to admit that her nervous trembling was due to being afraid that Bert would be caught. For she was sure it was him who had been wearing the mask.

I'm not going to waste five shillings on a taxi, she thought, not when I've already got my train ticket home. As she sat on the train going home she wondered how and where Bert had got hold of a gun.

I hope he gets rid of it, she thought, nasty horrid thing.

Bella was very cross with Hattie that night; even when she'd explained what had happened, her sister sulked and refused to speak to her.

"I was given five shillings to get a taxi home, but I didn't spend it as I'd already got my train ticket," said Hattie, "would you like to come to see a film one night this week?"

Bella still refused to speak to her. But Hattie knew how

177

to wheedle her way back into favour.

"There's that new Lilian Gish film *The White Sister* on at the Plaza next week. I've seen the posters. She's got a new leading man called Ronald Colman. He's ever so good-looking."

Bella's face softened. She still didn't say anything but Hattie knew she'd won.

Next day Hattie bumped into Alice on her way to church.

"Oh, Hattie!" she said. "I'm so glad I've seen you. I understand Bert told you all about losing the necklace."

"Yes he did. How could you have been so careless?"

"It was the clasp; it was broken. Anyway, did Bert tell you that our friend had seen it and picked it up? He gave it back to us on Wednesday."

"No he didn't. Why didn't he give it back to you straight away?"

Alice looked a bit shamefaced.

"Bert and I were having a row and he didn't like to interrupt."

"Oh?"

"Yes. I want us to get engaged but he says we should wait until we've saved up some more money."

"I can see why your friend wouldn't want to interrupt, but he could have waited and given it back to you later."

"Apparently he forgot."

"Isn't that just like a man?"

"Yes, I was out of my mind with worry about it all weekend. Still it's all sorted now. Milady has her necklace back and no harm done. See you soon, Hattie." Alice waved farewell and scuttled off after her employers to get into the dogcart with the footman and the housekeeper.

"I wonder what Bert will do with all that money he stole?" Hattie asked herself as she walked back home. "He can hardly take it back. He's not giving it to me to take back either, and it wouldn't be right to keep it." Hattie laughed at her thoughts. It wasn't right to take it in the first place whether it went to replace the necklace or not. She supposed he would put it towards the savings to get married.

She didn't see Bert till the following weekend. He was looking rather sheepish.

"I've got a bone to pick with you," she said.

"I know. I've come to apologize to you for all the worry we caused you. I really am sorry."

"You gave me the fright of my life."

"It shouldn't have frightened you all that much. You weren't involved at all." Bert seemed bemused.

"So what are you going to do with all that money?" Hattie asked.

"What money?" Bert stared at her in amazement.

"The six hundred pounds you stole from my shop last Saturday."

"But I didn't steal from your shop." Bert looked flabbergasted.

"I'm not daft you know. I saw you. I work there, remember?"

"But I didn't go anywhere near your shop last Saturday."

"And where did you get the gun? It scared me half to death."

"Gun? Wherever would I have got a gun from?"

"You mean it wasn't you? I was so sure it was."

"Well it wasn't." Bert looked very offended.

Memory of the robber, his wildly threatening gun and the fear she had felt flooded back into Hattie's mind. This time her faint was genuine.

Ann West has been writing for about ten years. Her first short story to be published was also in a charity anthology for Breast Cancer. Since then she has had a number of stories published in *People's Friend* and *Weekly News*. She also has a story currently in the *Yours Yearbook*. Ann Lives in a very small village in North Kent with her husband and two cats.

The Clockmaker's Daughter
by Penelope Alexander

ANNIE PROUD CLOSED THE bevelled glass, and stepped back, dusting her hands. She'd checked the last clock, an elegant grandfather, which struck the quarter hour as if Doomsday had arrived. Annie took heart from its forthright chime. Smoothing her hair into her bun, and straightening her frilled cuffs, she walked to her counter. It was Tuesday, the morning she planned everything should change.

As a child, she'd sewed beside the insistent *tock* from the mantelpiece, slept to the soft tick of many longcase clocks, and woken to the shrill of the metal alarm. When smiling Will Applegarth, then her father's young assistant, had first arrived it became a joke between them that even blindfolded she could tell where she was anywhere in the house by the sound of the nearest clock.

Annie had another game, too. The one where she would imagine people as clocks. She decided Will was the one on the mantelpiece. Square and dependable, but liable to jump if over-wound. They'd quickly become friends.

Her mother said Will was an excellent assistant, but in a way that told Annie very clearly it was all she ever expected him to amount to. The picture that came into Annie's mind was her mother as the fussy ormolu timepiece she'd once glimpsed in a grand drawing room. Annie's mother had also hinted – often – that Will's temperament meant he wasn't "a stayer". True enough, soon afterwards, Will was offered other work. But to Annie's unspoken relief, after days of anguish, he'd told them he knew where he was best off.

After her mother died, Annie enjoyed helping her father. When the sound of the great cathedral bell floated down to the cobbled streets where she ran errands, Annie knew that inside her father's shop, at exactly the same moment, the clocks would be chiming.

Throughout the town Jacob Proud was entrusted to set timepieces great and small, and his name became a by-word for accuracy.

Edgar Bullman called on Annie after her father died. As a formality between old business acquaintances, his first visit had been as stiff as a piece of buckram. But even in her mourning state, Annie had caught the gleam in his bright, brown eyes. It was no surprise he called again. And again. Proud's had been a successful business. Bullman's, he told her, was "interested".

'In clocks?' Annie said, surprised.

They were together deep inside her conservatory. Edgar looked almost endearing in all-over green, but Annie knew that was a trick of the light. Somewhere a drip of water fell, and Edgar loosened his tight collar with a large finger.

'Your father and mine were both successful in their different ways.'

'Very different,' agreed Annie, thinking of Bullman's cloth factory, a red-meat-chunk of a building on a steep hill outside town.

'We have much in common,' said Edgar. He craned his neck as if to be sure no servants were visible, and reached for Annie's hand. 'I think we should pool our resources. I would be honoured if ...'

He looked mortified as his fingers grasped only air.

'I am not considering marriage,' Annie said.

'A pretty girl like you?' Edgar asked. At that moment,

despite some sympathy for his position, Annie characterised Mr Bullman as the overbearing clock on the Town Hall.

'Mr Bullman, you are blessed with too much imagination! I am nearly forty, and even my father – the kindest of men – thought me plain.'

'Then he was wrong. Marriage to you would suit me very well …'

'But not me!' said Annie.

'I hate to see you struggle on like this, Annie Proud. Don't say you're planning to continue your father's business alone.'

'I've run it alongside him since I left school.'

'I say this for your own good, but continuing this situation will be very unpopular in the town. With a sole female in charge, I'd give your business less than six more months,' said Edgar, flatly.

'You forget Will!' snapped Annie.

'Your failure would leave any assistant jobless,' said Edgar. 'You know Applegarth doesn't deserve that.'

Annie slumped in her seat, and twisted her hands in her lap. The humidity trapped beneath the glass panes of the conservatory seemed suddenly oppressive. She hadn't fully considered her desire to run her father's business might become a danger to Will's livelihood.

Her father's only advice before he died had been for her to do whatever seemed best. And here was Edgar Bullman, arms folded, suggesting her 'best' would never be good enough. Annie wondered how he knew what she'd only recently admitted to herself – that there had been difficulties in the year since Jacob had died. Nothing she couldn't overcome, but enough to tempt. Was Edgar an opportunist? Or did he genuinely care?

'I shall need time to consider,' she said, at last.

Edgar, agitated, fumbled for the repeater watch which Annie knew was still in Proud's workshop.

'I can allow you until Tuesday,' he told her. 'I shall be

183

catching a train at ten-past-ten that morning, and will call to collect my watch at nine-forty. Give your answer then, whatever you decide. If that's convenient?'

Or even if it's not, I suppose, Annie thought with a sigh. She was relieved when Edgar gave an uncertain smile, and left.

'Now what?' Annie asked Will Applegarth. They stood together inside the workshop, where Will was feeding tiny drops of oil into the back of a fluttering mechanism.

'I can sell the business to Bullman's and survive, if it comes to it, but what would you do?' Annie asked.

'Don't you worry about me!' said Will, pinging up his watch-mender's eyepiece and brandishing the oil-dropper. 'I reckon you've got enough to worry about.'

Annie, alarmed by Will's vehemence, rested one hand on his arm to calm him and instantly found her fingers covered by his. His hand was very warm.

'But I won't abandon the only place and the only people I've ever loved without a fight!' said Will Applegarth, sweeping his free hand into the air for emphasis.

Feelings like that could certainly set a couple of mainsprings loose, Annie thought, shocked. She didn't know what to say, so she pursed her lips and said nothing. She remained steady, too, as Will's hand caught the corner of the cloth spread on the workbench and scattered the innards of the large watch to the floor.

'Oh dear,' she said, inadequately.

She knew her words weren't helpful, but on the other hand someone had better keep calm. Will was an excellent watchmaker, but outside the workshop his fiery nature had a habit of putting a stop to rational discussion. Annie realised she needed to think coolly for them both, and on that account, Will wasn't much help.

Taking a deep breath and retreating into the shop, Annie came face to face with an old grandfather clock, her father's

184

joy. She stared at it in a daze for some moments before she felt a smile lifting her lips and a plan shaping in her mind.

From early on Tuesday morning, Annie kept Will fully occupied with repairs.

After dusting her hands, she'd already moved behind the counter as the final humming notes from the grandfather clock died. Annie had checked, and re-checked. All her clocks told the same time. She was sure none would let her down.

But what she'd just done to them caused her to feel as if a weighted pendulum had settled in her stomach.

'When is Mr Edgar Bullman collecting his watch, Miss Proud?' Will called, from the workshop.

'At twenty minutes to ten,' Annie called back. 'Prompt.'

Will Applegarth popped his head around the door. He was frowning. For a moment, Annie feared the worst.

'The man's nothing but a bloomin' piece of clockwork at times,' he observed. 'Or a train. Only knows how to run when there's a printed timetable.'

'Now, Will …' said Annie. 'Remember, our business is time. There's not a place in town that doesn't depend on the accuracy of our clocks, Bullman's factory included. And there'd be no use for timetables without them!'

Will pushed the stub of a pencil into his wiry hair, and retreated, still muttering.

'As your father always said, time should be our servant. But, to be fair, Mr Bullman is nothing if not a good businessman. I suppose if he takes over and changes us all into automatons, we would keep working. But I think this business can survive, if you and I are determined. Goodness knows, together we've been in it long enough …'

'It's not certain Mr Bullman is taking over, Will,' Annie said. Her hands were shaking, and Will wasn't making things any easier.

'No, it's you he'll bid for, and then he'll get everything

for free ...' Will muttered.

Annie suddenly found it necessary to lean forward and grip the edge of her wooden counter.

'Let me tell you, Will Applegarth, I haven't said yes to anyone, much less chosen to put my signature to any piece of paper!'

She forced herself into stillness, and hoped the next few minutes would prove her instincts were right. Otherwise her plan was going to look very foolish indeed.

Just as Annie imagined that even the punctual Edgar Bullman would be late, at nine-forty the door rattled and he arrived.

'Your watch is ready, sir,' she said. 'I'll collect it from the workshop ...'

'I have plenty of time, Miss Proud,' said Bullman. He was wearing a heavy coat for the journey he was due to make that morning, and he looked as handsomely at ease as Annie had ever seen him.

'Here we are ...' Annie returned, wrapping the watch carefully and placing it in a box. She shut the lid. 'Is there anything else ...?'

Bullman frowned.

'Dammit, Annie Proud. You know there is! What about that answer you promised me?'

'What answer?' Annie asked. She spread her hands on the polished counter. There should only be another minute to wait, at most.

'To my offer!'

'I don't recall any *business* outstanding between us,' Annie said, thoughtfully. She was almost holding her breath.

'You must remember!' Bullman said. 'I asked if you would consent to be ...'

As if she'd only just thought of it, Annie looked at the clocks ranged around her walls, and gasped.

186

'Mr. Bullman, didn't you say your train leaves at ten past ten?'

Edgar made an easy, charming gesture.

'I can spare ten minutes!'

'I don't think so,' Annie said, breathing out at last. She'd heard the first clock. In a rush, there followed the Westminster, the Whittington and the St Paul chimes. Every grandfather, mantel, wall and carriage clock in the shop joined the cacophony, and cheekily over all came the insistent chirping of six carved cuckoo clocks. Proud's shop in full voice regularly drowned attempts at speech for a full minute.

'Ten o'clock already?' Bullman bellowed, above the racket.

'Jacob Proud clocks are *generally* accurate,' Annie shouted back.

'But I had time to spare when I left home …!'

'Time has flown, hasn't it?' said Annie. 'I believe you may catch your train if you leave immediately. Unless waiting for my answer is more important, of course. If it isn't, then by my reckoning you have eight – no, *seven* – minutes, to reach the station …'

She spoke to the empty air. With a hurried apology, Bullman had left, and the door slammed behind him.

Will Applegarth wandered into the shop, holding his personal timepiece to the light, and squinting at it.

'What's all the noise?' he demanded. 'Never known this Proud little darling to be out by so much as a minute …'

Annie pressed her cold hands to her burning face.

'Oh, Will …' she said.

'If that man's caused any bother …' said Will, hurrying towards Annie. 'What's he been saying to you?'

Will pulled out a chair. Annie sank gratefully onto the seat, and took a deep breath, knowing her Tuesday morning plan was not yet complete.

'He wanted me to choose a life with him!' she said, watching Will's face carefully. 'But he's just proved to me exactly what kind of husband he'd turn out to be!'

'Well, you know in this town you could do worse – for you, and for the business,' said Will, reasonably.

'No! I do not know that!' said Annie, fiercely. 'This is a new century, Will, our dear Queen is dead, and things are changing. I want to make my own choices.'

'Which are …?' Will asked. He'd placed his watch on the polished counter. It spun twice, very slowly. Annie watched the gleaming metal as if fascinated.

'To marry you, Will Applegarth.'

'Just because you don't want Bullman?'

'No, Will. Just because you would be best for the business,' said Annie, smiling. She hoped her tone would tell him that wasn't all he would be best for.

Will stared at Annie for a long time, then he took her hand in both of his and kissed her palm.

'Then I accept,' he said. 'Just because I've always loved you.'

As they stood in the middle of the shop, hands clasped, the solitary booming bell of the cathedral clock struck ten in the streets outside.

Will, puzzled, began moving around the shop to check each of Proud's timepieces against his watch.

'I just knew there was something wrong,' he said, slowly. 'What's happened to our famous accuracy?'

'I think you'll find all the clocks are somehow ten minutes ahead, my dear,' said Annie, calmly. 'Perhaps you could re-set them?'

The Clockmaker's Daughter was originally published in *People's Friend*, April 14th 2007 as *In The Nick of Time*

Penelope Alexander was born in beautiful Bristol, but now lives in the Rose of the Shires – Northamptonshire – with her husband. She is a retired teacher with a grown-up family who has always enjoyed writing. These days she feels blessed to have both time and opportunity to tackle anything from poems and articles to short stories and serials. She also helps run local writers' meetings, where the support of the library service is much appreciated.

Travelling Light
by Jill Steeples

AS SOON AS CHLOE stepped out of the plane and on to the tarmac, the warm Mediterranean air engulfed her, welcoming her to the island and lifting her spirits.

During the flight, she hadn't been able to settle at all. Instead she'd fretted as she gazed out of the window, her best friend Allie's words ringing in her head.

'Are you mad? Why would you want to go on holiday alone? I mean, what will you do? You know you can always come away with Ian and me.'

It wasn't Chloe's first choice to come away alone, but what was the alternative? Staying at home with only the prospect of some decorating to entertain her? She didn't fancy that and although Allie meant well inviting Chloe to join them, she really didn't relish playing gooseberry for a full two weeks. In previous years, Michael had arranged the holidays with his usual meticulous precision; fell-walking in the Lake District, kayaking on the River Wye and sailing on the Isle of Wight. No longer did she have to tiptoe around a bad-tempered boyfriend and this year Chloe was looking forward to pleasing no one but herself, lazing around the pool with a good book and a long cool drink.

Collecting her case from the carousel, she felt a renewed sense of freedom and enthusiasm for this holiday and arriving at the hotel just confirmed that she'd done exactly the right thing. Her room was spacious with a lovely balcony overlooking the swimming pool. Perhaps she'd go for a quick dip now, she thought excitedly. She hauled her case up on to the bed, flicked open the catches and then stopped with a start.

'Oh no, please no!' she groaned.

The case was exactly the same colour and the same design as hers, but those were definitely not hers, she thought cringing, picking out a pair of boxer shorts gingerly. Her fingers sifted through the unfamiliar clothes, T-shirts, shorts, loud swimming trunks, flip-flops, all of the male variety. No, there was definitely nothing of hers in there and, it seemed, no clue as to the owner of the case. She rifled deeper into the bag and pulled out a very old battered teddy.

'Ugh, what kind of man brings his teddy on holiday with him?' she muttered, sinking onto the bed with Ted.

Just then a phone buzzed into action and Chloe snatched it up from the bedside cabinet.

'Hello?'

'Miss Brown? Reception here. There seems to have been a mix-up. We have your case and a gentleman here is hoping you've got his?'

'Oh yes, thank goodness, I'll come straight down.'

Chloe quickly zipped up the case, thinking it probably belonged to some spotty adolescent, judging by the contents, and hurried down to reception.

'Ah-ha,' said a dark-haired man who looked neither spotty nor adolescent, as he spotted Chloe trundling along with the case behind her, 'the wanderer returns'.

'Yes, that's my case, thank you.' Chloe felt riled that he looked so nonchalant standing there with her bag. 'Here's yours.' She dropped it at his feet. 'It would have been helpful if you'd filled out the contact details on your tag. It was a good job one of us did,' she said, haughtily.

'Yes well, no harm done, eh?' The man smiled lightly and Chloe gave him a tight smile back. 'Enjoy the rest of

191

your holiday, won't you?' he called after her.

Perhaps now she could get on with exactly that. She'd have a quick freshen up, change into her bikini and then grab a couple of hours by the pool before dinner. She was just applying a light covering of mascara when there was an urgent rapping on her door. What now? Chloe threw on a sarong and opened the door.

'Ah, hello, sorry to bother you again, but I think you may still have some of my property.' It was Mr Missing Case.

Chloe shook her head, bemused. 'No, I'm sorry, there was only the one bag.'

Mr Missing Case peered around the door and into the room, his eyes alighting on the scruffy teddy which was looking very comfy set against the pillows.

'There!' he said, pointing eagerly.

'Oh, right.' Chloe felt her cheeks flush, wondering what all the fuss was over an old teddy. 'I must have taken it out when I was looking for your contact details. Sorry. Here you go,' she said, handing the bear over.

'Archie,' said the man.

'Chloe,' she said, desperate now to get rid of him so she could get on with the business of holidaying.

He threw back his head and laughed. If Chloe hadn't known about his unnatural obsession with his teddy or had an intimate introduction to the contents of his wardrobe, then she might have found him attractive. He was tall and broad, with dark curly hair, brown eyes and a lazy expression.

'No, my name's Tom. The bear's name is Archie.'

'Oh, I see.' Well, if he thought she was about to speak to a bear, then he could think again.

'Well thanks again,' he said, 'I'll leave you in peace now.'

She was thankful that she managed to avoid Tom over the next few days. Getting up for a late breakfast, she'd help herself to some fruit and yoghurt from the buffet before heading down to the pool to wile away a few hours lost in her book. Occasionally she'd take a dip in the pool or take a wander down to the beach.

On the fourth day, in a change from her routine, Chloe decided to join the coach excursion up into the mountains. She found a window seat and was adjusting her ipod when she heard a familiar voice.

'Hello there. Mind if I join you?'

It was Tom, smiling broadly. Thinking it might be nice to have some company for the trip, Chloe looked up, nodding her agreement. They'd clearly got off on the wrong foot. Maybe if she spent some time getting to know him they'd find some common ground. After all, they must be about the same age, thought Chloe. She watched as he placed his camera case in the rack above their heads and almost gasped aloud when she spotted his rucksack. Not that wretched teddy bear! There it was peeking out over the top of the cover. Chloe's eyebrows jumped high into her forehead. Any attraction she might have felt towards Tom disappeared on the sight of that teddy.

'So how are you enjoying your holiday, then?' he asked, plonking down into his seat.

'Great,' said Chloe, deciding he was probably just emotionally immature. A bit of a mummy's boy. 'It's lovely to be able to come away and leave all those everyday stresses behind. And all this wonderful sunshine, I can't get enough of it!'

'I know what you mean, it's lovely, isn't it? I could get used to these long leisurely days doing nothing.'

Chloe could too. She was reminded of Michael and all those holidays they'd spent together, planned like military operations with no time for all the things Chloe enjoyed doing, like wandering around admiring the scenery, exploring the local shops or just sitting in a cafe watching the world go by. Tom seemed much more laid back.

After a bumpy journey up into the hills they got off the coach and went their separate ways. Chloe visited a beautiful 17th-century church and then sat outside in a sun-doused square, savouring an ice-cream. She was just thinking she ought to make her way back to the bus when she bumped into Tom who had a familiar harassed look upon his face.

'Are you okay, Tom?'

'Not really,' he said, running his hands through his hair. 'I've only gone and lost Archie somewhere. He must have fallen out of my rucksack. You haven't seen him, have you?'

Chloe felt her mouth twitch. She wanted to laugh, but looking at Tom's crestfallen expression she realised that probably wouldn't be the best reaction. No wonder the guy was holidaying alone. Any girlfriend would need to be a saint to put up with Tom's slavish devotion to his teddy.

'No,' said Chloe, trying her best to look sympathetic. 'Maybe if you retrace your steps you'll come across him.'

They walked together back to the bus with Chloe trying to ignore the sighs and groans coming from Tom.

'I've got to find him. I'll never forgive myself if I don't.'

'Look, over there!' cried Chloe, feeling ridiculously relieved at the sight of the teddy lying underneath a bush.

'Oh, thank goodness,' sighed Tom, rushing to pick it up. 'Thanks Chloe. You're a lifesaver.'

Now if only she could find herself a man who cared as much about her as Tom clearly cared for his teddy, she thought, smiling wryly.

'You wouldn't do one more favour for me, would you, Chloe, before we get back on the bus?'

'Um, yes, if I can,' she said tentatively, feeling only the slightest sense of unease.

'I wonder if you could just take a photo of Archie and me. Perhaps over here,' he said, marching across to a stone wall. 'You'll be able to get the mountains and the sea in the background. It'll be perfect.'

He foisted the camera upon Chloe and then sat down on the wall clutching Archie in his grasp, looking shamelessly pleased with himself.

'You want me to take a photo of you with your bear?'

'Yes, please. And if you could get a move on, the bus will be leaving soon.'

It was just her luck, Chloe thought. When she eventually gets to meet a good-looking available man he turns out to be a pathetic loser.

'There you go,' she said, taking a couple of snaps. 'I hope they come out OK.' It would be something to show his mother, she thought uncharitably.

'I hope so too,' said Tom, guiding Chloe towards the bus. '5B will give me a really hard time if I don't go back with some decent photos.'

'5B?' asked Chloe.

'Yes, they're my kids. I'm a primary teacher and Archie is the class mascot. He's been all over the world. America, Australia and Scotland. Every time someone goes away they get the chance to take Archie with them. Of course, they have to take a photo of Archie on his adventures. We've got a whole wall full of photos showing his travels. This year the kids decided he should come away with me.'

'Oh, right,' said Chloe, seeing Tom for the first time in a totally different light.

'To be honest, it's a bit of a responsibility. I've been terrified of losing the little blighter.'

Chloe laughed, as she settled back into her seat on the bus.

'Well, I did wonder. I thought perhaps you and Archie had something special going on.'

Tom turned towards her, their legs touching briefly and Chloe felt her cheeks flush, surprised at the reaction his touch invoked.

'I know I'm a sad old singleton who's holidaying alone,

but I promise you,' he said, his eyes twinkling fondly, 'I'm not that sad.'

'Well, if you're a sad old singleton, that makes two of us,' smiled Chloe.

'Listen,' said Tom, giving Chloe the benefit of his dazzling smile, 'I can't help feeling we got off on the wrong foot. I was thinking of trying out that little taverna down in the harbour tonight. Would you like to come?'

Chloe smiled, thinking her holiday was about to get a whole lot better.

'I'd love to,' she said. 'On one condition.'

Tom raised a quizzical eyebrow.

'You promise to leave that pesky bear behind!'

Tom stuck out his bottom lip petulantly.

'Archie, sorry mate,' he said, stuffing him into the bottom of his rucksack. 'Don't tell the kids, but I've just had a much better offer!'

Travelling Light was originally published in *Take a Break's Fiction Feast* July 2010

Jill Steeples loves writing short stories, particularly those with a twist in the tail, and her work has appeared in the popular women's magazines in the UK, Ireland, Scandinavia and Australia. She was also a contributor to four of the *Sexy Shorts* charity anthologies published by Accent Press. She lives in Leighton Buzzard, Bedfordshire with her husband, two children and a mad English Setter and is currently working on a romantic comedy novel.

The Sunday Team
by Catherine Burrows

I NEVER EAVESDROP. OUR marriage is based on the principles of honesty, trust, respect and privacy. It was his hushed and strained voice that alerted me. Graham was talking to his best friend, Lewis, and had no idea that my ear was pressed against the study door. He had just returned home from the doctor's.

'I'm taking it as well as I can, Lewis.' There was a pause.

'It's very serious indeed, very serious.' There was another pause and then his tone deepened,

'This could be it. The end.'

Feeling certain that Graham could hear the thump of my heart, I fled to find peace in the garden, desperate to gulp at fresh air and steal some time for my racing thoughts. It was hard to believe this was happening to us. We were such a normal and happy family. Graham was an exemplary husband and father, his zest and enthusiasm infected everyone he met. In those five snatched minutes, standing on the patio in the stark June heat, I attended his funeral, told the children he was dying and held his hand as he lay on his deathbed, several times over. My mind was spiralling out of control.

'What time did you say we had to pick the kids up from the party?' Graham stepped through the French windows, with no hint that he had just had such a terrible conversation with his friend.

'Two o'clock. I'd better get going.' I needed to shake myself back into the whirl of the family weekend.

'I'll come with you,' he offered, 'and since it's Father's Day, let's grab a pub lunch after we collect the little monsters and then walk it off together,' he rubbed his hands and grinned, thinking of the afternoon ahead. The pain was already unbearable for me. He never spent Sunday afternoons with us. Something had clearly changed in his life. He just couldn't tell me, perhaps unable to inflict worry and pain on me. Maybe he didn't have the right words.

'What about football practice?' I asked, almost frightened to hear the answer. He shrugged, brushing my question off.

Our children, Tom and Maisie, scrambled into the back of the car when we collected them. They filled the car with a flurry of party bags, cake crumbs and knock-knock jokes. Their excitement was uncontained when Graham announced we were off for lunch, ice cream included, and then for a long walk in the glorious sunshine. We found a lovely pub. Graham had chosen one off the beaten track that we used to visit every weekend before the children came along. There was an empty table in the beer garden perfectly placed in the shade. We sat and watched as the children guzzled cold lemonade and continued to laugh at their silly jokes and mocking insults. It would have been perfect, particularly because we never spent Sundays together, or much of the weekend for that matter. Saturdays were dedicated to the frenzied shipping of the children to and from their clubs, restocking the groceries and catching up on desperately dull household chores. Sundays were no different with more parties and activities for Tom and Maisie, although the afternoon was Graham's sacred time. He absolutely never missed his football practice. There was nothing I could think of that would ever keep him from the Sunday team, nothing except for something truly dreadful like a serious illness.

'Graham, please don't go today,' I would nag, 'by the time you get home and have a shower, the day has gone. We don't have any time to be together as a family. It's not fair.'

'Darling, I work hard all week and I would do anything for you and the kids. The football's my selfish passion though. I love it. I forget about all my troubles and sweat it all out on the pitch. Please don't make me feel rotten for doing the thing I love,' he used to reply, trying to field my selfish grievances. We were in a dreadful situation now and I wished I could take away all the complaints and just let him be. Every time I looked at Graham or heard him speak, all the regrets hammered through my mind. I watched Graham, analysing his words and actions, looking for clues that betrayed his illness. It was good to see his appetite hadn't been damaged, he ploughed his way through the three-course Father's Day menu with gusto.

'Come on then gang,' he drained the dregs of his pint and stretched languidly like an oversized cat, 'let's walk off the calories.'

It could not have been more idyllic. The park opposite the pub was in the full throes of summer and as we walked the children raced about like young foals freshly turned out into their paddock. This was exactly how Father's Day should be with Graham wallowing in the delights of his family, ignoring the black clouds that were gathering in our lives.

'Tom, on the head?' Graham was watching Tom dribble the ball as we walked and it was impossible for him to resist the call of the game.

'Fancy a kick, Dad?' Tom tossed the ball to his father and the magic overpowered Graham. Father and son raced into the middle distance, patting the ball between them as Maisie and I trailed behind.

Then it happened. Without any warning, Graham's legs

folded and he pitched to the ground like an axed oak. It was so wrong, my Graham was too solid, too strong to be cut down like this.

'Graham,' I screamed his name and ran from Maisie's side towards the boys, driven by fear. By the time I was at his side, with his head on my lap, his skin had become transparent and his face was crumpled with agony.

'Graham, please don't do this. What's wrong with you? Please, darling, speak to me?' I was trying to stay calm and rational but nothing could stop tears of panic and confusion streaming down my face. Graham could hardly speak with the pain. His eyes appealed to me for help to make it all better. Tom and Maisie watched wordlessly, they had never seen their parents so vulnerable and human. It must have been very frightening. I tossed my mobile at Tom, 'Darling, we need an ambulance for Dad.' Tom nodded and started to fiddle with the keypad of the phone. It was then that something amazing happened. The pain, the agony and the groaning stopped. Graham opened his eyes and looked at me with concern and confusion,

'An ambulance?' he repeated.

'Graham, I know what's going on. I heard you tell Lewis. I understand and I think we really need to get you to a hospital.'

'Darling, what are you talking about?' Graham sat perfectly upright. 'The tendon's finally gone. I knew it would, it was just a matter of time.'

'Tendon? Is that it?' I yelled, relief flooding my world.

'Tendons are pretty important darling and very painful too.' He winced as he tried to demonstrate his injury.

'I thought it was serious, Graham.'

'It is serious. Why do you think I went to the doctor's? I even had to come home and ring Lewis to tell him I couldn't play football for the foreseeable future. That's how bad it is. Pretty catastrophic.' Graham had barely finished speaking before I leaned over and planted a firm kiss on his

200

cheek, ruffling his hair, like I would Tom's.

'Graham, I'm so sorry. You love your football don't you? If you ever start playing again, I promise I'll come to the matches with Tom and Maisie. We'll yell like crazy from the sidelines.' Graham smiled and smudged away my tears with his hands,

'Darling, I don't care. This has been great today. Really special, better than a thousand football games, in fact. I'm not even sure if I'll go back to playing every Sunday.'

I never eavesdrop. Our marriage is based on the principles of honesty, trust, respect and privacy but this time it was the buoyant laughter that made me listen. He was happy to phone Lewis and tell him that he'd enjoyed a fantastic Father's Day and that when some things end, other great things begin.

The Sunday Team was originally published by *The Weekly News* in 2008.

Catherine Burrows feels like the world is her playground. She travels through time and space, meeting new characters every day. That's why she writes, it's all in her imagination. Her stories have appeared in *The Weekly News, Allas* and *That's Life* (Australia). Placed in several writing competitions, her work has been published in the *Daily Mail,* the *Guardian, Take a Break* and *That's Life.* Catherine's book, *'Postnatal Depression – The Essential Guide'* is published in December 2010.

Love and Chocolate
by Della Galton

CHOCOLATE IS A SUBSTITUTE for love. Isn't that what they say? Having had half a bar for breakfast, and now finding myself contemplating having another few chunks for elevenses, I'm beginning to think they might be right.

I woke up this morning feeling terribly sad. It wasn't difficult to pinpoint the reason. The house had a silence about it – a one-person feel.

No-one's feet but mine to spark off the creaky floorboards, no tuneless humming alongside the whistle of the kettle or the slam of a door to tell me I'm not alone.

It's a horrible sound, the silence of a one-person house. It has a desolate finality about it, although I haven't always thought like that. When I first started living on my own, I loved it. In those days I heard independence, freedom, peace. I wonder when that changed. I haven't known you all that long. When did our lives begin to overlap each other's and merge – so that when the edges were separated again there was a tearing apart, like sticky plaster coming away from skin?

I'd imagined the pain would be fleeting. One quick rip, a slight sting and it'd be over. But it doesn't feel like that now. Even though it's what we agreed yesterday.

Yesterday was bittersweet. You see, even though I know you're right, we can't carry on as we are – you still make me feel exactly like you did when we first met. You make

202

me feel like it's summer inside me. That, whatever the weather outside, it's all blue skies and sunshine in my heart. Dead corny, I know. I'd never say it to you. In case you thought I was being pushy or asking for more than you can give.

Mad, isn't it, to feel like this. Especially when we're not really anything more than friends. No, I don't think that's true, actually. We are more than friends. We might not have done more than share the odd peck on the cheek and a hug, but we know each other – in that deep-down inside kind of way you don't get with people very often.

I know how to make you laugh. I know how to put that light in your deep brown eyes. And you know how to say exactly the right things. They're not always what I want to hear. But they are the right things. I also know we could be much more than friends if circumstances were different. And I think you know it too. But they're not different, are they?

You want to live in Spain. You dream of a gentler pace of life, a white-washed villa with shutters opening on to skies that are permanently blue. Golden beaches and the hot dust of unmade roads and the horn blares of Spanish drivers yelling at each other.

No more rat-race, rain and rented rooms. No more scrimping and saving and trying to get back on a property ladder of which even the lowest rungs are out of reach. It's not easy to begin again at fifty, with one failed marriage and two grown-up kids whom you spend your life running around. You love them desperately. You're rebuilding your relationship, which was shattered when you split up with their mother – an endless uphill struggle. There probably doesn't seem an awful lot to smile about sometimes.

I can see why you want to escape and live in Spain. But I have England running through my veins. I love the wet grey mornings of winter, the crisp white skies of autumn, the seasons turning on their endless wheel. I love the buzz of people, the shine of rain on wet tarmac and the rhythm of traffic outside my window. I love my work. I love the feeling of roots: the kind that run deep into the damp blackness of English soil.

I can't imagine leading a drifter's life. Not for longer than a week or so. I like structure and routine and a life filled with appointments and lunch dates and friends. Yet, neither can I imagine life without you.

It's not as though we haven't always known these differences about each other. How foolish then to fall in love at all. But perhaps it's just me who is in love. Neither of us has ever said the words. There didn't seem much point when we knew our futures lay in different countries.

Do you remember the first time we met? It was at one of those fiftieth birthday parties where the relatives sit on one side of the room and the friends the other. I knew Aisha because I worked with her. You were a friend of her brother's. When I walked into the room, you were playing with Aisha's daughter, a dark-haired tot of a girl in a scarlet dress. She called you Uncle Des and I thought you were her real uncle, but later you explained you weren't – just a friend of the family who liked kids.

I liked that about you. Not many men are so easy around kids. Or at least not many Englishmen. I glanced at your flashing dark eyes and olive skin and decided you probably weren't English. Not completely. As soon as you opened your mouth, your cockney accent contradicted the image. It was intriguing. You were intriguing.

We got chatting. We were easy in each other's company – much easier than strangers – and you asked me if I wanted to go out sometime. The pub where we'd planned to go for a drink was closed for refurbishment, so we drove along to the next one. It was a Friday afternoon and the place we found was almost empty. A dingy room filled with a pool table and a juke box and tables too close together. It felt like someone had put a tube in through the window and sucked out all the atmosphere.

So we sat in the garden, on a picnic bench, alongside an empty kiddies' play area. It was a freezing January lunchtime. But it didn't matter. The warmth of our conversation made everything else irrelevant. I had never felt so at ease with someone, nor so attracted to them. It was a magical time out of time. At some point during that afternoon, you put summer in my heart. And it's stayed there, ever since.

It's very hard to say goodbye.

But that was really what yesterday was about, wasn't it? We held hands across the old wood roughness of my kitchen table, and we said we'd meet again. When you'd sorted out some of the things that needed sorting in your life – like making sure your kids were settled, one at Uni, the other with a new job.

Like getting your passport renewed.

Half of your heart was in England – your mother was English, your father, Spanish. And although you'd been brought up in London and had settled and married there, you ached to be in Spain: grew a little more restless with each passing year; felt that if you didn't go there soon, you never would.

I think we both knew that yesterday was goodbye. But it was easier not to say the words. To pretend we would meet again – on some unspecified date in the future.

I think about it as I make myself a cup of tea and break off another four squares of chocolate to go with it. Its sweetness is comforting, perhaps they're right about it being a substitute for love. Yet when I look out of the window, I'm not so sure. The roses are in full bloom. The long grass needs cutting and the warmth of the sun hits my face through the glass. But the summer inside me has disappeared. Inside it might as well be winter.

I put the chocolate in the fridge, right back behind the milk, where I can't reach it too easily, and set about clearing up. I hate Saturdays. They are catch-up times. Catching up on housework and paperwork and planning my next week's work. They are not times to be lounging about eating chocolate and feeling sorry for myself.

The very actions of unloading and restacking the dishwasher, and wiping down worktops and hanging out washing make me feel better. It's hard to be sad when you're busy.

Later, I survey my tidy house and think perhaps I should cut the grass. The garden looks bigger when I have finished, as it always does. I like green grass. Not for me the arid dryness of foreign soil. I'd hate to stare out of my window at palm trees and cacti and bougainvillea.

My friends – the few I've told about you – say I'm mad. What's wrong with living in a hot climate? What's wrong with permanent summer? As I empty the lawn mower, and breathe in the scent of cut grass I know I could never do it. Never again to run through autumn leaves, or see a winter sea, or have a snowball fight. It wouldn't work. I know it wouldn't. I would ache for the cool green fields of England. And you're right – as you so often are, we can't sustain a relationship with thousands of miles between us. Better not to start one at all.

That's why we've never become lovers.

"It's so much harder to say goodbye to a lover than a friend, Sally." You said those words a long time ago. And I agreed with you. Yet we couldn't quite let go. For seven months, we still met a couple of times a week to chat, to learn a little more about each other To see if there was any way we could compromise. There wasn't. Yet now the fact that we never became lovers in the traditional sense doesn't help with the grief of goodbye. It doesn't help at all.

Weeks pass, and I wonder where you are. What you are doing. If you are even still in this country. I said you should send me a postcard – if you ever got to Spain. Now I hope you don't because I'd rather think you are still in England, still somewhere not too far away. I think a postcard might finish me off altogether. And perhaps you realise this too because a postcard never comes.

It's a Saturday evening in autumn – and I am watching the last of the migrating birds gather on the pylon wires at the bottom of my garden, when there is a knock on my door.

At first I can't believe it's you. You look thinner, browner, more serious. And even though you are smiling that lopsided smile, your eyes are uncertain.

"Hi, Sally. Is it convenient to come in?"

"Of course it is." I pull back the door and follow you down the hall into the kitchen. Your footsteps sound tired.

"I thought you'd gone," I murmur, as we stand in my kitchen, eyeing each other like wary strangers. I'm not looking my best. I'm not wearing make-up, and I've put on weight – all that chocolate. A bar of fruit and nut lies unopened on the kitchen table.

I wasn't expecting visitors. I certainly wasn't expecting you.

"I did go to Spain. And then I came back. I missed you."

"Was it not as good as you thought it would be?" Hope rises in me like winter snowdrops pushing through frozen soil.

"It was everything I thought it would be. It was great. I loved it."

So much for hope.

"But you weren't there, Sally. I don't want to be without you." There are tiny cracks in your voice. They make me want to weep.

"I don't want to be without you either."

We stand at the same old impasse. Nothing has changed. Yet something has, I realise, as we move towards each other like two characters in one of those soppy old black and white films.

We've changed. It feels so good in your arms. It feels so good to have your breath in my hair, the warmth of your lips on my neck, the warmth that carries on going right through me, spreading sunshine into my heart. Who needs snowdrops when you've got daffodils and maybe even a bit of bougainvillea? I could even get used to palm trees and Spanish drivers. I could get used to anything, as long as you're by my side.

My friends were right. I have been mad. And it's taken a whole season of feeling winter within me to realise it.

As we finally draw apart and look at each other with unguarded eyes for the very first time, I know we can no longer pretend we're just friends. Or that we can live without each other.

You take my hand and kiss my fingers, one by one, and I glance at the fruit and nut in its pristine purple wrapper, and decide they're wrong about chocolate, too. There is no substitute for love.

Love and Chocolate was originally published in *Woman's Weekly* in 2007

Della Galton is a freelance writer and tutor. She is best known for her short stories, and sells in the region of 90 short stories a year to magazines in the UK and abroad. She also writes serials and her first two novels, *Passing Shadows* and *Helter Skelter* were published by Accent Press. Her non-fiction book, *How to Write and Sell Short Stories*, is on its second reprint and her next book, *The Dog with Nine Lives* is out in October 2010
www.dellagalton.co.uk

Butterflies
by Dawn Hudd

MAGGIE AND I MET in High School on the first day at St
Matilda's. I stood at the back of the hall where we'd been
told to assemble. I was eleven years old and too big to be
escorted by Mum. I'd shooed her away before we reached
the school gates – a decision I was regretting just ten
minutes later. I was lost, quaking and close to tears when a
voice squawked near my ear.

'You new too?' The mass of ringlets and freckles in
front of me shocked me back to reality. I choked back my
tears and nodded. 'So what do we do?' the creature before
me asked. I just shrugged, still unable to find a voice.

'I'm Maggie.' said the ringlets. Maggie grabbed my
hand and pulled me forward. 'Let's go find out, then.'

That was my introduction to Maggie. She marched me to
the end of one of the queues that were forming in the centre
of the hall. At the front of each queue was a table. At each
table sat an older pupil. We reached the front of our queue
and Maggie squawked at a boy.

'We're new. What do we do?'

Looking bored he said, 'Name?'

'Maggie Duston.' She screeched

'Margaret Duston?' he asked.

'If you like,' she replied, her voice lowering a little.

'Class 1D. Room 31.' He handed Maggie a sketchy map.
She stood to the side, waiting for me.

'Name?' snapped the boy. The badge on his lapel said Prefect. I'd heard that in High School some pupils became prefects. My mum, in her fussing with my school tie that morning, had told me that if I was good, behaved well and worked hard at my studies that I could become one of these strange creatures. If this is what they were and what they did I wanted no part of it, and looking at him I was glad that girls wouldn't join up with boys for another three years.

'Catherine. Kate,' I stammered. 'Kate Smith.' Compared to Maggie I was a mouse in all ways. Standing only to her shoulder with my short blonde bob, my voice was never going to light up a room like hers.

'Class 1D. Room 31.' He pushed the same hand drawn map towards me, ticked my name off a list and I was dismissed.

'Great!' squealed Maggie. 'Same class as me. Best friends for ever.' She grabbed me in a big bear hug. And that was Maggie.

Throughout High School and on into employment Maggie was always one step ahead of me, but I didn't mind. I hid behind her voice and her personality. She took me to my first disco, my first pub. She gave me my first – and last – cigarette. She organised my first 'grown-up' holiday, a weekend camping just outside Weston-super-Mare. How she persuaded my mother I never did find out. I was still only seventeen and not a girl of the world.

Maggie, on the other hand, was older than me by five months – already eighteen and streetwise. It wasn't that she was more trustworthy. Quite the opposite, really. If trouble happened, she was the first one they looked for. Her voice was often heard emanating from the Headmaster's office protesting her innocence. No, it was just that she was more forceful, insistent, that people found it hard to say no to her.

This forcefulness was probably the reason I found myself in a fluffy pale blue meringue at her wedding while she slid down the aisle in cream satin, hand-stitched with the tiniest of butterflies. And then eighteen months later holding a puce, screaming bundle called Eric in church promising, as his Godmother, to help care for him and help him walk in the way of a faith I had little belief in.

A few years later, I found myself jumping out of a plane strapped to a rather dishy instructor. At least I had Maggie to thank for introducing me to my husband, but she probably engineered that as well. The marathon we ran two years later was easy by comparison.

Two years after Eric was christened I was back in the same church making the same promises for Edwina. Maggie's choice of names. Dave, her husband, was another who never could say no to Maggie.

It was a shock when, one year after Eddie's christening, the same church was the setting for a far sadder affair. Dave's funeral was beautiful and tragic at the same time. Maggie would accept no help. She threw herself into the organisation, speaking to no one.

And now, here I was again, still unable to say no to Maggie. Only now Maggie wasn't squawking or squealing. She spoke quietly.

'Please say you will?'

I looked across the coffee shop at Eric and Eddie, now nine and seven. They sat at a separate table from Mummy and Auntie Kate. Far enough away to feel grown-up but close enough to feel safe.

'But Maggie,' I said, 'What you're asking ...'

'Isn't beyond you,' she interrupted. 'They don't have anyone else. At least, not anyone I trust.'

Maggie was estranged from her own mother now. I never knew what argument set it off, but I always wondered if she had at last said 'no' to her daughter. I thought about Dave's mother and her starchy, immaculate home. She'd made it clear from the start that Maggie wasn't good enough for her son and since his death her contact with her grandchildren had been limited to birthday and Christmas cards.

'I'll make it legal. We'll see a solicitor and make you their guardian. Then, if anything does happen …' She left the 'anything' unsaid.

For the first time in my life I wasn't saying a straight yes to Maggie. I didn't need to confer with anyone since my divorce and the end of my own childless marriage.

'I need time to think,' I said to her. 'It's a huge responsibility. Give me twenty-four hours. I want to sleep on it.'

Maggie nodded. She didn't look upset or put out as I thought she would. At the same time she didn't look as self-assured as she usually did. Did she think I was rejecting her? Her children?

I looked again at the two of them sitting with their milkshakes. Eric and Edwina, both so like Dave and so unlike their mother. Then I saw it. A twinkle from Eddie as she whispered something to Eric. Eric glanced around before grabbing a handful of sugar packets and slipping them into his pocket. A glimmer of Maggie in her daughter, a child someone couldn't say no to.

I took Maggie's hand across the table. 'I've decided. I don't need time. See your solicitor. I'll look after them.' Maggie smiled. She understood.

I found out about her scare by accident a week later. I was standing at the entrance to the hospital, waiting for my mother, when I saw her. She didn't notice me at first. She walked with her head down. Something I'd never seen her do. As she got closer I could see she was crying. Then she saw me. She squealed. Or squawked. I could never tell the difference with Maggie.

'It was nothing!' Her voice echoed across the car park. 'Nothing! I'm clear!' Her tears were tears of relief. As she explained, I felt an urge to hit her. Reach out and slap her across the face. For what I wasn't sure. For not telling me she thought something was wrong? For leaving me, her best friend, out of things? For making me think, just for a moment, I could lose her?

She still went ahead with the legal guardianship. In some ways I understood. She didn't want to leave her children unloved and unwanted, not that they would be. I was their Godmother anyway and I had always done my best to be a good example to them, whatever that was.

The church was packed. I was close to Maggie but I never really realised how much of an impact she'd had on so many other people. I don't believe I expected her to go before me. Not like this. She was still too young. I looked at Eric and Eddie. They sat holding hands, Eric the stoic one, Eddie crying quietly. Next to them sat Maggie's mother, the argument resolved, thankfully, a year before. Before she knew what was coming.

Eric was a handsome twenty-one year old, Eddie now nineteen. Maggie never did need to call on me to take on the responsibility of two young children, but she'd lived secure in the knowledge that I was there if they needed me to be. I looked again at Maggie's children as they stood and followed the coffin to the churchyard. I slipped to the back of the church and to the cupboard that the vicar had said I could use, then I rejoined the group at the graveside.

As the coffin was lowered into the ground I let go of the balloon. Cream and decorated with tiny butterflies. We all watched as it disappeared into the distant clouds, silently and gracefully. It was what she'd asked for. One last request. I could only say yes.

Dawn Hudd gets much of her inspiration from nature. She wrote butterflies after a visit to a zoo where she saw the most exquisite gossamer-winged butterfly. She lives in Hereford with numerous cats, dogs, guinea pigs and children. She gained a BA (Hons) in Creative Writing after six years of 'mature' study and now teaches as well as writes – when she has time after clearing up after her busy household!

Cross Stitch in Time
by Kelly Rose Bradford

HE WAS ON THE train again. Sitting opposite, engrossed in a broadsheet, all floppy hair and little round glasses. My tummy gave a slight flip as I squeezed myself into a vacant standing position opposite him.

At my age I should know better, of course, going weak at the knees over a stranger on a train. He was probably married, and even if he wasn't, the only times he'd ever glanced in my direction were when I'd trodden on his toes or been pushed into his knees by the early morning commuter chaos. My time would be much better spent trying to finish Great-Aunt Annie's present than drooling over my fellow passengers. I felt my calves press against the carrier bag wedged between them and gave a smile of satisfaction as I thought about its contents – an almost completed cross-stitched picture of Railway Cottage.

I'm not really the kind of person you'd expect to do cross stitch. I mean, it's usually associated with, lets be fair, *old people*, isn't it? A case in point being my Great-Aunt Annie. Annie is – in her words - an '80-something'.

"Well, Theresa, you and your girlfriends all call yourselves 30-somethings, so why can't I say 80-something?" she'd once asked me. No reason at all, I suppose, except, when it suited her, Great-Aunt Annie was quick to point out she was in fact 87 – 88 come August.

*　　　　　　*　　　　　　*

Despite her failing eyesight and her fingers not being quite as nimble as they used to be, Annie loved her stitching. And, what's more, she expected everyone else to love it as well. My little boy Harry had a room full of, well, frankly sinister-looking framed cross-stitched bears, several of which Annie had neglected to stitch eyes onto. "I am 87, Theresa, my eyes are not what they used to be," she'd told me.

It was because Annie was '88 come August' that I had indulged in a spot of stitching myself. She'd shown me an advert in one of her stitching magazines for a company who would turn any photograph into a cross-stitch grid for you to stitch. "I'd love to get one done of the cottage," she'd said wistfully, "but it'd be too much for me to stitch these days – all those fiddly rose bushes in the front garden. I'm fine with big blocks of colour, but I'd never manage that."

I didn't have a clue as to how anyone could cross stitch a rose bush, but, ever the dutiful niece, decided to send the company a photo of Annie's cottage and have a bash at stitching up the image for her birthday. After all, how difficult could sewing crosses be?

That had been in May – I wasn't banking on it being a quick project and had given myself plenty of time to master the craft. It wasn't as though I had anything better to do in the evenings. Now it was the middle of July and the cross stitch was almost finished – and what's more, it didn't look too bad, even if I did say so myself. Harry, with all the eloquence of his seven and a half years, had simply said "Yuk, its Annie's cottage, eugh, all flowery. Couldn't you have done the trains instead?"

As well as spending my evenings stitching away, I was taking the work in progress to the office with me every day, managing a bit on the train on the rare occasion I got a seat, and doing a little bit in my break and at lunch time. My pride in my work was twofold – firstly, I knew just how much Annie was going to love her gift, a far cry from the usual lavender-scented bath-cube-and-talc-combo she got each Christmas and birthday, and secondly, because I had actually embarked on, and (almost) completed a project! That in itself was completely unlike me – I was notorious for starting something and not finishing it – and what was more, I had made a fairly good job of it too.

Annie was always quick to mention my lack of 'staying power' as she called it. The failed diets, the dropping out of night-school classes, the abandoned correspondence school courses, and of course the Big One. The Failed Marriage.

"You've missed the boat now," she always said, convinced that as a 'thirty something', with a small son into the bargain, I was blighted to a life of singledom and spinsterhood. "On your own with a child to raise, you'll not have time for men." But I had time for them all right, it was just that men, it would seem, did not have time for me. I had dated of course since Dave and I split up, but, after five years of being on my own, I was starting to wonder if Annie had a point. Perhaps I was destined to a life as 'spinster of this parish' and from here on in my nights would be filled with nothing more than homework supervision, *Coronation Street*, oh, and cross stitch.

I couldn't resist pulling the cross stitch from the bag to admire it on the train. Given the confines of the compartment and the close proximity of my travelling companions, this probably wasn't a good idea. It was nearly finished. I had one rose bush, a pint of milk on the door step and Annie's neighbours' cat left to stitch, then it just had to be framed and inscribed on the back with suitably gushy sentiment. I knew Annie would love it. The Object of My Desires however, whose lap I and it ended up in as the train gave a sudden lurch, probably wasn't so keen.

"I am so sorry," I spluttered as I prised myself from his lap and removed the rough Hessian cloth from his face. The impact had forced his trendy little specs down his nose and off at an angle. I couldn't help but laugh. Fortunately he did

217

too.

"It's OK," he grinned, "commuter injured in freak tapestry accident. It happens all the time."

"It's cross stitch," I corrected, "Not tapestry."

"What's the difference?" he asked, straightening his glasses and smoothing the imprint of my fall from his broadsheet.

"I, erm," I pulled a face, "who knows?"

He laughed again and made to get up. "No, please, I'm fine, I wasn't hurt," I insisted as he vacated his seat. Good-looking and good manners, a rare combination.

"Er, no, actually, this is my stop," he said as the train juddered to a halt.

I blushed scarlet.

"But, please, do have my seat," he looked at me for a long time and shook his head and laughed. "See you again," he said and kind of saluted at me with his newspaper. I wondered if it was a statement or a question.

I thought about the bespectacled charmer a lot more than usual that day at work. Had he flirted with me that morning, or was he just being friendly? He didn't wear a wedding ring, though that didn't mean anything. What did he mean by "see you again"? Oh grow up, I told myself sharply, what do you think he meant by "see you again", just that – he could have said it to any of the other passengers we journeyed with every morning. "See you again," a throwaway statement that meant nothing. Except in my smitten little mind.

I spent the whole lunch break analysing those three little words. The result being a cat with partially stitched ears, half a left leg and not a lot else.

"Right," I told Harry as I scooped beans onto toast that night. "I didn't get to finish Annie's present today, so I need to do it tonight so I can take it to her tomorrow. That means, kiddo, that you can do the washing up and drying tonight, because I am going to be a busy bee."

"Dunno why you couldn't have just bought her a box of chocolates," Harry moaned.

"No," I thought, "Neither do I."

But I finished it. Bleary-eyed and sore of finger, the masterpiece was pushed into a frame at 2.30 that morning. "To Great-Aunt Annie," I calligraph-ied on the back, "Happy 88th Birthday, from your loving niece Theresa".

The following morning I was so tired I could barely see straight. I hastily shoved the cross stitch into a bag with Annie's birthday card, ran with Harry all the way to the childminder's and then sprinted on to the station. I just made it on to the train as the doors were closing and the guard was blowing his whistle. I was so tired I didn't even look for Him. I squeezed into a seat next to a sleeping bearded man and joined him in the land of nod for a blissful ten-minute snooze.

It was when I alighted at my destination and the train rolled out of the station that I realised something was missing.

"My cross stitch," I shouted at the departing train, "Stop, my cross stitch is on there!" But the train rolled on. Calm down, I told myself, go and tell the man at the ticket office and he can make contact with the next station and they can get someone to get on the train and retrieve it.

But of course the ticket office was closed. My cross stitch! Two months of work, probably lost for ever, no doubt trampled on by hordes of feet in the rush to get the elusive vacant seat, or kicked out of the doors by the throng of passengers coming and going.

I got to my desk and phoned the station. The station master had never even heard of cross stitch, let alone found one on one of his trains. "You need to contact Lost Property," he told me, and gave me a central London number. "Ring back in a week," they told me, "It takes a while for things to reach us." I put down the receiver and cried. And at lunch time I went into town bought Great-Aunt Annie another birthday card and a set of lavender-scented toiletries.

As I boarded the train that evening I walked its entire length, scanning under the seats of every carriage for my carrier bag. I didn't even know it was the same train of course, but I had to do something. I just could not believe that all that hard work had been for nothing. Annie would never know all the trouble I'd gone to, and now, instead of a lovely framed work of her chocolate-box cottage she had nothing more than some lavender smellies which she'd probably give away for the Church tombola.

Annie's cottage faced the railway, and as I crossed the footbridge miserably kicking a stone in front of me, I squinted at the house in the fading evening sun. I really had made a good job of my cross stitch! It was an exact copy of the cottage, from the lattice of the leaded windows to the latch on the front gate. I kicked the stone viciously down the last of the steps and cursed under my breath.

"It's only me Annie," I called with as much cheer as I could muster as I let myself in through the back door. I heard voices coming from the sitting room.

"… never been once to finish anything has my Theresa … oh this must be her now …"

I opened the door to the face of Great-Aunt Annie and the back of a gentleman visitor.

"Sorry – I didn't know you were having company – I've brought your birthday present," I stuttered.

"Have you now?" Annie replied with a smirk, no doubt able to smell the lavender bath cubes from halfway across the room.

"Actually, my dear, strictly speaking, Robert here isn't my visitor but yours."

The man rose from his chair and turned to face me. He had on a smart suit and trendy little specs.

"You!" I gasped, "How do you know Annie?"

He laughed, "I don't – well, I do now of course, but I didn't before."

"Before what?"

"Before this!"

He picked up a carrier bag from the coffee table and handed it to me. My cross stitch!

"You left it on the train this morning – I tried to call after you, but it's a bit difficult when you don't know a person's name – I tried Oi! But you just ignored it."

"I didn't hear you," I stammered, "I've been worried sick about this all day! How did you know to bring it here?"

"Well, it wasn't difficult once I looked in the bag and saw what it was – the train passes the cottage every morning and I recognised it straight away, so I brought it round after work expecting it to be you who lived here – I hadn't noticed the inscription on the back."

"It's very good, Theresa darling," chipped in Annie, "I was just telling Robert here how you never finish anything usually – what with being so busy with Harry."

"Annie!" I blushed deep scarlet – I bet there was now nothing Robert didn't know about me and my life of failure.

"Your aunt has been telling me all about you," he smiled, "answering all the questions I've been trying to pluck up the courage to ask you each morning on the train in fact …"

He reddened and we all stood in awkward silence for a moment of two before Robert spoke up again.

"I, erm, hope you don't think I am being too forward, but, er, as it is Annie's birthday and all, why don't we all go down to the Railway Tavern? – I hear their restaurant is first-class."

My heart skipped a beat – but I quickly came back down to earth. "I'd love to, but I can't, I need to collect my little boy from the childminder at six thirty."

"Bring him along too?" Robert ventured.

221

"I don't know …" I bit my lip and glanced at Annie. She had her eyebrows raised with expectation.

"You've missed the boat now," I could hear her saying in my head, "on your own with a child to raise, you'll not have time for men."

"I'd love to," I finally said. "I'll go and get him now."

"Wait, wait," Annie interrupted, "you go and fetch the lad and bring him back here – you two go off and enjoy yourselves."

"But it's your birthday …"

"And I'll get a lot of pleasure spending it with my great-nephew – he can help me hang my beautiful present – go on, off you go."

I didn't need telling twice. I might be a thirty-something, but I practically skipped all the way to the childminder's.

Perhaps cross stitch wasn't just for oldies after all …

Kelly Rose Bradford is a freelance journalist and writer. Her work appears regularly in the *Daily Mail,* the *Express* and the *Sunday Telegraph.* She is also a columnist for AOL's *Parentdish,* where she chronicles the ups and downs of life as a Semi-Detached Parent. Kelly has a seven-and-a-half-year-old son and lives in west London. When she is not writing or parenting, she drinks red wine. Copiously.

George and the Dragon
by Angela Johnson

IT WAS FRIDAY. GEORGE could take his time over his Weetabix. Then he would have toast with Marmite on one half and honey on the other. On Fridays, Mum said, he didn't go to nursery, and they could do fun things together like go to the park and go down the slide. He liked the zipping sound his bottom made as it slithered down.

Sometimes, Mum came down the slide with him, and he would put his arms round her waist and his head on her back and they would giggle down together. All the world around them changed and the trees and the people were different shapes, and he and Mum were special people in a different world of rushing colours and shapes, and he wanted it to go on for ever.

The other mums didn't go on the slide. They sat on the seats and talked to each other and every now and again one of them would call out:

"Samantha darling, it's time to go home now" or "Mummy is going to get very cross if you do that again, James, and you'll have to sit on the naughty step when you get home."

Mum was different from the other ladies, she wore long skirts and scarves, and her hair was dark and curly and very long, and smelt of fresh air and the sun when she kissed him at night, and her voice was crackly, and sounded like singing. When his far-away nan and grandad came to stay she spoke to them in a different language which went very fast and was full of strange sounds like clearing stuff from your throat when you had a cold. There was one very long word which Mum sometimes said to amuse him. It sounded amazing, but it was only the name of a place that people lived in, like he lived in Rochester.

The only thing that he didn't like about going to the park was that he wasn't allowed to take Fred.

"People will stare and get scared and they might run away from him and you know how upset he gets when people don't want to be friends with him," Mum said every time he asked. People stared at Mum too, but not in a scared way, more that she was something special that made the world better; like the sun coming out.

He wouldn't be going to the park much longer. He stopped munching the Marmite side of his toast as it didn't taste so nice any more. After Easter he was going to school. He liked Easter. He liked all the chocolate and painting eggs for breakfast. And best of all searching in the garden for secret eggs, with Fred lolloping behind him making big snorting sounds as he breathed. You had to make sure that Fred didn't get too close to the eggs. Easter was good, too, because Dad would be home all day and would take him out in the car and they would go to McDonalds and eat naughty food. And it would be their special secret.

Best of all was when the three of them went out to the woods together. The woods had a special smell to them, of damp and secrets, and of a long time ago. Mum would run around picking plants and herbs which she said were better than medicines, and she would make special tea out of them which she drank while Dad drank coffee with sugar in it. She moaned at him, but they smiled their secret smiles at each other, and George was warm in a blanket of happiness.

He wasn't going to think about after Easter. He'd been to school for a morning to try it out. It had been all right, and a lady with big teeth had smiled and talked a lot, but he wasn't sure whether he wanted to go back there and be without Fred and Mum for a very long time, a whole morning and a whole afternoon.

"I've finished, Mum, can I get down now? What's Fred got for breakfast?

He looked up at Mum. She had a big bump in her tummy. When he put his hand on it now, it sometimes kicked him, and he knew that the kick was his new brother or sister. He didn't want to think about it very much. It was like this business of going to proper school, Mum and Dad didn't ask him what he thought about it. He'd go and tell Fred about it. Fred always listened even though he never said anything, but he snorted extra loud to show that he understood.

He sometimes went to his friend Joshua's house after nursery, and they played with his new kitten, Jemima. She was lots of fun but you couldn't talk to her like Fred because she was too naughty and wouldn't sit still.

Joshua had a new baby sister and she was no fun at all, and Josh said she was a pain because she made everybody tired and cross. Everybody made a big fuss of her. He and Josh couldn't see why. He hoped the bump wasn't going to be like that.

George got down from the table. "Can I give Fred his breakfast now?" He took a plate of breakfast scraps on the special tin plate off the work surface.

"We're going shopping later, but you can play in the garden for a little while, it's a lovely morning."

George didn't feel like playing, he wanted to talk to Fred about school and bumps which became babies.

He liked going down the garden, it was long with lots of trees to hide in and secret places where you could make camps. Perhaps the bump would play camps. Fred liked camps, although he was a bit clumsy about carrying things and was a bit of a nuisance when he swished his tail too hard and broke things. Mum had been very cross when

225

George borrowed a garden chair to play nurseries and Fred sat on it and it was never the same again, and Dad had to take it down the dump and he was cross and said that he would take Fred down there next time.

Dad didn't like Fred very much, and Fred wasn't allowed in the house since he went funny watching the washing machine go round and round. And Dad had to spend the whole weekend redecorating the kitchen instead of playing rugby which was his favourite thing.

The garden was full of yellow flowers which bowed to him with big smiling faces and he pretended he was king of Rochester and he waved to the flowers like the important lady on the television that Nanny liked, but Mum said was a waste of space.

Perhaps he and Fred could play palaces before shopping. Fred would have loved the big shop and pushing the trolley and smiling at all the people, but George knew that there was no point in asking. Fred would have to stay at home. They could carry on their game this afternoon.

Funny, Fred's face wasn't at the window waiting; he was always very hungry in the morning and sometimes got very impatient. Dad had been very cross about the marks on the shed door that time when George was late with Fred's breakfast, and he preferred not to think about the time the firemen came and they said words which he wasn't allowed to say.

The shed was empty. The door was open. Fred was gone. The choking and swallowing feeling before crying came, and he ran round the garden shouting, "Fred, Fred come here, breakfast's ready. Come and play."

There was no snorting reply, no branches swaying as Fred brushed clumsily against them.

Fred was gone.

"Mum, Mum, Fred's gone, Fred's gone, Mum find him."

She saw the agony of first loss on his face, and as the new child moved inside her she wept inwardly;

acknowledging the limits of motherhood.

"Come and sit down and I'll tell you a story." There was the first scepticism hardening the baby contours of his face and there, like a subliminal flicker, was the young man he would become.

"Fred's gone away because he's needed somewhere, because he's so special. Remember the story I told you about King Arthur who's sleeping in a cave till his country needs him,? Well, we looked after Fred till his country needed him and now they do, and he's very grateful to you for being his very special friend while he was waiting. Now would you like to go to McDonalds?"

He knew that Mum hated McDonalds, so she was being particularly nice to him, so that he wouldn't be so sad.

They had a nice day. He had a happy meal, and afterwards they went down the slide in the park, and the trees whistled at him. In the afternoon Joshua came and they arranged a camp to play palaces in, but Josh didn't want to be a princess, so they played fighting instead.

After his favourite supper of spaghetti Bolognese he was allowed to stay down longer and watch *Coronation Street* which he watched with Nan sometimes. He liked the funny voices. Mum and Dad talked all through it about a grand slam. He was still feeling sad.

Dad took him for a long walk next day and he was a little bit less sad when Dad asked him if he would like a puppy, and they had a very nice talk about whether to get a puppy which would grow really big, or whether they'd get one which stayed small.

That afternoon he was tired, and had a sleep after baked potato with cheese for lunch, and when he came down all sleepy and dozy Mum and Dad were watching television.

"Wales have won the Grand Slam," Mum said, looking happy, and he looked at the television.

"Fred!" he shouted, and there he was, on the big flags waving, on the T-shirts of the people who were shouting and singing. Fred was everywhere, smiling and snorting, breathing his flames of happiness; all over Wales.

George and the Dragon was shortlisted for the H.E.Bates Memorial Prize in 2008.

Angela Johnson studied Creative Writing at the University of Kent and has won the Folkestone Arts Festival Poetry Prize. She has completed two novels and is currently working on a third and is a student at the Write Place in Dartford, Kent.

The Good China
by Katharine Swartz

IT WAS CREAM PORCELAIN with a twining ivy pattern around the gilt-trimmed edge. *Cottage Garden*, long since discontinued.

Laura remembered picking it out. Andrew hadn't come, of course. Picking out china was neither his interest nor his expertise. Her mother had accompanied her, in a twin set and pearls, a metal-clasped handbag bobbing on one wrist as she ran her gloved finger along the edges of the display saucers.

"Now you want something simple," she lectured. "Elegant. Enduring. I can't abide these modern fancies, this fiestaware in garish colours that will be gone tomorrow."

Laura, twenty years old and jumping with nerves and excitement, the ring solidly on her finger, the announcement in the newspaper, the wedding in three months, nodded obediently.

"Right. Elegant."

Had she been the one to pick out this pattern, Laura wondered now, tracing one worn thumb along the twining ivy. Funny that she couldn't remember. Most likely her mother had directed her to it, pointing imperiously at the simple pattern, the elegant structure of the plate, the cup, the soup bowl.

None of them really used, even after forty years of marriage. They'd languished in the dusty bottom of the welsh dresser she'd inherited from her grandmother, the cupboard with the stuck door that she rarely opened.

She'd used them in the beginning, hadn't she? The first time she and Andrew had company over, the couple from downstairs. She'd been so proud. The cheap cutlets and wilted beans had looked incongruous on the elegant plates. She hadn't been much of a cook then, and besides they hadn't had the money.

She'd got them out for birthdays, but there was something lonely about two pretty plates that were meant for a dinner party, a crowd of chattering guests. And besides, they were the good china. They weren't really *meant* to be used.

When the children came along, the good china had been retired from its brief service. Jack had managed to open the stuck door and smash the gravy boat, Laura remembered, although she hadn't been as bothered as she'd thought she should be. She'd never been a dab hand at making gravy.

When the children had entered their teens, she'd brought it out again, for birthdays and Christmas. No point impressing any company they had over, Laura thought wryly, they weren't really dinner party sort of people.

Somewhere along the way they'd stopped using it at all. Birthday dinners turned into pizza parties or sleepovers, not china material. Christmas dinner had been at the local for the last decade. It was easier, and everyone enjoyed a night out.

There just had never seemed any point. And, truth be told, she'd forgotten about the good china.

Laura leaned back on her heels, inspecting the plate in her hands. She wasn't sure why she'd chosen to tackle the old dresser today. Perhaps it was just another symptom of the empty nest syndrome she'd been suffering since her youngest child Richard had finally got a proper job and moved out two weeks ago. She hadn't expected to feel this unsettled, uncertain. Lonely.

Andrew came into the dining room from the garden, his old trousers grass-stained and muddy, his hands still encased in garden gloves.

"Take your wellies off," Laura said almost absently, her mind and eyes still on the plate.

"I'm just coming in for a second," Andrew protested. "Forgot the shears."

"They're not in here."

"I know." He looked sheepish as he asked, "Any chance of the kettle being put on?"

Laura couldn't help but smile at his hopeful look. "And the biscuit tin out, I suppose. All right." She was about to put the plate back in the cupboard, but then left it out instead.

"What's that?" Andrew asked.

"Our old china." The good china. Her mother had put out a place setting, along with all the other wedding gifts, on the dining room table, so all the guests could admire Laura's booty. How many settings had she received in the end? Ten, twelve? Far too many.

Sometimes Laura wondered if her mother had insisted on the good china for her own sake. She'd had a small, rather dreary wedding, very few gifts, and certainly no good china.

Laura's wedding, by comparison, had been spectacular. Laura had felt a bit of a spectator in it all, watching the parade of guests and presents, bewildered by the sudden change her life had taken.

Yet what had she imagined would happen? She and Andrew had been sweethearts all through school, and when Andrew had gone to university she'd taken a job in a local shop, waiting for Andrew to return and propose.

Her mother had wanted her to go secretary school, 'just in case', but Laura hadn't bothered.

She was going to get married. She knew Andrew would come back, and that was enough. Any dreams or thoughts

231

she might have had for something else, school, a proper job, were so far buried under her expectation and love for Andrew she hadn't even been able to name them.

When he had proposed, the happy whirlwind had begun, and Laura had smiled in satisfaction.

"Haven't seen that in years," Andrew said, peering at the ivy pattern. "Forgot we had it, actually. Did we ever use it?"

"No, not really." Laura stood up, brushing off her skirt, and went briskly into the kitchen. "It's a bit old-fashioned now, isn't it?"

"What? The pattern? Looks all right to me."

She filled the kettle and turned it on, took down the biscuit tin and took out a handful of bourbons which she arranged on a plate. She knew how Andrew liked things, especially since he'd retired.

"Not the pattern. The custom. A second set of china, good china, just to be used on special occasions. No one does that any more."

"Don't they?" Andrew snuck a biscuit from the plate. Laura took out the teapot, the box of tea bags, and two mugs.

"Ella didn't when she got married." Her oldest daughter's wedding had been three years ago, and they'd done it all themselves. A handful of guests, the ceremony on a beach, and no gifts in sight. 'Ella and Steve would prefer a donation to Save the Seals instead of wedding gifts' had been written on the invitation. They'd been living in their own flats for years, hadn't needed all the requisite appliances and dishes, linens and cutlery.

Not like when Laura had been married. Had she even thought beyond the wedding, back then? Considered what direction her life would take?

She had to admit that such thoughts had never crossed her happy mind. Marriage, children, were ends in themselves. They were enough.

The kettle hissed and then clicked off. Andrew rubbed his hands in expectation. Laura smiled at the sight. He was like a little boy, enjoying simple pleasures with the freshness of childhood. No more fifty-hour work weeks, trudging home at the end of a long day to flop in front of the telly.

He was enjoying his retirement.

But where's mine?

The thought surprised her. Laura poured the boiled water in the teapot, swishing it around as this new thought performed the same motion in her mind.

She hadn't had a job, not a proper one, really, ever. Married at twenty, first child at twenty-two, and then two decades of nappies and muddy football boots, sleepless nights and teacher conferences. Her youngest child was twenty-seven, so those days were long over.

No excuses, now.

"Laura?"

Laura smiled briefly at her husband and then set about pouring the tea. Even after the children had moved out, there had been things to occupy her time, if not her mind. Committees, housework, volunteering …

She'd never considered getting a job, doing something else. She'd been happy as she was, and they hadn't needed the money.

And yet … life was different now, and not just about dishes. There was no need to continue trudging down the same path as before, was there?

But I'm not trudging, she thought ruefully. *I'm happy.*

Yet she still felt the desire, like a flame flickering inside her, to do something else. Something more. Not a job, she didn't need to prove herself that way.

I don't need to prove myself at all.

She just wanted … something else. Something new.

Where were these thoughts coming from? She was *happy*. She loved Andrew. She didn't need to retire; there

233

was nothing to retire *from*.

"Do you think we should get rid of it?" she asked abruptly. Andrew looked mystified, so she clarified, "The good china. We never use it."

"Seems a shame, really. It's rather nice. But if we don't use it, as you said it ..." he trailed off, shrugging, wanting her to make the decision.

Laura's eyes travelled over the worktop to the plate she'd left on top of yesterday's post. Nothing but bills and flyers. She'd looked over one, absently, never really thinking ...

"We don't ever use it," she said now, taking a sip of tea. "As you said. We never really did." The sensible thing was to get rid of it, keep things as they were.

Laura didn't feel like being sensible.

"Funny, some things are too good to be used," Andrew mused. "Doesn't really make sense. Except, of course, if we used it every day, it wouldn't be special, would it?"

"So special now, it's kept in a dusty old drawer," Laura replied with a wry smile. Her gaze rested on the plate, on top of the discarded post, again.

"Well, thanks for the cuppa." Andrew, ever thoughtful, rinsed his mug in the sink. "I'm off again, battling the azaleas."

"Good luck."

Laura watched him tramp purposefully through the dew-damp grass. Since his retirement six months ago, Andrew had made the garden his personal mission. What would it be after that? He'd drawn up a list his first day as a free man, full of plans to transform their little square of lawn, then clear the garage and make a woodworking area, even though he barely knew one end of a saw from the other.

Laura smiled. Andrew had plans. Dreams, even, but what about me?

Laura picked up the plate. It was dusty, forty years old, and yet it still looked almost new. Barely used. Ready to be

234

taken out.

She could bin the whole lot, of course, give it to a charity shop. She didn't think any of her children would want it. If they weren't having takeaways, they were using serviceable dishes, plain ones, or even paper plates. Life was different now.

Or she could use it.

She picked up the flyer from yesterday's post. 'Adult Education Classes. Sign Up Today!'

She'd picked the pattern, now she remembered. Her mother had wanted something simpler. "Just an edging, Laura, or what about the fleur du lis? Ivy, really, it's so common."

"I like it," Laura had said firmly. "We'll be happy with this china." And she'd envisioned her future, as bright as the gilt trim on the plates.

That evening, Andrew looked down at the ivy patterned plate with its scoop of shepherd's pie in bemusement.

"You decided to keep it, then?"

"Yes. There's no reason we can't enjoy it every day, even if it's a little late."

"It's never too late," Andrew said robustly, and Laura smiled.

"Just what I was thinking." She would tell him about her enrolment later, how she was finally taking the art course she'd wanted to forty years ago, except it hadn't been sensible since she was getting married.

The dream she'd buried without ever realising it.

Just like the good china, she thought, talents never used, never enjoyed.

Now they would be taken out and dusted off.

It would take Andrew a while to get used to it, she knew. Get used to her doing something else, learning something new.

Eating off the good china.

With a smile, she traced the ivy on her plate then dug

into her shepherd's pie.

The Good China was originally published in *People's Friend*

Katharine Swartz has written short stories and serials for various women's magazines, and she also write for Mills & Boon under the name Kate Hewitt. She loves to touch readers' lives with stories of love and redemption. She lives in New York City with her husband and four young children.

The End of the Pier
by Lynne Hackles

CELIA GOT OUT OF the car and carefully lifted the old square tin off the passenger seat. She turned it in her hands. Once it had held biscuits but that was a long time ago. Now it held … Well, no one would ever guess what its contents were on this windy morning.

Balancing the tin on the car bonnet, Celia locked the door of Ken's old Astra and zipped up her jacket. It was blowing a gale and it would be worse at the end of the pier. It couldn't be helped. Today was the day she had to do it and the weather wasn't going to stop her. She didn't want the contents of the tin hanging around the house any longer.

A dozen or more seagulls had already landed near the car and were swaggering expectantly towards her, their beady eyes on what she was carrying.

They must recognise the damned thing, she thought.

She clutched the tin to her chest and began walking away from the car-park and down the tarmac slope towards the sea. How many times had they done this? Her and Ken? Probably hundreds. How many hours had she spent sitting on the rickety exposed bench on the end of the pier watching him fish? Probably thousands. It had certainly felt like it.

'How about a nice day out?' Ken would say, and she would shudder knowing what was coming next. 'We'll go fishing.'

Why hadn't she ever refused? Why hadn't she stuck up for herself? Because of Ken's temper, that's why. It had always been easier to give in and do what he wanted than to face a row and a week of him sulking and slamming doors.

So, fishing it would be. While Ken got his rods and bait ready, Celia would stand in the kitchen, buttering bread to make sandwiches and cutting fruit cake into manageable slices, wrapping the picnic in greaseproof paper before packing it into the old biscuit tin. She'd longed for a proper picnic basket, one of those lovely wicker ones lined with gingham and complete with wine glasses, proper china plates and cups and stainless steel cutlery. Once she had suggested buying one and you'd have thought she was considering purchasing a second home. The fuss he made!

'Always wasting money,' he'd accused her. 'Frivolous, that's what you are.'

Frivolous? Chance would be a fine thing. Subdued was a more fitting word to describe Celia. Over the long years of their marriage she'd given up trying to change him. All she wanted was an easy life with no arguing.

The wind tugged at her hair as she reached the bottom of the slope. Now she could turn left and walk on to the beach or go right and climb up the steps to the pier. She hesitated for a moment. Today Ken wasn't with her. He'd never be with her again. A massive heart attack had seen to that. Now she could do what she liked. She could make the decisions, please herself. Her dream had always been to walk along the beach, to feel the warm sand between her toes, collect shells and paddle in the shallows. She'd pictured herself, sitting in the shelter of the rocks, sipping white wine and nibbling on smoked salmon sandwiches from the wonderful wicker basket. No, that would have to wait. She couldn't do it. Not yet.

'Tomorrow,' she whispered, clutching the old tin more tightly, knowing what was going to happen to it once it was empty and no longer needed. The wicker basket was already bought and at home, waiting for her to take it out and christen it.

She turned to the right and climbed the steps on to the pier. Beneath the wooden slats she was standing on, the waves crashed. Above her head the gulls circled, screaming at each other, still loud above the noise of the wind. How Ken had hated those birds. It wasn't only the picnic food that had attracted them. They were always close by when Ken was fishing, hoping to steal his catch and dine on fresh mackerel.

Celia could see her husband now, flapping his arms madly at the birds, swearing and cursing them, stamping his feet and chasing them away. They'd been the thing he hated most in life. 'If I could get away with it I'd shoot the damn lot of them,' he'd often threaten as they strutted past him, up and down the pier.

Celia liked watching the birds. Sometimes it was the only thing she could do to pass the time. Her wooden bench was open to all weathers and it was often too windy for her to sit and read or knit. Her magazines or wool would get blown away. And if it was sunny it was too bright to concentrate on her reading. Sunglasses would have helped but they cost money and were totally unnecessary, according to Ken. So she would sit, watching the antics of the gulls and dreaming of how life could be if she ever had enough courage to strike out on her own. Now, she didn't need courage to leave Ken. He had left her and his leaving was irreversible.

She reached the end of the pier. Her bench was empty. It usually was. 'One last time,' she said, sitting down on the damp wood. It was strange being there without Ken, knowing she could get up and leave whenever she wanted to. Her fingernails were turning blue. It was cold. Soon she would leave and today she would do something she'd never done before. There was a little cafe on the top of the hill. She was going to have lunch there. Haddock and chips. It was another of the little treats she'd planned for herself. One of many.

For a full five minutes she sat silent and motionless, staring out to sea, the tin on her lap. Across there, across those waves, were other countries and she was going to see them. She could afford it now. The only thing that was stopping her was the lack of a passport and even that would soon be on its way. She'd filled in the forms and sent them off not long after the funeral. Oh, how life was going to change. How life had changed. The house was at this very moment being totally redecorated. Everything belonging to her late husband, including his fishing tackle, had either been sent to the local charity shop or burned. She'd enjoyed that bonfire. Now there was only one thing left to do. Get rid of the tin and its contents. She looked down at it. The original red colour was faded, the pictures of custard creams and shortcake circles barely visible. Celia, staring at the distant horizon, ran a finger absent-mindedly around the rim of the lid.

This had been Ken's favourite place. The end of the pier. He'd often said that if anything ever happened to him he'd like his ashes to be scattered off it. Celia sighed, remembering how much red tape had been involved for such a simple procedure. After a wait of several weeks the proper authorities had sent her an official letter telling her that permission for the disposal of Ken's mortal remains had been denied. Celia had glared at the urn on the sideboard and wished she'd never bothered asking but doing things properly had become the habit of a married lifetime. No-one would have been any the wiser if she'd simply taken him and casually sprinkled him into the sea. Now, they might be watching her to make sure she didn't pollute the water with the heap of grey dust that had once been the bad-tempered control-freak she had called husband.

Her nail snagged as she prised off the lid of the tin. Celia smiled down at the perfect Victoria sponge cake nestling inside. The gulls hopped closer, sensing food. 'Shoo!' she hissed at them, as she stood up and walked towards the railings.

She supported the tin with a protective arm as it teetered on the top rail. It was destined for the dustbin. But the contents, the cake, she had other plans for that.

Celia's smile spread to her eyes. She felt a new woman. She felt clever. If the powers that be were standing next to her they would never guess she was defying them. And, at the same time, she was having her revenge on Ken, even though she was only carrying out his wishes.

The wind swirled around, blowing her newly-coloured hair into her eyes. 'Poor Ken,' she said aloud. 'Victoria sponge was always your favourite but you never thought you'd be baked into one.'

As the cake fell downwards Celia turned and marched quickly away. She didn't see the gulls swoop.

The End of the Pier was originally published in *Take A Break's Fiction Feast.*

Lynne Hackles has been writing full-time for 15 years. Her regular columns appear in Writing Magazine. She has had over 400 short stories published, written a novel for children and several non-fiction books about writing. The latest book, about how to ghost write, will be available in early 2011. Lynne is also known as one of the most courageous players ever on Channel 4's *Deal Or No Deal.*